A DREAM
FULFILLED

OTHER BOOKS BY AL LACY

Angel of Mercy series:
A Promise for Breanna (Book One)
Faithful Heart (Book Two)
Captive Set Free (Book Three)

Journeys of the Stranger series:
Legacy (Book One)
Silent Abduction (Book Two)
Blizzard (Book Three)
Tears of the Sun (Book Four)
Circle of Fire (Book Five)

Battles of Destiny (Civil War series):
Beloved Enemy (Battle of First Bull Run)
A Heart Divided (Battle of Mobile Bay)
A Promise Unbroken (Battle of Rich Mountain)
Shadowed Memories (Battle of Shiloh)
Joy From Ashes (Battle of Fredericksburg)
Season of Valor (Battle of Gettysburg)

A DREAM FULFILLED

BOOK FOUR

AL LACY

MULTNOMAH BOOKS

6431

A DREAM FULFILLED
© 1996 by Lew A. Lacy

published by Multnomah Books
a part of the Questar publishing family

Edited by Rodney L. Morris
and Deena Davis
Cover design by David Uttley
Cover illustration by Ed Martinez

International Standard Book Number: 0-88070-940-5

Printed in the United States of America.

For information:
Questar Publishers, Inc.
Post Office Box 1720
Sisters, Oregon 97759

Library of Congress Cataloging-in-Publication Data

Lacy, Al.
   A dream fulfilled / by Lew A. Lacy.
      p. cm. -- (The angel of mercy series ; 4)
   ISBN 0-88070-940-5 (alk. paper)
      I. Title. II. Series: Lacy, Al. Angel of mercy series ; 4.
PS3562.A256D74 1996   96-21134
813'.54--dc20   CIP

96 97 98 99 00 01 02 03 — 10 9 8 7 6 5 4 3 2 1

For Cheryl Reinertson, TDQ.

Who else tells me I'm her favorite author,

laughs at all my jokes, and

takes my wife shopping so she can spend all my money.

Love you, kid!

2 CORINTHIANS 1:2

PROLOGUE

CARE OF THE SICK HAS BEEN A NECESSITY of life since the beginning of man's history. From time immemorial, all societies have set up ways to deal with illness.

Because it is an elemental need, care of the ill, the infirm, the injured, and the wounded has been linked with the economic and social development of the human race. Hence, the need of a centralized place to care for such...and the establishment of the hospital.

History's first hint of anything resembling what we know as a hospital is found in Egypt, circa 1280 B.C. A few of the temples provided housing and care for the physically and mentally afflicted. In addition to their religious service, the priests engaged in medical practice.

The most famous of the temples that provided care for the sick was the Temple of Amen-Re in Karnak, Egypt. It still stands today on the east bank of the Nile River. The most striking feature of the temple is Hypostyle Hall, which occupies fifty-eight hundred square yards in the temple complex. The hall is surrounded by fourteen massive pillars which stand seventy-eight feet high.

The Greek word *hypostyle* means "pillared." It was in this hall where the sick and infirm were housed as "guests" of the temple priest-physicians and given treatment.

If you look at the word *hypostyle,* you will almost pick up *hospital.* It's interesting to note that the English word *hospital* came from the Latin *hospitale,* a place for guests. It is believed that the ancient Romans picked up *hypostyle* from the Egyptians, since it was in Hypostyle Hall where the "guests" were kept, then passed it on to the Anglos, who came up with *hospital* in English.

The position of women in ancient Egypt was higher than in other Eastern lands. They enjoyed considerable freedom and dignity, thus we read of priestesses or "temple women" who performed nursing duties.

In China, the history of medicine goes back to 2900 B.C., but it wasn't until almost 300 B.C. that they had anything resembling hospitals. Those hospitals were small buildings adjoined to the Buddhist temples, and were known as "Halls of Healing."

Hospitals were established in India during the thirty-two-year-reign of King Asoka (269-237 B.C.). These hospitals were constructed by government order, serviced by government-paid physicians, and supplied by government stores. Under Asoka, state medicine became a reality in India.

The first hospital to appear in Europe was in Greece around A.D. 325. As time passed, the Romans established hospitals in Italy. And by the beginning of the Middle Ages (A.D. 500), the idea of establishing hospitals spread all over Europe. In England, great numbers of hospitals were built during the thousand years of the Middle Ages.

The establishment and growth of hospitals in colonial America was slow. When the American Revolution against England took place in 1776, there were only three hospitals in existence.

The earliest American hospital on record was established in New Amsterdam in 1658 (the name was changed to New York City in 1664) on Manhattan Island by the Dutch West India Company.

Charity Hospital of New Orleans, Louisiana, was second. It was founded in 1737 with funds provided by wealthy French seaman, Jean Louis.

The third was founded in Philadelphia, Pennsylvania, in 1751 through the efforts of Dr. Thomas Bond and other Philadelphia physicians.

After the United States had secured its independence from England, the establishment of hospitals began to accelerate. Most of them were financed, as was the hospital in Philadelphia, by private donations.

The first hospital established after the Revolution was Bellevue Hospital, also built on Manhattan Island, in 1794.

From there, other fast-growing cities from the East Coast to the Mississippi River began to establish hospitals. There was nothing but unexplored wilderness from the west bank of the Mississippi to the Pacific Coast. On the West Coast, however, were two cities—San Francisco and Los Angeles—that were starting to boom. Both had been established by Spaniards in the late eighteenth century.

San Francisco grew mightily in the Gold Rush of 1849, and Los Angeles began to show rapid growth a year later. It stands to reason, then, that hospitals had been established in both of those cities by 1860.

As for the Wild West (the territory between the Mississippi River and the Pacific Coast), there were no hospitals established until the population began to grow after the Civil War ended in 1865.

We once again join our angel of mercy, Nurse Breanna

Baylor, and observe the establishment of a hospital in her home town of Denver, Colorado, in 1870. The story begins on the Pacific Coast.

STEFANIE ANDREWS REMOVED HER APRON as she watched Alex Baker and Harry Mitchell wheel the unconscious patient from the operating room. Alex looked over his shoulder and said, "Soon as we deliver her to the recovery room, I'll head for the front door, Stefanie. See you there."

Stefanie glanced at the clock that hung between two kerosene lanterns. "Oh, my! How did it get to be almost ten o'clock?"

Harry chuckled. "You don't have to hurry for him, Stefanie. He'd wait all night to walk you home."

Alex cuffed his friend playfully on the shoulder. "You stay out of it, pal!"

The two friends continued down the hall with their patient, keeping their voices low as Harry teased Alex.

Everyone on staff at San Francisco's City Hospital knew Alex's crush on Stefanie was one-sided. She regarded him as a good friend, nothing more. Alex had just turned twenty, and Stefanie, who had earned her Certified Medical Nurse certificate at that age, was five years his senior.

A strong smell of ether lingered in the operating room as Stefanie walked toward Dr. Girard Patterson, who was washing up.

He picked up a towel and dabbed at the sheen of perspiration on his face. "Unusually hot tonight."

"Mm-hmm. I've lived here for thirteen years, and I've never known the Bay Area to be so hot in early August."

They heard footsteps and voices in the hall as nurses and attendants came on duty for the 10:00 P.M. to 6:00 A.M. shift.

Head nurse Isabel Grady walked into the room, looking fresh and ready for work. She sniffed the air. "Smells like somebody just performed an operation in here."

"Hello, Isabel," Stefanie said. "Why, I did an emergency appendectomy on a lady about your age. Dr. Patterson assisted me."

"Yes, Isabel," Dr. Patterson said, keeping a straight face. "I think that if I can just assist Surgeon Andrews a few more times I'll be able to try one by myself."

The three laughed together, then the doctor said, "Well, Mrs. Patterson is expecting me home presently, and I don't want to disappoint her. If you're ready to go, Surgeon Andrews, I'll walk you to the lobby."

They bid Isabel goodnight and left the operating room. As they strolled the quiet corridors, greeting hospital staff along the way, Dr. Patterson said, "Stefanie, I'm glad you have Alex to walk you home."

"I'm really not afraid to walk the three blocks, Doctor, but since Alex and I are on the same shift, and since we both live in the same boarding house, it's nice to have his company."

"Especially with that maniac on the loose."

"The Bay Area Strangler? So far he's been stalking women only on Telegraph Hill and Russian Hill."

"That doesn't mean he can't broaden his field of operation."

"I know. But I doubt he would come all the way downtown."

"Maybe not. But just the same, I'm glad Alex walks you home."

They greeted two more nurses, then Patterson said, "Wasn't Dr. Carroll's wedding a beautiful one?"

He was referring to Dr. Matthew Carroll and Dottie Harper, a young widow with two children, eight-year-old James and six-year-old Molly Kate. Dr. Carroll, whose wife had died of consumption over two years previously, was not yet forty. He was a brilliant psychiatrist, surgeon, and physician, and was chief administrator of San Francisco's City Mental Asylum. He also served as a staff physician at City Hospital.

"It certainly was," Stefanie said. "I especially liked the way Pastor Hall talked to James and Molly Kate during the ceremony. I'm so glad Dr. Carroll's going to adopt them."

"He'll make a good father."

"Yes, I'm sure of it. And it's so wonderful to see how the children adore him already."

"I'm sure they'll all be very happy."

They rounded the corner into the lobby and saw Alex Baker standing at the front door. "Well, Surgeon Andrews, your escort is ready to go," Patterson said.

Stefanie giggled, then smiled at Alex. She was about to speak to him when suddenly the front door burst open and two uniformed officers carried in a young woman who was semiconscious.

Dr. Patterson hurried to her side and scanned the young woman's dull, heavy-lidded eyes and the marks on her neck. "Don't tell me—"

"Yes, sir," one of the policemen said. "It was the Strangler, all right! Except this time, his victim is alive!"

Patterson turned to Alex. "Get a cart! Hurry!"

As Alex dashed down the hallway, the doctor motioned the

policemen toward a couch in the reception area. "Lay her over there."

Stefanie followed and looked on the young woman with compassion as Dr. Patterson knelt beside her. The young woman rolled her head back and forth and coughed. Her lips moved between coughs as if she was trying to say something, but her words were unintelligible.

"Where did this happen?" Dr. Patterson asked, closely examining the rope burns on the woman's throat.

"On Telegraph Hill. He would have strangled her, but two men accidentally surprised him only a moment after he attacked her. He ran away, leaving her like this."

A rattle of wheels filled the hall as Alex rounded the corner on the run. Everyone made way as the cart came to a halt beside the couch.

Isabel Grady followed right behind. She took one look at the victim and blurted, "The Bay Area Strangler!"

Patterson nodded solemnly, then started to lift the young woman.

"Here, sir, let me do that," Alex said. He picked up the young woman as if she weighed no more than a feather and laid her on the cart.

As he did so, one of the officers said, "Doctor, we need to talk to her as soon as she's able. This could be the break we've needed to catch that monster. If she saw him—"

"I understand. But right now I've got to do a thorough examination. I don't like the sounds she's making. Her larynx may be damaged, as well as her trachea. Can one of you wait here?"

The officers exchanged glances. "I'll stay, Bob. You go make a report at headquarters. Tell the captain that as soon as I can find out who she is, I'll be there. We've got to let her people know what's happened to her and where she is."

Bob nodded and dashed out the door.

Patterson said to the remaining policeman, "And you are Officer—"

"Leonard Proctor."

"All right, Officer Proctor. You wait here, and just as soon as the lady is able to identify herself we'll let you know."

"I'll need to talk to her myself, Doctor. If she can give me a description, we can go to work on catching him."

Officer Proctor stood gazing down the hall as the cart was wheeled away. Like the rest of the San Francisco police, he was eager to find the man who had murdered seven women in a period of three weeks. So far the investigations had provided no clues to the man's identity.

The police knew the murderer was quite strong and that he used a slender hemp rope on every victim. They assumed that because all the victims were attacked in the same neighborhoods, he probably lived on one of the hills. Other than this, they knew nothing more about him.

Residents on Telegraph Hill and Russian Hill were terrified, and the police had assigned more men to patrol the areas. Officer Proctor thought this might drive the murderer to strike elsewhere. So far, it had not.

This latest victim, who was fortunate to be alive, was attacked in Telegraph Hill's most affluent residential section. Proctor figured by the way she was dressed that she might be a maid or a housekeeper.

When the sounds of rapid footsteps and the cart's spinning wheels died out, Proctor sighed and sat down on the couch to wait.

↑

As the most recent victim of the Strangler was wheeled into an examining room, a young nurse rushed up to head nurse Grady. "Isabel! We need you in room twenty-one! Old Mr. Watson is in a bad way, and Dr. Clower isn't here yet!"

Isabel excused herself and dashed away.

Alex transferred the woman to the examining table, then stood looking on as Dr. Patterson bent over her with Stefanie by his side.

"Doctor," Stefanie said, "I'll stay with you. When she comes fully conscious, it will help if there's a female present to comfort her."

Patterson paused in his examination. "But, Stefanie, you're tired. You've done your shift. Certainly we can free up one of the other nurses to—"

"They're all quite busy at the moment. I don't mind at all, Doctor."

Dr. Patterson smiled and said, "Well, if you insist, Stefanie. I agree. This poor young woman has been through untold horror. You'll be a great help to her, I'm sure."

"Uh…Stefanie…" Alex said.

"I know you need to get home, Alex. Don't worry about me. You go on."

"But I don't want you walking the streets alone. I—"

"I'll take her home," Dr. Patterson said. "There's no reason for you to stay."

Alex thanked the doctor, bid Stefanie goodnight, and left.

Seconds later, Dr. Neal Clower, who was in charge of the hospital for the night shift, came in out of breath. "Sorry I wasn't here when they brought her in, Doctor," he said to Patterson. "Had an emergency with a next-door neighbor. He was eating a bedtime snack and got a chicken bone stuck in his throat. I talked to Officer Proctor out front. How is she? Hello, Stefanie."

Stefanie smiled a quick hello, then focused her attention back to the victim, who was still coughing and gagging, though it had subsided a little. "Dr. Patterson, should I give her some water?"

"Yes, but only a tiny amount." Patterson glanced at Clower. "She's not in good shape. She may have some tracheal damage and possibly some damage to the larynx."

"I see. Poor thing. Must've been horrible."

"Yes. I think they may need you down at room twenty-one, Doctor. Mrs. Grady was just called down there. Some kind of emergency."

"You don't want me to take over?"

"No. You go ahead and see about Mr. Watson. Isabel may need help, but she hasn't called for me because she knows what I'm dealing with here."

"But the evening shift is over. Won't your wife worry?"

"Bea knows we have emergencies. She won't worry."

"All right." Clower backed toward the door. "I'll go see about Mr. Watson."

Stefanie dribbled water past the young woman's lips while Dr. Patterson held her mouth open. She gagged on it and spewed some out, but the rest went down her throat. Then Stefanie held a kerosene lantern by the patient's mouth while Dr. Patterson used a mirror on a head strap to study the victim's throat. Still only semiconscious, she fought him, trying to roll her head from side to side while making angry grunts as he propped her mouth open with a metal instrument.

"What do you see, Doctor?"

Patterson didn't answer for several seconds, then said, "I

can't see any serious damage, but it could be lower in her throat than I can probe. There's quite a bit of swelling in the trachea, which is causing her to gag. There could be serious damage. The pressure of the rope on the trachea could have put a tremendous strain on the larynx. She's fortunate to be alive."

"Yes, but thank God she is," Stefanie said.

Patterson removed the metal apparatus from the woman's mouth. "Give her some more water now."

Stefanie moistened the victim's throat once again. She seemed to settle down and her coughing and gagging subsided. Finally she became quiet and closed her eyes.

Dr. Patterson asked Stefanie to hold the lantern as he lifted the woman's eyelids one at a time. "She'll come around shortly," he said, relief evident in his voice. "Let's cover her up so she doesn't get cold."

When the patient was resting quietly, doctor and nurse sat down to wait.

"I hope her trachea isn't damaged seriously," said Stefanie. "I've studied about the trachea a little. Fascinating. Just like the rest of the marvelous human body."

"Greatest machine there is," Patterson said.

"Yes, isn't evolution wonderful?" Stefanie said.

"Only a self-deceived fool could convince himself that this universe, the earth, and all that's on it came from an accidental explosion. Besides, who struck the match, anyhow?"

Stefanie laughed. "Good question!"

Patterson shook his head. "How any medical doctor could study the human body and say it had no Designer behind it is beyond my comprehension. Everything we know in this world has perfect order, beauty, and design. Think of the stars. Their constancy allows seamen to chart courses by them. And plant life here on earth. How could anyone study a rose petal and say it happened accidentally? And the animal kingdom—"

"No end to it, is there?" Stefanie said. "Only a fool would say there is no God—that it all happened by accident. In fact, the Bible says it quite clearly. Twice in the Psalms it says, 'The *fool* hath said in his heart, There is no God.' Evolution is an ignoramus's folly."

The doctor laughed. "We were discussing the trachea. That, by itself, would be enough to convince me there is a Creator."

Stefanie glanced at their patient, who still lay quietly, then said, "And it is this same God, Doctor, as I have told you before, who sent His Son into this world to die on Calvary's cross for a lost, sinful human race. The Lord Jesus Christ paid the full price for our sins when He shed His blood, died, and rose from the grave. That's why you need to open your heart to Jesus. There is a hell at the end of this life for those who die in their sins."

Dr. Patterson was trying to find some way to change the subject when the woman on the examining table groaned and ejected a scream. She put her hands to her throat and shook her head as if she were trying to pull something from her neck.

2

"NO-O-O! NO-O-O! LET GO OF ME-E-E!"

Doctor and nurse bent over the terrified young woman who continued to fight off an imaginary assailant.

"Maybe she should hear your voice first, Stefanie," Patterson whispered.

Stefanie nodded and leaned over the young woman. "It's all right, miss," she said in a soothing tone. "You're safe now."

As she spoke, Stefanie caressed the woman's face and stroked her hair. "It's all right. You're at City Hospital. Nobody will harm you."

As Stefanie's words penetrated the woman's mind, she stopped wailing and tried to focus on the voice that sounded so firm and reassuring.

"I'm Nurse Andrews. You're safe now. We know what you've been through, but it's all right. It's over. No one's going to hurt you."

The patient frowned in confusion, blinking against tears.

Stefanie looked directly into the young woman's eyes. "There, honey. Can you see me now?"

The patient swallowed hard, choked a little, and whispered, "Yes. I…I'm at City Hospital?"

"Yes."

"How did I get here?"

"Two policemen brought you." Stefanie took both the woman's hands in her own and squeezed gently. "The Bay Area Strangler tried to kill you, but he was foiled. I'll explain it all later."

Stefanie looked toward the doctor, who stood close, and added, "This is Dr. Girard Patterson. He's here to take care of you."

Stefanie shifted her position slightly to allow Patterson to step into full view, yet kept hold of the patient's hands.

"Hello," Patterson said, with a smile. "Your throat has been damaged some, young lady, and there are some rope burns on your neck. You already know it's painful to talk. I'm going to treat your burns right away. I examined your throat as thoroughly as possible, and at this point I can't say what the extent of your injuries are. It'll take a little time to tell. Hopefully there's nothing permanent.

"Now, miss," Patterson said, "we need to know your name and where you live."

"Oh...yes. Of course. I'm Lucy Campbell. I work as a live-in housekeeper for the Clifton Harbrook family on Telegraph Hill."

"I see," Patterson said. "One of the officers who brought you in is waiting to talk to you. He wants to notify your family about this incident and let them know where you are. Do you feel like talking to him?"

Lucy swallowed with difficulty. "I...I guess so. But I have no family. The Harbrooks are my only family."

"All right. I'm going to dress your rope burns with a special salve. Then we'll bring the officer in to see you."

Five minutes later Dr. Patterson left Stefanie with the patient and went to get Officer Proctor.

Stefanie held Lucy's hand. "I'm so sorry this awful thing happened to you, Lucy, but thank the Lord you lived through it."

Lucy managed a smile. "Yes. Please forgive me, but I can't remember what you said your name is."

"Stefanie Andrews."

Lucy smiled again.

"Lucy, when you said you have no family but the Harbrooks, did you mean in San Francisco, or no family anywhere?"

"My parents are dead. I have no siblings nor grandparents. There are some aunts, uncles, and cousins in Massachusetts or New Hampshire somewhere, but I don't know any more than that. I...I only wish my parents were alive. I need them right now."

Stefanie leaned down and kissed Lucy's cheek. "I understand, honey. Like you, I have no family. I—"

"Right in here, Officer," came Dr. Patterson's voice.

"Lucy, this is Officer Leonard Proctor. He was one of the officers who carried you here from Telegraph Hill."

"I'm glad to see you awake and looking better, Miss Campbell," Proctor said.

Lucy's voice cracked a little. "Thank you. And thank you for bringing me here. How...how did I escape the Strangler?"

"Two men happened to come along just after the Strangler attacked you. He got scared and ran."

"Do...do you know the names of the two men?"

"Yes. Jim Vasco and Troy Ronson. They said they didn't know you."

"Their names are not familiar, but I do want to thank them."

"I'm sure you'll get the chance. Dr. Patterson tells me you

are the Harbrooks' live-in housekeeper."

"Yes, sir."

"Now, I know you are very tired, and your throat hurts, so I won't stay long. In fact, I need to get a message to the Harbrooks and let them know what happened and where you are. But I do need to ask you a question or two."

"Yes, sir?"

Stefanie gave Lucy's hand a squeeze of encouragement.

"Miss Campbell, I need to know if you saw or heard anything that could help us identify the Strangler. Did you get a look at his face?"

"No, I didn't see him at all. He came at me from behind as I was walking home from an errand for Mrs. Harbrook. I was in front of the William Kendrick mansion when he attacked me. That's less than half a block from home."

"You didn't hear anything before you were attacked?"

"No. The Strangler must have come from Kendrick's lawn. I heard no footsteps. The first thing I knew, the rope was over my head, squeezing down painfully on my throat. I—" Lucy closed her eyes.

"What is it, Miss Campbell?"

"I just remembered. I quit trying to pull the rope loose and reached back and clawed his face with both hands."

Stefanie raised the hand she was holding and examined Lucy's fingernails. "You sure did, Lucy. Look there, gentlemen."

Doctor and policeman saw some loose skin beneath Lucy's nails.

"Good for you," Stefanie said. "I'm glad you left some marks on him."

"Those wounds will aid our search," Proctor said.

"Anyway," Lucy continued, "the last thing I remember is reaching back and clawing his face. The next thing I knew, I was here in this room with Nurse Andrews."

Proctor rubbed his chin. "Since you reached back and found his face, how tall would you say he is?"

Lucy thought a moment. "Well, I'm almost five feet five inches. He wasn't much taller than me. Probably five feet eight or nine."

"Mm-hmm. Could you give me any idea how he's built? You know, thick-bodied, medium, thin?"

Lucy thought quietly for another moment. "Well, his face seemed to be fleshy...round. He definitely did not have protruding cheekbones like a slender man would."

"Okay. I didn't want to plant anything in your mind by telling you that Vasco and Ronson saw him clearly for a few seconds as he ran away. Your description fits exactly what they saw. He was short and stocky."

"Did they get a look at his face?"

"No. Apparently the Strangler heard them approaching a few seconds before they realized what was happening. He was already running when they saw him. They said he passed by a street lamp, and they got a quick glimpse before he disappeared around the corner. Rather than chase him, they attended to you. One stayed with you while the other ran for the police."

Deep lines furrowed Lucy's brow. "I'm sorry I can't tell you more, Officer Proctor."

The uniformed man patted her arm. "You've told me quite a bit, considering the fact that you never saw him. Until now we've had absolutely nothing to go on. Now we know he's short, stocky, and has claw marks on his face. Judging from the amount of skin under your fingernails, you must've cut him pretty good. He'll have scabs there for quite a while."

Lucy smiled, then coughed and choked. Stefanie went to the cupboard and returned with a cup of water. "Here, honey," she said, "drink as much of this as you can."

While Lucy sipped the water, Dr. Patterson said, "Officer, we'd better call this to a halt. She needs to rest."

"Of course. Miss Campbell has given me plenty to go on. I'll go tell the Harbrooks what has happened. No doubt they're wondering where she is by now."

Dr. Clower and Nurse Grady entered the room just after Proctor had gone, saying the emergency was over and the elderly patient was resting well. Dr. Patterson told them he wanted to keep Lucy in the hospital a couple of days for observation to make sure her trachea and larynx had not been seriously damaged.

When Stefanie was satisfied Lucy was settled and comfortable in her private room, she said, "Nurse Grady will give you some powders to help you sleep. Get some rest and I'll see you tomorrow."

Tears filled Lucy's eyes as she gripped Stefanie's hand. "Thank you for being so kind to me."

"Don't have to thank me for that." Stefanie squeezed her hand tightly and said goodnight.

Dr. Patterson looked over Stefanie's shoulder. "And goodnight from me, young lady. Nurse Grady will look in on you through the night."

"Thank you, Doctor."

Dr. Patterson kept his buggy at the hospital stable at the rear of the building. He quickly hitched his horse to the buggy, helped a weary Stefanie Andrews aboard, and drove her home.

The next morning the San Francisco newspapers carried Lucy Campbell's story on their front pages. Jim Vasco and Troy

Ronson were lauded for having run the Bay Area Strangler off and saving Lucy's life. There was a bold statement in the article from Police Chief Randall Myers, warning the Strangler that his days were numbered.

The afternoon sun brightened Lucy Campbell's room as she sat up in bed, reading her story on the front page of the *San Francisco Chronicle*. Her door stood open, and she could hear the nurses and male attendants who were finishing their shift greet their replacements.

Lucy's head came up when she heard a familiar voice from somewhere down the hall. Seconds later, Stefanie entered, wearing a white pinafore over a light-blue dress. Her brunette hair was pinned in an upsweep, topped with tiny ringlets that were partially covered with her white nurse's cap.

"Well! I'm told our Miss Lucy Campbell in room seven is doing quite well today."

"I'm even better now that my favorite nurse is here." Lucy's voice was still hoarse but somewhat improved. Her color had definitely improved.

Stefanie leaned close to look at Lucy's neck burns. "I'm glad I'm your favorite nurse, because right now, you're my favorite patient." She studied the red marks through the clear salve and added, "These burns are looking better, too. Still feeling some pain?"

"Not where the burns are, but inside my throat."

"Mm-hmm. I would expect that. As Dr. Patterson said last night, it's going to take some time." Stefanie noticed the *Chronicle*. "I read that same paper this morning. Chief Myers spoke plainly to the Strangler, didn't he?"

"Plain enough. He wants him on the gallows."

Stefanie leaned behind Lucy and fluffed up her pillow. "Well, that long drop to the end of the rope will keep him from strangling any more women, that's for sure."

A stocky form appeared at the door and caught Stefanie's eye. "Oh, hello, Alex."

"Hi. They tell me this young lady is doing better."

"She sure is. Come in. I want her to meet you."

Stefanie introduced Alex, explaining to Lucy that he had transported her from the lobby to the examining room the night before.

At the same moment, a tall, graying man of fifty entered the room.

"Hello, Doctor," Stefanie said, smiling.

"Hello, Doctor," Alex echoed.

"Good afternoon," Dr. Clayton Wyler said. "I'm filling in for Dr. Patterson on this shift. He asked me to examine this young lady's throat and rope burns first thing."

Alex excused himself, saying he would walk Stefanie home as usual at the end of their shift.

Dr. Wyler did a thorough examination of Lucy's throat and told her she would recover from the laryngitis within a few days. He was optimistic there was no permanent damage to her larynx or trachea, and the rope burns were showing signs of healing. She should be able to go home the next day.

Lucy was pleased with the news. When the doctor was gone, Stefanie said, "Lucy, did the Harbrooks come to see you?"

"Yes. Twice. They came last night as soon as they knew where I was. Because I'm a close friend of the daughter to whose house I ran the errand, they didn't worry about me until about eleven o'clock. Then Mr. Harbrook went to the neighbors to see if I was still there. He arrived home, upset, just as Officer Proctor was knocking on the door. They were back about eight this morning to check on me."

"That's good."

"And about nine-thirty, Troy Ronson and Jim Vasco came to see me."

"So you got to express your appreciation to them."

"Yes. They're nice men."

"Good. Now, I want you to lie down and take a little nap. You've been through a lot, and I want you to get some rest. Besides, my other patients might start complaining that I'm neglecting them."

"All right." Lucy laid aside the newspaper and eased down on the fluffy pillow. "When will you be back?"

"Probably not until after supper. Things will slow down by then, and I'll come and spend some time with you."

"I'll look forward to it, Nurse Andrews." Lucy reached out and squeezed Stefanie's hand.

"Tell you what," whispered the nurse, bending low. "You can call me Stefanie."

"All right. I'll look forward to seeing you later, Stefanie."

After supper that night, Lucy was sitting up in a chair beside her bed when Stefanie entered the room.

"Well, lookee here! My favorite patient is out of bed!"

"Mm-hmm. Nurse Grady was in about an hour ago. She asked if I felt like getting out of bed and I told her I did. So, here I am."

Stefanie leaned over and hugged her. "That's wonderful! Can I get you anything?"

"No, thank you. I'm fine. Are…are you free for a while?"

"Well, sort of. My other patients are settled down. So unless something comes up, I can stay with you for about an hour. Then I'll have to do a routine check from room to room before lights out. Is there some special reason you asked?"

"Yes. I want to know more about you."

Stefanie smiled. "Well, there's not much to tell. I—"

"Last night you said that, like me, you have no family. You started to tell me about it, then you were interrupted when Dr. Patterson brought Officer Proctor in. I'd really like to hear your story."

Stefanie pulled up a chair and sat down. "You want to know because maybe there's solace in talking to someone else whose life has known the same sorrows?"

Lucy nodded, smiling. "Something like that."

One of the nurses interrupted from the doorway. "Stefanie, Mrs. Worthington needs her feet rubbed."

Stefanie rose from the chair and told Lucy she would return.

Twenty minutes later, Stefanie found her patient still sitting in the chair. "Well, let's try again," she said. "Let's see. Where should I begin?"

"How about the beginning? Where were you born?"

"I don't know."

"Really?"

"My first memories are of my father, Will Andrews. I was four years old. We lived in Mexico."

"Just the two of you?"

"Yes. I'll tell you about my mother in a moment."

Stefanie adjusted her position on the hard wooden chair. "Daddy and I lived in a small adobe house. I think it was on the outskirts of Tijuana. He did construction work—houses and store buildings—in Tijuana, Mexicali, and Ensenada, just south of the California border. Sometimes he did carpentry work, making cabinets and furniture. Before I turned five, Daddy and I moved to San Diego, where he did the same kind of work. Things changed when we moved to San Diego, however."

"In what way?"

"Well, I remember that Daddy would leave me with neighbors and be gone for days, sometimes weeks at a time. He told me he was doing construction in other parts of southern California and had no way to keep me with him."

Lucy shook her head slowly. "What a life for a little five-year-old—living with neighbors. I assume your mother had died."

"Yes. Her name was Ellen. Daddy told me she died when I was two years old. I don't remember her at all. Daddy didn't have any photographs of her, so I have no idea what she looked like. As I grew older, I remember asking Daddy many questions about my mother, but he told me very little. It seemed too painful for him to talk about her. Though I can't remember my mother, there's a natural yearning in my heart for her. And you know what?"

"What?"

"Though Ellen Andrews is dead, and though I don't remember her, I love her. I really do. I love the dear one who bore me in her womb and went into the jaws of death to give me life, as every mother does when she brings a child into the world. Can you understand that?"

"Oh, yes. My mother and father were killed by robbers when I was seven. But even if I had never known Mom, I would love her just because she's my mother."

They lapsed into silence for a few moments, then Lucy

asked, "What about your father? When did he die?"

Stefanie's countenance clouded and tears filmed her eyes. "Lucy, I don't even know for sure that he *is* dead."

"You mean there's a possibility he's alive?"

Stefanie picked up her story from when she was five years old in San Diego. There was trouble of some kind, and her father had to leave San Diego in a hurry. She never did know what the trouble was about. For several years they lived in small towns and villages in southern California, slowly moving up the coast.

The pattern was the same. Will Andrews would leave his little daughter and be gone for days or weeks on end. He left it up to the neighbors who kept her to see that she went to school. At times he would act nervous and upset when he returned, then they would pack up and move farther north.

In 1855, when Stefanie was ten, they moved to Los Angeles. During the two years they lived in the "City of Angels," Will Andrews continued his construction and carpentry work. As usual, he left her with neighbors when he went away.

Just before Stefanie turned twelve, they moved to San Francisco. One time when her father had been gone nearly three weeks, Stefanie came down with a severe case of influenza. The people who were keeping her took her to their family physician, Dr. Edwin Hazlett. The doctor put her in City Hospital.

Will Andrews came home to learn that his daughter was in the hospital. He visited her and was told that Stefanie was improving but would need to stay for another week. Andrews embraced her, saying he was glad she was in such good hands.

"And, Lucy, that's the last…the last time I saw my father—when he walked out of that hospital room thirteen years ago."

"You mean he just never came back?"

"That's right. Dr. Hazlett and the hospital staff kept expecting him to return. When it was time for me to be released, Will Andrews could not be found. The apartment where we lived had been rented to someone else, and Daddy had vanished. I was horribly upset. I couldn't understand why he would just abandon me, but he most certainly had. That is, unless he was dead. The police did a search of the city and surrounding areas, but found no sign of him."

"What did you do?"

"I fell apart. I must've cried for more than an hour before Dr. Hazlett or any of the nurses could talk to me. When I finally gained control of myself, Dr. Hazlett asked if I had any family who could take me in. I explained that I had no family at all, except some aunts, uncles, and cousins in New England that Daddy had mentioned. I didn't know their names. And Daddy had never told me where I was born, except that it was not in Mexico. There was no way to trace any relatives, if others existed. I asked Daddy several times where my mother was buried. Every time I asked, he just clammed up and wouldn't talk to me for hours."

"So what happened? Apparently *somebody* took you in."

"Yes. Dr. and Mrs. Hazlett. Frances—Mrs. Hazlett—had never been able to have children. They were now in their seventies. They asked me to come and live with them, and their home became my home."

"Oh, you must've been happy to actually have a permanent place to live."

"It was wonderful to have a real home and someone I could depend on. The Hazletts were like parents to me." Stefanie brushed tears from her cheeks. "As the years passed, living in a physician's home, I became interested in medicine. When I graduated from high school at seventeen, Dr. Hazlett started me in a medical program to become a Certified Medical Nurse. Two years and four months later, I had my certificate. I was hired immediately here at City Hospital, and I've been working here ever since."

"Well, Stefanie, you certainly found your place in life. You're a wonderful nurse."

"Thank you."

Stefanie went on to explain that just nine months before she received her certificate, Frances Hazlett became ill one Sunday afternoon, and by Monday morning she was dead from congestive heart failure. Less than a year after she received the certificate, Dr. Hazlett took ill and died. Stefanie then moved into a boarding house three blocks from the hospital in downtown San Francisco. She had lived there ever since.

"It must have been almost like losing your parents all over again to lose the Hazletts," Lucy said.

"It was."

"Stefanie...down in your heart...do you believe your father is really dead?"

"I have to."

"Why?"

"Because if he were alive, he wouldn't have abandoned me. Something happened to him. He's dead, all right."

Lucy leaned forward and took Stefanie's hand. "I'm so sorry for all the heartaches you've gone through. And I'm sorry you're all alone and have no family. I know exactly how that feels."

"You know what, honey? I really do have a family."

"Oh? What do you mean?"

"Have you heard of Dr. Matthew Carroll? He's chief administrator at City Mental Asylum, and he's also a staff physician at this hospital."

Lucy's eyes brightened. "Yes, I've read about him a few times in the newspaper. He seems to be quite a humanitarian...and quite active in his church."

"That's right. Dr. Carroll is a fine Christian man. Two years ago he talked to me about the Lord Jesus Christ and my need to be saved. Do you know what I'm talking about?"

"Well, sort of. I know about Jesus, of course, because of Christmas and Easter. And I had a friend in school when we lived in Los Angeles who used to talk a lot about being saved. She used to quote Scripture to me once in a while."

"Good for her. That's what Dr. Carroll did with me over a period of several weeks as we met in the halls of the hospital. He explained that I must be born into the family of God in order to miss hell and go to heaven."

"Sounds exactly like what my friend told me. I think she called it being *born again.*"

"That's it. You see, I often fill in where I'm needed at City Mental Asylum on my days off. One day, while I was working at the asylum, Dr. Carroll took me into his office and showed me from God's Word how to be born again—born into the family of God. I did what the Bible said to do, and now I'm in God's family. Even though I have no earthly family, I have brothers and sisters in the family of God to fellowship with. Every person who has been born again is part of the family of God."

Lucy blinked and said, "But I thought everybody in the world was God's child."

"No. Every person is God's *creation,* but not everyone is His child." Stefanie jumped up, headed for the door, and called over her shoulder that she'd be right back. Less than a minute later she returned, carrying a Bible. She flipped some pages, and when she had found John 1:10–13, she said, "Listen to this. It's talking about the Lord Jesus:

He was in the world, and the world was made by him, and the world knew him not. But as many as *received* him, to them gave he power to *become* the sons of God, even to them that believe on his name: Which were born, not of blood, nor of the will of the flesh, nor of the will of man, *but of God.*

"You see, the Bible says we are all God's creation, but we are not all God's children. You become God's child by turning from your sin of unbelief and receiving Jesus into your heart. When you turn from sin to God, that's repentance. We are born *of God.* It's God who gives the new birth when we call on Jesus, acknowledge that we are guilty sinners in need of cleansing and saving, and receive Him into our hearts. Do you understand?"

Lucy's eyes filled with tears. "Strange how it's all coming back to me. Margie—that's the friend I referred to—used to say the same things. It just didn't sink in. I always figured as long as I lived a decent life that God would take me into heaven when I die. But…but if I'm not saved…if I'm not a child of God, I can't go to heaven."

"That's right, Lucy. If you believe that Jesus died for you on the cross and rose from the dead, as the Bible says, then all that stands between you and being a child of God is to receive Jesus into your heart. When you do, the Bible says He will write your name in the Lamb's Book of Life. Every person whose name is in that book is a child of God."

Tears streamed down Lucy Campbell's cheeks. Her voice grew even more hoarse as she said, "Stefanie, will you help me? I want to call on Jesus and be saved."

Stefanie thought she'd burst with joy. She took hold of Lucy's hands and said softly, "Yes, I'll be glad to help you."

3

CERTIFIED MEDICAL NURSE Breanna Baylor leaned toward the window as the train's whistle signaled its approach to Denver. Billows of black smoke rode the airwaves, dissipating as it drifted higher. Breanna smiled at a herd of antelope that bounded away from the shrill sound of the whistle, showing their white rumps.

Next to Breanna was her fiancé, John Stranger. The mysterious man in black, with twin jagged scars on his right cheek, sat on the aisle. It was high noon, and the Rocky Mountains rose majestically in the blazing sun, taking a jagged bite out of the azure Colorado sky.

John and Breanna had traveled together from Montana where John had tracked down a gang of outlaws for the authorities in Deer Lodge and Jefferson Counties. Breanna had served for several weeks at the new hospital in Billings to help get it running. By the Lord's hand, they met up in Billings.

Breanna knew someone would meet them at the depot, since she had wired her sponsoring physician, Dr. Lyle Goodwin, from Cheyenne City, Wyoming, advising him she and John would arrive on the noon train.

The front door of the coach opened, the conductor entered. "Denver-r in fifteen minutes! Denver-r in fifteen minutes!"

Breanna turned to the man she loved. "It's been so good to

have some time with you, darling. I'm going to miss you."

"I'll miss you, too, sweetheart." John raised her hand to his lips and kissed it.

Breanna laid her head against John's muscular shoulder. "Hard to say where Dr. Goodwin will be sending me next."

John pressed her head against him. "If Chief Duvall doesn't need me right away, I'll wait till you leave town. Then I'm heading into the mountains to see some people I helped out of a financial problem a few months ago. I want to see how they're doing."

"You wonderful man. You're so generous. Before I left for Billings, Dr. Goodwin told me something few people know."

"What's that?"

"That you've put more money toward Denver's new hospital than any other individual, even more than Drs. Goodwin, Wakeman, and Stratton put together."

"Oh, he did, did he?"

"Yes."

"Well, he's a tattletale. I gave that money anonymously. Only the three doctors are supposed to know about it."

Breanna giggled like a schoolgirl. "Well, Dr. Goodwin said he didn't think you'd mind if *I* knew about it since we're… ah…engaged and all."

John chuckled. "I guess I'm not upset. As long as it's *you* and nobody else."

Movement outside the window caught Breanna's attention. Several teenage boys on horseback galloped alongside the train, waving their hats and whooping a greeting to the passengers who stared at them through the windows.

"Oh, to be a kid again," John said.

Breanna laughed.

The train started to slow down, and houses on Denver's

northern outskirts came into view as the young riders pulled back and galloped away. Moments later they were in the heart of town, and the big engine chugged into Denver's Union Station, its bell clanging loudly.

"Dinner tonight at the Diamond Palace, Breanna?"

Breanna looked up and explored his face. "I'd be delighted."

"Then it's a date."

As the train squealed to a halt, passengers began to reach for their hand luggage and file toward the nearest door. John retrieved his and Breanna's carry-on items from the rack overhead, and Breanna preceded him onto the coach's platform. Her eyes caught sight of a familiar face.

"John! It's Dr. Goodwin!"

"I didn't expect him to pick us up."

"Nor did I." John descended the steps ahead of Breanna and gave her his hand.

At the same moment, the tall, graying physician greeted them. "Hello, lovebirds! Glad to have you home!"

Breanna gave him her customary daughterly embrace, and Stranger shook his hand.

"To what do we owe this exceptional gesture, Doc?" John said. "We never dreamed you would come after us yourself. Things slow at the clinic?"

"Are things ever slow at the clinic? I just wanted to take you and Breanna by the new hospital and let you see how well the construction is going."

"Oh, we'd love it, wouldn't we, John?"

"Sure, I'd like to see it."

"I'd think so," Goodwin said, "seeing as how you've put a lot of money toward it."

John elbowed the doctor playfully. "Yeah. I hear you've been tattling on me."

Goodwin glanced at Breanna then grinned at John. "What do you mean?"

"You know what I mean. My gift to help build the new hospital was supposed to be anonymous except to you and Drs. Wakeman and Stratton."

"Oh, it is, John. Uh…that is, except for Breanna. I felt that since she's engaged to marry you, she ought to know what an unselfish and generous man she's marrying. Can you find it in your heart to forgive me?"

"I'll think about it."

The three laughed together and Lyle Goodwin led them toward his buggy. Soon they were pulling away from the depot and entering Denver's dusty streets.

John scanned what he could of the town and marveled at all the new construction. "Looks like the town's booming, Doc."

"That's putting it mildly. Our little town is soon going to be a big city."

John glanced toward the Platte River, then raised his eyes to the mountains. "Well, I don't blame people for wanting to live here."

"This is why we need the new hospital, John. The population growth demands it. The three clinics can't keep up with all the accidents and sicknesses that naturally come with such an influx of people."

As they drove into the center of the business district, the streets were at full boil. Street vendors announced their wares, and people moved up and down the crowded thoroughfares on foot, on horseback, in buggies, surreys, carriages, and wagons.

The brightly painted buildings stood shoulder to shoulder, their false fronts making a ragged up-and-down pattern. Lots that had stood vacant when John and Breanna had last seen Denver were now under construction. Piles of lumber and other building materials lay along the streets where new buildings were going up. The sounds of hammer and saw kept up a steady tone, intermingled with the hurdy-gurdy piano music coming from saloons.

"My, my," Breanna said. "One doesn't dare stay away from this town for long, or they wouldn't know it when they returned."

"I can't believe my eyes, Doc," John said. "Where is everybody coming from?"

"Back East. I think they want to get away from the humidity and breathe some clean, dry mountain air."

Breanna drew in a deep breath. "Good clean mile-high air. No wonder Denver's on the grow."

Breanna's traveling schedule was arranged, or at least approved, by Dr. Goodwin, since he was her sponsoring physician. He gave her a sidelong glance. "Breanna, I've fixed it so you can stick around town for a while."

"Oh?"

"Mm-hmm. I've scheduled you to stay and work at the hospital for the first three months of its operation."

"Wonderful!"

Even as Breanna was expressing her delight at the prospect of working in the new hospital, the buggy turned onto Wynkoop Street, and there before them stood the imposing two-story edifice with a sign in front that read:

Drs. Lyle Goodwin, Glen Wakeman, and Newt Stratton,
along with many generous donors
proudly present Denver's new
Mile High Hospital.

Next to it, a smaller sign informed the passersby that the hospital was being built by the Cullen Construction Company of Denver.

"Oh, I like that name, Doctor!" Breanna said. "Mile High Hospital."

"Martha came up with it," Dr. Goodwin said.

He pulled rein and stopped the buggy near the front entrance. The roof was on, the walls were completed, and the north end had already been painted a glistening white. The windows were in on the north end, too. The front entrance faced east, with the Rockies as a magnificent backdrop.

John noted the crew of men moving about the building, carrying lumber inside, and others working on the exterior. Two men were on a scaffold above the front entrance, getting ready to attach a ready-made overhang to heavy timbers embedded in the wall.

"Doc, this Cullen Construction Company has to be new," John said. "They weren't here before, were they?"

"The company's headed up by a fellow named Russ Cullen. Recently moved his company here from El Paso, Texas, hoping to get in on Denver's boom. Cullen made a lower bid than Denver's other three construction companies, so we gave him the job."

"Well, I guess there's room for another construction outfit, the way things are going in this town."

"Want to take a look inside?" Goodwin asked.

"Sure do!" Breanna said. "I can't believe how quickly the building is going up!"

The doctor paused for a moment and pointed to the unpainted, unfinished exterior at the south end. "As you can see, what we're doing is finishing the north end first so we can go ahead and get the hospital in operation. We'll finish the south end after we're already in business. The construction noise in the daytime will be a slight problem, but the other doctors and I agree that it'll be worth it to get the place open and functioning as soon as possible."

Breanna eased closer to Goodwin. "Um, Dr. Goodwin, have...ah...have you hired the new chief administrator for the hospital yet?"

Lyle Goodwin smiled, his eyes crinkling. He reached inside his coat pocket and pulled out an unopened white envelope. "I was wondering if you were ever going to ask me about Dr. Carroll. I think this letter from Dottie will have some vital information. It came to the office for you two days ago."

Breanna squealed with delight when she saw her sister's name followed by the name "Carroll" in the upper left-hand corner and an address on San Francisco's fashionable Nob Hill.

"Oh, John, look! They did it! Matt and Dottie got married!"

"Wonderful!"

Breanna ripped open the envelope and unfolded the letter. She started to read, then stopped and looked up at John with tears in her eyes. "They were married on August first. Let's see...that was a Saturday. Dottie says she wishes you and I could have been there."

Breanna continued to read and then stopped abruptly. "Dottie says Matt has been hired as chief administrator of Denver's new Mile High Hospital! They plan to arrive by train on August twenty-fourth. That's...that's two weeks from this coming Monday! And Matt is going to legally adopt the children as soon as they get settled in Denver!"

John folded Breanna in his arms. "Sweetheart, that's wonderful. Praise the Lord!"

"Yes!" she said, hugging him tight. "Praise the Lord!"

Breanna turned to the smiling physician. "Dr. Goodwin, you scamp! You were holding out on me! Why didn't you tell me at the depot?"

Goodwin threw back his head and laughed. "I was just having a little fun, Breanna."

She gave him a quick hug. "Well, since I'm so happy, I'll forgive you!"

"Dry your tears, now, little lady. I want to take you inside so you can get a look at Dr. Carroll's new place of employment."

John and Breanna followed closely on Goodwin's heels as he led them toward the double doors at the front entrance. As they approached, a bearded, middle-aged man in dusty work clothes came out. He was bareheaded, and his thick head of hair was salt-and-pepper gray. The man smiled at seeing Dr. Goodwin.

"Hello, Russ," Goodwin said. "I want you to meet Breanna Baylor and John Stranger. Breanna is the visiting nurse who works out of my office. John and Breanna...Russ Cullen of Cullen Construction Company."

Cullen nodded at Breanna. "Ma'am. Glad to meet you." Then he extended his hand to John. "Did I understand correctly? Your name is John *Stranger?*"

"That's it," John said, gripping his hand.

"Never heard of that before."

"It's pretty rare. I want to commend you for what I recognize as quality construction."

"Thanks. You been in construction work?"

"Not professionally, but I've been in on building houses, barns, and an office building or two. Just helping out, you understand."

The four were standing directly beneath a scaffold, which

was some twenty feet above the ground. Suddenly a hammer came hurtling through the air directly in line with Russ Cullen's head.

Breanna's eye caught the movement.

"Look out!" she cried, and shoved Cullen out of the way. The hammer struck her left forearm and clattered to the ground. Breanna ejected a tiny cry and grabbed her arm.

John looked up as the man who had dropped the hammer called down, "Hey, I'm sorry! Hope nobody's hurt!"

"It struck the lady's arm," Stranger said, then turned to Breanna, putting a protective hand on the small of her back.

"Here, Breanna," Dr. Goodwin said as he took hold of her arm. "Let me look at it."

Dr. Goodwin examined Breanna's forearm as the two men from the scaffold scrambled down. "Ma'am, I'm awfully sorry," said the worker who had dropped the hammer.

"It's all right," Breanna said. "Accidents happen. You didn't drop it on purpose."

"Clay, you blundering idiot!" Russ Cullen said. "That hammer would've hit me on the head and split open my skull if this lady hadn't pushed me outta the way. I oughtta fire you on the spot!"

"Boss, I'm really sorry," Clay Meldrum said.

"Mr. Cullen," Breanna said, "it's all right. Clay apologized to me. Obviously, he didn't drop the hammer on purpose. Please don't fire him."

Cullen kept his gaze on Breanna for a moment, then turned to Clay and said, "Because the lady has pleaded your cause, I'll let you keep your job. But no more slip ups or you're outta here!"

"Yes, sir. Th-thank you, sir." And to Breanna, he said, "I really am sorry you're hurt, ma'am."

"Don't worry about it. I'll live."

"Breanna, we need to go to the office and tend to this," Dr. Goodwin said. "I'll give you the tour later."

"Did it break the bone, Dr. Goodwin?" Clay asked.

"Doesn't appear so, but she's going to have a mighty sore arm for a few days."

4

JOHN HELPED BREANNA from the buggy while Dr. Goodwin tied the reins and greeted two elderly women who were just leaving the clinic. Both wore flowered cotton dresses and sunbonnets to match. Sadie Perkins and Cordelia Beckwith tottered toward Goodwin with their arms locked together for support.

"Did my nurses take good care of you?" he asked.

"Oh, yes," Cordelia said. "That new little nurse is as sweet as a lump of sugar. What's her name? Ah…Sissy. That's it! Sissy. I can't remember her last name."

"O'Day, honey," Sadie said. "And it's not Sissy, it's *Missy.* Now that you're nearly ninety-four, you can't remember anything. Her name's Missy O'Day."

"Oh, yes. That's it. McKay. Sissy McKay."

Sadie rolled her eyes.

Dr. Goodwin knew better than to ask Cordelia how she was feeling. She would talk for half an hour. Just then Cordelia looked beyond him. "Oh, Sadie! Look!"

Both women converged on Breanna, asking where she'd been and what she'd been up to.

When Cordelia turned her attention to John, she tilted her head back and said, "Oh, you're a tall one, aren't you? What's the stranger's name, Breanna?"

"Do you want to tell her, darling?"

"Sure," he said, not quite suppressing a chuckle. "That *is* my name, ma'am. *Stranger.* John Stranger."

Cordelia squinted up at him. "I couldn't have heard that right, Sadie. It sounded like he said his name is *Stranger.* My hearin' is really gettin' bad."

Dr. Goodwin stepped in. "Sorry ladies, but Miss Breanna has been injured. I've got to get her inside and take care of her." He whisked the couple away and held open the clinic door for them.

The waiting room was packed, mostly with women and children. Dr. Goodwin's regular nurse, Letha Phillips, stood at the desk making notes on a patient's record. She caught sight of the doctor out of the corner of her eye and started to talk while still writing notations. "Oh, Doctor, I'm glad you're back. Missy and I have handled most everything, but we have a little boy in the back with a dislocated shoulder—" Then she looked up and noticed the couple with him. "Oh, Breanna! Welcome home. Hello, John. Nice to see you."

Before either could reply, Dr. Goodwin said, "Breanna's got an injured arm, Letha."

"How bad is it? How'd it happen?"

"We'll explain later," Goodwin said. "I want to get her arm into some cool water, quick. What else do we have in the waiting room?"

Letha assured Dr. Goodwin that she and Missy could handle the other patients, but they had been waiting for him to take care of Tommy's dislocated shoulder.

"All right. I'll have Missy tend to Breanna while I work on Tommy. You take the next patient."

✦

Eight-year-old Tommy Hargrove lay on an examining table with two pillows under his left arm. His mother stood next to him.

Nurse-in-training Missy O'Day was talking to the little boy in soothing tones as the door opened. "Oh, Dr. Goodwin! Am I glad to see you! I told Tommy you'd be here soon." Then her eyes strayed to John and Breanna, and she noticed the pain in Breanna's eyes.

"Breanna! Mr. Stranger! What's happened?"

"Long story," Dr. Goodwin said. "I'll tend to Tommy first, Missy. You've given him some powders for his pain?"

"Yes, sir. He's a bit drowsy now."

"Good. Hello, Mrs. Hargrove."

"Hello, Doctor. I'm so glad you're here."

"Dislocated shoulder, eh?"

"That's what Nurse Phillips says."

"She's seldom wrong. Tommy…"

"Yes, sir," came a dull voice.

"Ol' Doc Goodwin will take care of you, son. Be right there. Missy, I want you to give Breanna some powders for her pain, then dip that arm in cool water and keep it there till I say different. She'll explain what happened while you're taking care of her. I want that swelling to go down and the blood to coagulate under the skin as fast as possible."

"I understand, Doctor. Come on, Breanna. It's about time somebody took care of you for a change."

John stayed close to Breanna as Missy sat her down next to a small table and hastened to the cupboard for water. She poured the water from a bucket into a metal basin and brought it to the table.

Breanna winced as she submerged her arm, then looked up at John. "I'll be all right, darling. Don't look so worried."

"I just can't stand to know you're hurting," he said.

Missy smiled at him. "That's sweet, Mr. Stranger. Clint is like that with me. You'll both make good husbands."

Breanna had met Missy O'Day and Clint Byers when the three were held captive, along with other kidnap victims, in a canyon west of Denver where an illicit gold mine was operating. John Stranger had led a band of Arapaho Indians into the canyon and rescued them. Clint was now employed with the Union Pacific Railroad, laying track in southern Colorado toward Santa Fe, New Mexico, and Missy was studying for her Certified Medical Nurse certificate.

Dr. Goodwin administered a small amount of laudanum to the boy, then waited a few minutes for it to take effect. Within half an hour Tommy's shoulder was back in place and a sling applied. He was still quite groggy as John Stranger carried him to the Hargrove family wagon.

Dr. Goodwin gave Esther Hargrove some powders to administer when the laudanum wore off and apologized that he had no way to keep Tommy for a day or two in the clinic. That kind of problem would be solved when the new hospital was finished.

As the wagon rolled away, the two men turned back toward the clinic. "Have you got a target date for opening the hospital, Doc?" John asked.

"Not an exact day, but we want to open it the first week of October. We've got another doctor coming to Denver to set up his own practice and be a staff physician at the hospital. His name is Eldon Moon. In fact, Dr. Moon is now on his way here from Kansas City."

They moved back inside, and Dr. Goodwin worked on the

next patient who needed his attention, while Missy tended Breanna. Letha handled the rest of the patients, and soon the waiting room was empty.

Goodwin was pleased that the swelling in Breanna's arm had gone down. He applied salve to the bruise and watched while Missy bandaged it.

"Breanna," John said, "Doc told me outside that there's another doctor coming to Denver to serve as one of the hospital's staff physicians."

"Wonderful! Do I know him, Dr. Goodwin?"

"Dr. Eldon Moon of Kansas City."

"Oh, yes. He has an excellent reputation."

"I didn't get a chance to tell you, John, that Dr. Moon is also bringing three C.M.N.s with him. One for his office, and two for the hospital."

"How many nurses do you plan to start out with?" Breanna asked.

"We'd like to have three for each shift. That's all we'll be able to afford at the start. It means they'll have to work seven days a week till we can expand the nursing staff."

"I assume you have others lined up to come," John said.

"Yes, and I've already put Breanna to work in the hospital for the first three months."

"And I'm happy about that!" Missy said.

"We also have three nurses from Women's Hospital in New York and two from Philadelphia Hospital. They're all C.M.N.s with a great deal of experience. One of the nurses from Philadelphia is Mary Donelson. She has an outstanding reputation. She's been head nurse of Philadelphia Hospital for fourteen years."

"I assume she'll be head nurse at Mile High Hospital," Breanna said.

"Yes, but we'll have to pick two others to work as assistant head nurses so we'll have one on duty for each shift."

Breanna winced slightly as Missy tightened the bandage with a finishing touch. "How were you able to get Mary Donelson?" she asked.

"Well, I've known of her for some time, and on a whim I wrote and offered her the head nurse job at our new hospital. Since one donor has been very generous in giving to the hospital fund, I was able to offer Mrs. Donelson the same salary she's getting as head nurse in Philadelphia."

Breanna managed not to look at John until she noticed Letha and Missy were busy straightening up. Then she flashed him a smile.

"And to my surprise and pleasure, Mrs. Donelson accepted the offer. She's a widow with no children and is excited about coming to Denver."

"Getting this kind of quality personnel will really help the hospital," Breanna said.

"Your brother-in-law feels the same way. Since he's going to be chief administrator, I've been wiring the information on all the nurses to him for his approval. He likes them all, but he's especially happy about Mary."

Breanna pondered what she had heard for a few seconds, then said, "Even with me included, Doctor, aren't you one nurse short? Two from Kansas City, three from New York, and two from Philadelphia. That makes eight of us."

"Oh! I forgot to mention that Dr. Carroll has his eye on a C.M.N. who works at San Francisco's City Hospital and also works for him at the asylum on her off days. As of yesterday he hadn't talked to her yet, but if she'll accept the job, he and Dottie will bring her with them when they come. He tells me she's young, single, and very dedicated to her work."

Breanna smiled. "Well, if Matt—Dr. Carroll—likes her, you can be sure she's good at her work. But what if she doesn't want the job?"

"Then Dr. Carroll says he has some other ones in mind. If he should hit a snag with all of them, he'll let me know. He's supposed to wire me within a day or two and let me know if his number-one choice accepts the offer."

Breanna looked toward heaven and said aloud, "Thank You, Lord, for making it possible for Dottie and her family to move to Denver!"

"Amen to that," John said. "I can't wait to meet them."

Dr. Goodwin left Letha Phillips and Missy O'Day to look after the clinic long enough to drive John and Breanna to her small cottage behind the Goodwin house.

John unloaded Breanna's luggage, leaving her with Martha Goodwin, who loved Breanna like a daughter. Then Goodwin drove John to the hotel where he always stayed while in town, and returned to the clinic.

After placing his luggage in the hotel room, John went to the stable where he had boarded his black gelding, Ebony, since leaving for Montana several weeks previously. Ebony had sustained a bullet wound when an outlaw tried to kill John from ambush. The magnificent animal was healing well and was glad to see his master.

From there, he walked to the office of Chief U.S. Marshal Solomon Duvall at the Federal Building on Tremont Street. John often took assignments from Duvall without compensation when the chief was low on deputies and high on outlaws. Duvall liked to have the man in black working for him. He never failed to get the job done.

Duvall welcomed John into his office and wanted to hear the details of his time in Montana. Duvall was happy to know that every one of the gang members John had caught had either been hanged or was behind bars in the Montana Territorial Prison at Deer Lodge.

John tilted back his flat-crowned hat and exposed a thick head of coal-black hair with tiny slivers of gray. "How's the U.S. marshal business these days, Chief?"

"Tougher than ever, John. Seems we're getting more law-breakers in the West all the time. A lot of them are men who fought in the Civil War and can't seem to settle down to a normal life. They got used to violence, and even though it's been five years since Lee and Grant met at Appomattox, many of them can't seem to live without it. I wouldn't care if they'd just kill each other off, but instead they rob and maim and kill decent, innocent people."

Stranger nodded. He knew full well what Duvall was talking about.

"Right now I've got a red-hot one on my hands. There needs to be a man-hunt for a killer on the loose in western Kansas or eastern Colorado. But I can't spare even one deputy to hunt him down."

"Tell me about him."

Duvall leaned forward, placing his elbows on the desk. "You have any immediate plans, John?"

"Got some friends I need to see up in the mountains. But tell me about this killer."

"Well, I received word a week ago from the Kansas City U.S. Marshal's office that a fugitive named William Gregg is headed this way. He's wanted on several counts of murder in some states back east and in some of the states and territories out here…including California. His killing record goes back about twenty years."

"Twenty years and he's never been caught?"

"Nope. He's slick."

"How does the Kansas City office know Gregg's headed this way?"

"Chief Blaine says he has three sources, but they wish to remain anonymous. They fear for their lives."

"I can understand that."

"From the report I received, Gregg has been known to use aliases. He could be using one right now."

"Do you have a picture of him?"

"No, there are none available, but I have a brief description of him from the Kansas City office."

Duvall lifted a two-page telegram from the desk and hooked half-moon spectacles behind his ears. "He stands about five-ten and is thick-bodied and muscular. He's now in his early fifties, is known to wear a handlebar mustache, and has dark hair sprinkled with gray.

"Says here that Gregg is quick-tempered and plenty dangerous when he's angry. He's been known to gamble heavily. Most of the men he's murdered—those the law knows about, anyway—have been professional gamblers. Says here that Gregg has tried to make it as a professional gambler but lacks the finesse to come out on top at poker or other card games."

Stranger chuckled. "Some guys just aren't cut out for it, but they keep trying and end up in debt, either to another gambler or to the owners of the casinos and saloons."

"Funny you should say that." Duvall shifted to the second page of the telegram while looking into Stranger's gunmetal gray eyes. "It says here that he's killed several saloon and casino owners, blaming them for cheating him at the gaming tables.

Twice he's killed lawmen who tried to arrest him. And bear in mind, these are the killings we know about."

"I don't have any sympathy for people in the saloon and casino business," Stranger said, "but this bird has to be stopped."

"My sentiments exactly." Duvall rose from his desk and stepped to a cabinet. He returned with a handful of orange-colored posters. "These arrived this morning by rail from the Kansas City office."

Stranger read the top poster, which gave a description of William Gregg exactly as the telegram had described him. It also listed the names of the men he had murdered, including the two law officers he had killed. Stranger counted twenty-four men. "Too bad they don't have a picture of him."

"Yes. He'd be a lot easier to catch." Duvall looked down at his friend. "John..."

Stranger grinned up at him. "Okay, what do you want me to do?"

"Can your friends in the mountains wait?"

"Looks like they're going to have to. When you give me that wounded coyote look, I know you're desperate."

Solomon Duvall's time-seamed features broke into a broad smile. "I want you to ride from town to town in western Kansas and eastern Colorado with the posters and leave them wherever people gather. There are plenty more in the cupboard. Talk to local lawmen and ask in saloons and casinos if they've seen a man fitting Gregg's description. Who knows? Maybe you'll pick up his trail. If you do, work with the local law. Get Gregg arrested and bring him to Denver for trial. I'll give you an official letter to carry. Gregg can be tried in Colorado Territory because he killed two professional gamblers in Colorado Springs four years ago."

Stranger rose to his feet, towering over Duvall. "I'll be on my way toward Kansas at first light, Chief. I've been invited for supper at Doc Goodwin's house tonight, which means I can spend a little time with Breanna before I go."

"Can't fault you for that. She's one lovely lady."

Stranger headed for the door and then turned. "Ebony's hip wound is healing up real good, but he's not ready for a long ride yet. I'll need to rent a good horse from the hostler who's keeping him."

"How about letting me pay the rent for the horse?"

Stranger stopped and fixed him with his steady gray gaze.

Duvall threw up his hands. "Okay, okay. I should have known better than to ask."

"See you when I get back."

"And I know you'll have Gregg with you."

"I'll do my best."

It was customary for Breanna to take her meals with the Goodwins when she was in town, and since Missy had moved into the cottage, she too ate with the Goodwins, whether Breanna was home or not.

That evening, after Doc Goodwin had asked John to give thanks for the food, the conversation centered on the fugitive John would pursue at first light. Then Martha Goodwin said she wished, for Missy's sake, Clint could be there.

"Me, too," Missy said. "He's supposed to get a weekend off every month, but sometimes the work demands that he stay."

"Well, he's a fine young man, Missy," John said. "I'm sure glad my sweetheart stayed after him until she won him to the Lord. How's he doing spiritually?"

"Really well." Missy's shiny blond hair reflected light from the lantern chandelier. "Especially since there's no church for him to attend when he's on the line laying track. He reads his Bible every day, and when he does come home for a weekend, he's quoting Scripture and telling me all the things he's learned from the Bible since last we saw each other."

"Glad to hear it. And how's Sheriff Curt Langan doing?"

"Wonderful, John!" Breanna said. "He's growing in the Lord, as is Steve Ridgway, since he got saved. They switch off going to Sunday services. One of them goes on Sunday morning and the other on Sunday night. And Pastor Larribee has taken time to sit down with them during daytime hours at the office and teach them from the Bible."

There was a pause, then Breanna added softly, "My heart goes out to Curt. He's still carrying deep scars over the jolt Sally Jayne—or Morgan—gave him."

"One wicked woman," Missy said, "even if she was my cousin. I remember when my parents died and I went to live with Morgan. What a shock when she admitted she'd killed her father to gain that gold mine. I watched many of the men she'd had kidnapped die, and she didn't care at all. Nothing mattered to Morgan but gold and what it could buy."

"She sure had Curt fooled into thinking she was in love with him," Breanna said.

Missy nodded. "She used to come back from town and tell me how she had the sheriff eating out of her hand."

"I'll never forget the look on his face when he found out that the infamous Mr. Morgan was Sally Jayne," Breanna said. "I was shocked enough, myself, but Curt looked as if he'd seen a ghost. Recently he told me he doesn't know if he'll ever find a woman he can love and trust. He wonders if such a woman is only a dream."

"I know about a woman being a dream," John said, looking at Breanna. "Only this dream is real. Curt will find the right one when it's God's time."

Dr. Goodwin looked at Breanna with concern. "How's the arm feeling?"

"It's sore, but not too bad. It'll be better in a couple of days. John, maybe if I said it was hurting real bad, you wouldn't leave me tomorrow."

"Don't tempt me, sweetheart."

"But duty calls," Breanna said with a sigh. "And we both know your going after William Gregg is the right thing to do."

5

NURSE STEFANIE ANDREWS puffed a bit as she walked the steep incline of Telegraph Hill. She could see a few people in their tailored yards, and there were some buggies traveling the street. This was Strangler territory, but since it was daytime and people were in view, she felt safe.

It was late morning and the birds were warbling and flitting about the trees. She breathed deeply and murmured, "Even the air smells wealthy!"

Soon she was at the Clifton Harbrook mansion. Her heartbeat increased as she turned into the circular driveway that curved past the wide pillared porch and then returned to the street. There were four hitching posts at the porch, each with a lion's head on it. At the sides of the wide double doors, on pedestals, were marble statues of life-sized lions that seemed to watch her approach.

Stefanie mounted the steps and reached for the huge door knocker—the head of a lion in solid brass. She lifted the knocker and let it fall, its sound echoing across the yard.

Seconds later the door swung inward. A tall, thin, bland-looking man in his late sixties looked at her with pale eyes. He was dressed in a trim black suit with a stiff, high-collared white shirt and bow tie. He barely moved his mouth as he said, "Yes, mum?"

"Good morning, sir. My name is Stefanie Andrews. I'm a friend of Lucy Campbell's. Is she in?"

The butler almost smiled. "Oh. You're the nurse who took such good care of Miss Lucy. She has told me all about you. Please come in. I believe Miss Lucy is cleaning the kitchen. My name is Charles, mum."

"Happy to make your acquaintance, Charles." Stefanie moved past him into a broad vestibule.

"Please wait here, Miss Andrews. I will fetch Miss Lucy. Why don't you sit on the loveseat."

Charles disappeared down the hallway, leaving Stefanie to gaze in wonderment at her surroundings—the tapestried walls and paintings, the massive crystal chandelier. She felt as if she were in a king's palace.

Stefanie stood up as Lucy entered the vestibule with a stately woman at her side. Lucy wore a black dress with high neck, and a white pinafore.

"Stefanie!" Lucy opened her arms for an embrace.

"How is my favorite ex-patient?"

"Very well, thank you. It's so good to see you." Lucy released her and turned to the well-dressed woman by her side. "Mrs. Harbrook, I want you to meet Nurse Stefanie Andrews."

LeAnne Harbrook wore her long auburn hair parted in the center and swept into a sleek chignon at the nape of her neck. Her blue-and-white day dress was quite fashionable with open neck, high collar in the back, and sleeves that reached to the middle of her forearms.

She extended a prim hand. "Stefanie, we've heard so much about you from Lucy. To what do we owe this most welcome visit?"

"I just wanted to come by and see Lucy for a few minutes. If I've come at an inconvenient time…"

"Of course not. Let's go to the library and sit down. May I offer you some tea? It would only take a few minutes for Lucy to—"

"Thank you, but no," Stefanie said, with a smile. "I can only stay a few minutes."

They moved past the dining room where sunlight streamed through lace curtains and glistened brightly on the large mahogany dining table with matching chairs. A glass cabinet held elaborate china and crystal beneath another sophisticated chandelier.

Soon they passed through a wide door into the library. A rosewood grand piano stood in one corner next to a tall window adorned with crimson drapes and off-white sheer curtains. There was a huge walnut desk with stuffed leather chair in another corner and an intricately carved sofa midway on the inside wall. Brocade wing-backed chairs stood opposite the sofa with matching footstools. Directly in front of the sofa was a low walnut table.

The massive stone fireplace at the far end of the library was flanked with floor-to-ceiling bookshelves loaded with hundreds of volumes.

Mrs. Harbrook gestured for the nurse and housekeeper to sit together on the sofa while she took one of the wing-backed chairs.

"Stefanie, I appreciate what you've done for Lucy," Mrs. Harbrook said. "Her ordeal with the Strangler was so…horrible, but you seem to have nursed her through it with such compassion and tender care. You truly have found your calling in life."

"Thank you, Mrs. Harbrook. It has been my pleasure to care for Lucy."

"And speaking of the Strangler," Mrs. Harbrook said, "did you hear there was another young woman strangled on Russian Hill last night?"

Stefanie's face paled. "Yes. It's terrible. From what I heard early this morning, the police are in a frenzy. The Strangler seems to strike at will, no matter how many officers they have in the area. My landlady had already read the morning paper when I met her in the hall this morning. She said that even more officers will be on the two hills starting tonight."

Lucy shuddered with the memory of her own assault. "Oh, they've got to catch that beast before he kills again."

"I pray so," Stefanie said. "So far you're the only one of his victims who isn't dead. Your voice sounds almost normal. I'm glad there's no permanent damage. And your rope burns are healing all right."

"Yes, thank the Lord."

Stefanie rose to her feet. "Well, I really need to get going. Thank you for letting me see you."

"Thank you for coming by," Mrs. Harbrook said. She then excused herself, saying that she would let Lucy show Stefanie out. She invited Stefanie to come by anytime.

While the newfound friends walked toward the door, Lucy said, "Thank you, again, Stefanie, for leading me to Jesus. I'll look forward to seeing you at First Congregational Church on Sunday."

"And this Sunday is a special day at our church, too."

"Oh?"

"Have you heard of the evangelist, Dwight L. Moody?"

"Why, yes. Isn't he associated with the Young Men's Christian Association in Chicago? He used to be a shoe salesman in Boston, then became a preacher."

"That's right. He's preaching at our church this Sunday

morning and evening. I know his words will be a great help to you as a newborn child of God."

"Well, then, I'm looking forward to it even more."

At 1:45 P.M., Stefanie arrived at City Hospital for her shift. Alex Baker and Harry Mitchell had arrived just ahead of her and were talking to a pretty receptionist. Stefanie greeted all three and started to move on when the receptionist said, "Oh, Miss Andrews! I have a message for you."

Stefanie halted and approached the desk. Before she could speak, Alex said, "Walk you home as usual tonight, Stefanie?"

"Of course," she said and smiled.

Harry elbowed his friend and winked. "When you gonna ask her to marry you, Alex?"

Baker flushed and ducked his head.

"Harry!" Stefanie scolded. "You shouldn't talk that way to Alex. We're just good friends. You've embarrassed him."

"Well, you may be a few years older than him, Stefanie, but he's got a mountain-sized crush on you, and if you could only hear how he talks about you—"

"Harry, just leave it alone, okay?" Alex growled.

Mitchell laughed and moved on down the hall.

"I'm sorry, Stefanie," Alex said, in a low tone. "He's just got a big mouth."

"It's all right," she replied, patting his arm. Then she turned to the receptionist. "You said you have a message for me."

"Yes. From Dr. Carroll. He was here tending a patient a couple of hours ago. He said to tell you he'd be by this evening sometime between seven and eight o'clock. He wants to talk to you. Said it's important."

↑

At 7:30 that evening, Dr. Matthew Carroll entered City Hospital and found head nurse Isabel Grady in conversation with Dr. Patterson at the nurse's station.

"Isabel," he said, "I left a message for Stefanie Andrews earlier in the day, telling her I'd be by about this time to see her. I need a few minutes to talk to her. Do you think she'll have time?"

Isabel smiled warmly. "I'm sure we can arrange a few minutes, Doctor. Why don't you wait here and chat with Dr. Patterson, and I'll find Stefanie."

"Thank you."

The two physicians began talking about what was on everyone's mind—the Strangler's latest victim.

"That makes nine so far," Patterson said. "Eight dead."

"Well," Carroll said, "maybe putting an army of men in blue on those hills at night will result in the madman's capture. I sure hope so. This horror has got to stop."

"Seems like the police ought to dress an officer up as a woman and use him as a decoy," Patterson mumbled. "Maybe that's the way to catch him."

"Good idea. Why don't you go to police headquarters—"

"Stefanie says she'll be free in about five minutes, Dr. Carroll," cut in Isabel Grady. "She said she'd meet you at office number two."

"Fine. Thank you."

Dr. Patterson and the head nurse picked up their conversation where they'd left off, and Dr. Carroll headed down the hall to the small cubicles that served as offices.

Stefanie was coming out of a room farther down the hall. She gave Dr. Carroll a little "see you in a minute wave," then disappeared into another room. Two minutes later she emerged and headed toward the doctor.

"Busy night, eh?" Dr. Carroll said.

"Oh, just about routine. What did you want to talk to me about?"

"Let's sit down first," he said gesturing for her to enter the office. "I'm looking forward to Sunday, aren't you?"

"You mean hearing Mr. Moody?"

"Uh-huh."

"I sure am! And Doctor, I have some good news. I haven't seen you since Lucy Campbell was in here. I had the joy of leading her to the Lord!"

"Oh, Stefanie, that's wonderful!"

"And she's coming to church Sunday!"

"Stefanie, I can't tell you how pleased I am that you have such a burden for lost souls. What a joy to watch someone I've led to Jesus become a soulwinner! I'm so proud of you I could burst."

"Thank you, Dr. Carroll. I didn't know what the Christian life was really all about until I started witnessing for Jesus. What a delight to tell others about Him." Stefanie paused and cocked her head. "What did you want to talk to me about?"

Dr. Carroll cleared his throat nervously. "Stefanie, I...I'm resigning my position at the asylum and removing myself as a staff physician here. I'm going to be leaving San Francisco."

A tremor rocked Stefanie as Dr. Carroll's words registered in her mind. She loved this man who had led her to the Lord, and she loved Dottie and the children. She had gotten very close to James and Molly Kate.

Her mouth felt like cotton and her throat tightened. "But what are you going to do? Where are you going?"

"I've been offered the opportunity of a lifetime, Stefanie.

Denver, Colorado, as you may know, is a thriving, fast-growing town. Up to now, they've not had a hospital. But one is under construction. I've been hired as chief administrator of the hospital. Dottie and the children are very happy about it, not only for my career's sake, but Dottie's sister, Breanna, makes her home there. You remember Breanna."

"Yes, of course. A sweet Christian and an excellent nurse. I really liked her." Tears welled up and Stefanie's lower lip quivered as she said, "Dr. Carroll, I…I'm very happy for you. And for Dottie and the kids. I'm going to miss all of you terribly. When will you be leaving?"

"We plan to take the train from San Francisco to Denver on August twenty-first, which is only two weeks away. My departure won't be made public until this coming Monday. You're special to me and my family. I…I wanted to let you know before then."

Stefanie could no longer keep from weeping.

"Stefanie, I'm sorry to upset you. I—"

She shook her head and brushed tears from her cheeks. "Please don't blame yourself, Doctor. It's just that my life has been shaken so hard before. You and Dottie and those precious children have become my family since I became a Christian…and now I'm losing all of you, too. It's almost more than I can bear."

Dr. Carroll stood up and said, "Stefanie…I have one more thing to talk about. How would you like to move to Denver with us?"

"Move? To Denver?"

"Yes."

"What do you mean?"

"I mean you've got a job in Denver's new hospital if you want it."

"Me?"

"Yes, you! The board of Mile High Hospital is presently hiring nurses. Since I'm the new chief administrator, I've had to approve of each one before she was officially hired. Dr. Lyle Goodwin, who heads up the board, has sent me every application by wire. Believe me, we've kept Western Union in business!

"As it stands right now, we need one more good Certified Medical Nurse to complete the nursing staff for opening the hospital. I've already told Dr. Goodwin that I had an excellent nurse in mind to bring with me. He's waiting to hear whether you're coming or not. The pay would be exactly the same as here. And the cost of living is lower in Denver."

"You...you're formally offering me the job?"

"Yes, ma'am. It's yours if you'll take it."

A wide smile spread over her face. She popped her hands together and exclaimed, "Then I'll take it!"

"Good! Now, let me explain something. I've already obtained permission from the board of directors here to offer you the job. They reluctantly granted permission, but they don't want to lose you."

"Well, I'm glad to know they'd like to keep me around, but if I can work for you and be around Dottie and those wonderful kids, nothing short of a herd of wild elephants could keep me from going to Denver with you!"

"There's no herd of wild elephants within twelve thousand miles of here, so I guess I can tell the board you're going to Denver."

"You sure can! And I'll give notice at my boarding house right away that I'll be leaving August twenty-first!"

"All right, Nurse Andrews, you're hired! I'll wire Dr. Goodwin tomorrow and tell him our nursing staff is complete for opening Mile High Hospital. I...ah...I guess I'd better tell you that until we get the hospital going good, you'll have to work seven days a week. We'll rotate the shifts, though, so you can attend church either Sunday morning or Sunday night. You'll be paid extra for no days off. Still want the job?"

"Oh, yes!"

Dr. Carroll smiled and said, "I can't tell you how happy I am to know you'll be on my staff in Denver."

"Not as happy as I am." Stefanie thought a brief moment, then said, "Do Dottie and the kids know about this offer of yours?"

"Dottie knows, and right now she's on pins and needles at home, praying that you'll say yes. Now I can go home and tell everybody the good news. Oh! By the way..."

"Yes?"

"Dottie wanted me to ask if you would come to dinner with us after church on Sunday."

"I'd love to, Doctor, but I've only missed one Sunday eating dinner with you in the past month. Aren't the Carrolls getting tired of me horning in?"

"You are not horning in, young lady," he assured her. "We want you to come. Okay?"

"Okay."

He moved toward the hallway and then looked back over his shoulder. "I'll tell Dottie you'll be there. Molly Kate and that boy who hopes you'll wait till he grows up so he can marry you will be ecstatic when they find out you're going to Denver with us."

"Nobody's as ecstatic about it as I am, Doctor, but the way it's going for me, maybe I will be available when James is old enough to get married!"

Dr. Carroll laughed and started down the hall. He took less

than half a dozen steps before wheeling about. Stefanie was standing in the office doorway, looking at him with tears in her eyes. "Oh, one other thing," he said.

"Yes?"

"Dottie and I already discussed it. If you agreed to go to Denver with us, we'd pay for your railroad ticket."

"You wonderful people! I love all of you!"

"We love you, too," he responded warmly, then turned to leave.

"Doctor Carroll!" she called.

He turned to face her.

"Thank you...for everything."

"You're as welcome as the flowers in May, little gal," he said, then turned and walked away.

With a happy heart and a spring in her step, Stefanie went on with her duties, moving in and out of the rooms, taking care of her patients.

It was about an hour before the end of her shift when she met Alex and Harry, who were wheeling two small boys to surgery. Stefanie could smell burnt skin.

She watched them pass into the surgical wing, then went on about her business. Ten minutes later, she passed the doors to the surgical wing when the two attendants came out, pushing their carts.

"How bad are they?" she asked.

"Hair singed and hands burned pretty badly," Harry replied. "Dr. Patterson says they'll be able to use their hands again, but it'll be a while."

"How did it happen?"

"The boys were imitating their fathers when no one was looking—smoking cigarettes their fathers had pre-rolled. One dropped a lighted match into some cigarette papers. They tried to put the fire out with their hands."

Stefanie shook her head. "When will people learn that tobacco is a curse on the human race?"

Alex looked at the big clock on the hall wall. "Fifty-eight minutes, Stefanie. Meet you at the front door, as usual."

"Okay!"

Alex studied her eyes. "What're you so happy about?"

"Oh, I just got some wonderful news!"

"Well, tell me!"

"I can't share it with you right now. It has to remain a secret for a few days."

"There shouldn't be secrets between two people in love," Harry said.

Alex wheeled on him, eyes flashing. "Harry, I told you to shut your trap! C'mon. We've got work to do."

She waved them off, smiling, and headed the opposite way down the hall. Certainly Alex Baker knew that all they could ever be were friends. Besides, she was moving to Denver.

6

"MRS. KETTERING, WHY DIDN'T YOU USE the bell beside you to call a nurse?"

Stefanie held the hand of an elderly patient, who had fallen while trying to get out of bed, as Dr. Patterson examined her.

Elma Kettering gritted her teeth in pain. "I just didn't want to bother anybody."

"But that's what we're here for. Don't ever hesitate to call us for help. Understand?"

"Yes. I won't try to get out of bed by myself again."

"That's a good girl."

"Doctor—" came Isabel Grady's voice from the doorway.

"Yes?"

"Dr. Jeffrey Lynch's teenage son just came in to advise you that Dr. Lynch won't be able to work his shift tonight. He fell off a ladder this afternoon and sprained an ankle. Should I send one of the attendants for another doctor to take the shift?"

"No, I'll work it."

"But, Doctor, you're tired."

"Maybe we'll have a slow night and I can get some rest right here. Don't worry, I'll be fine."

"All right, sir." She nodded and left.

Dr. Patterson pulled Elma Kettering's gown over her hip and drew the covers up. "I don't think the hip is broken, Elma," he said. "We'll know more in a couple of days, but I'm pretty sure it's all right."

"Thank you, Doctor."

"Nurse Andrews will give you some powders to ease the pain and help you sleep." Then he, too, was gone.

Stefanie administered the powders and headed for the lobby to meet Alex Baker. When she rounded the corner by the reception desk, she saw Dr. Patterson and Alex helping two policemen place a bleeding man on a cart. Stefanie could see a police wagon out front.

Stefanie ran toward them and heard one officer say, "—stabbed in a saloon fight on the Barbary Coast, Doctor. We brought him as fast as we could."

An attendant who had just come on duty appeared as Dr. Patterson was telling Alex to wheel the man to surgery.

"I'll take him, Doctor. It's time for Alex to go home."

Patterson nodded, then called to Pauline Wilson, the head nurse for the new shift. "Mrs. Wilson, this man's been stabbed. Get him ready for surgery. I'll be right there."

"Yes, Doctor." Pauline hurried alongside the cart as the patient was wheeled away on the run.

"I guess we can go, if you're ready, Stefanie," Alex said.

Stefanie turned to Patterson. "Doctor, if you need me, I'll stay and help. Mrs. Wilson's going to have her hands full for the next half hour. I'll be glad to stay."

Dr. Patterson gestured to stand by for a moment, then turned to the policemen and told them he wanted the man's family contacted as soon as possible. The officers assured him they would take care of the matter.

Patterson turned back to Stefanie. "All right, you can stay

and assist me. I'll take her home when we're done with the surgery, Alex. You go on."

"Yes, sir," Alex said. "Good night, sir. Good night, Stefanie."

The operating room smelled strongly of ether mixed with whiskey breath. Stefanie made sure the man stayed under, while supplying Dr. Patterson with proper instruments, dabbing perspiration from his brow, and sponging up blood. After nearly an hour, Stefanie saw Patterson slowly shake his head.

"Complications, Doctor?"

"I'm afraid so. The chest wounds aren't so bad. They didn't go too deep. But it appears the knife went full-haft into his stomach. He's bleeding profusely internally and I can't get it stopped."

"All you can do is try."

Patterson nodded silently.

Suddenly there was no more rise and fall of the patient's chest.

"Doctor," Stefanie said, "he's quit breathing."

"See if you can get a pulse."

Stefanie placed her fingers on the side of the man's neck. "No, sir."

Patterson ran a sleeve across his sweaty brow, laid down the instrument in his hand, and removed his mask.

"You did all you could," Stefanie said. "I'll cover the body and have it removed to the corpse room. An undertaker can pick it up tomorrow. You go ahead and wash up."

Fifteen minutes later, Dr. Patterson was giving instructions to Pauline Wilson in case the man's family came to the hospital while he was driving Stefanie home.

"I'll handle it if they come, Doctor," Pauline assured him.

"Thanks. I'll only be gone a few minutes. Ready, Stefanie?"

"Yes, sir."

They were almost to the lobby when two attendants came around the corner in a hurry, wheeling a cart. A nurse named Nan Jones was moving along with it, holding the hand of a young woman whose face was smeared with blood.

"What was that you said earlier about maybe this being a slow night, Doctor?"

Patterson groaned. Then he rushed up to the cart and said, "What is it, Miss Jones?"

"Her husband beat her up and shoved her out a third-story window. She may have internal injuries."

"All right. Get her to the examining room. I'll be right there. Are you free to assist me?"

"Yes."

"Good. Go!"

As the cart disappeared around the corner, Patterson turned to Stefanie and said, "I'll get one of the attendants to walk you home."

"That won't be necessary, Doctor. I'll walk home by myself."

"Oh, no you won't. Not while the Bay Area Strangler is on the loose."

"I'm not afraid. He's limited his crimes to Telegraph Hill and Russian Hill. This is the center of town. I'll be all right."

Patterson set his jaw, shaking his head. "No. It's not good that a woman walk these streets alone at night, even without a killer on the loose. I've got to go see about that battered woman. Please. Let me send one of the attendants to escort you home."

"Doctor, I'll be all right. It's only three blocks."

"I don't like it, Stefanie," he said, heading toward the hallway, "but there's no more time to argue. You be careful."

When the physician had vanished around the corner, Stefanie squared her shoulders and exited the lobby. A cold breeze off San Francisco Bay blew along the street and raised goose bumps on her skin.

Downtown San Francisco was lighted better at night than the residential areas. Although the downtown blocks were almost half again as long as those in the residential areas, there were lanterns spaced a hundred feet apart on both sides of the streets. But even this spacing left dark areas midway between the lamps.

When Stefanie entered the first dark area, she felt the urge to turn back. Maybe she should have a male escort. She looked back toward the bold outline of the hospital against the sky.

At that moment, the clip-clop of hooves on cobblestone met her ears and stole the fear that had begun to play on her mind. A taxi had just entered the street and she could see its dual lanterns glowing in the night.

She drew a deep breath and resumed her normal pace, muttering, "Stef, get a move on. Nobody's going to bother you."

Soon the taxi passed her and the street grew quiet, except for the sound of her own soft footsteps. She was just passing through another dark spot when she saw a meat wagon from the packing house down by the bay cross the intersection up ahead.

She passed under the next street lamp, eyeing the distance to the cross-street ahead. After that she was almost halfway home.

She reached the next dark spot and kept up her steady

pace, letting her eyes roam the area around her. On both sides of the street were stores and office buildings. Their dark windows picked up the soft glow of the street lamps and reminded her of staring eyes.

"Lord," she whispered, "I know I'm not supposed to be afraid with You watching over me. Help me. Only two-and-a-half blocks to the boarding house. Just stay close, all right?"

The next block had apartment houses at the far end. She would feel safer in that area. There were people inside—people who would come to her rescue if someone tried to attack her. She hadn't screamed since she was a child, but she was sure she could do it if necessary.

She was in a lighted area now, and another taxi was on the street, this time coming toward her. She could see the first cross-street. Only one more dark area before she would be under two street lamps at the corner.

As the taxi went by, the driver gave her a long look, as if wondering why a young woman would be out on the street alone at this time of night.

Suddenly her attention was drawn to a shadowy form angling across the street at the corner. At first it looked like a young boy, but as he drew closer she saw that it was a young man, powerfully built, wearing an open-necked shirt. She was near the corner, and he was about to step onto the sidewalk. If he slowed his pace at all they would meet face-to-face before she could start across the street.

A quivering panic rose within her. There was nothing she could do but get ready to scream if the young man made a move toward her.

The night breeze whipped along the street and filled her ears with a faint whine that played on her nerves. She kept her gaze straight ahead as she came under the light of the corner street lamp, but she watched the man from her peripheral vision.

When they were but a few steps apart, he touched the bill of his cap, smiled, and said hello. He passed on by and headed in the direction she had come from. She sneaked a look back and saw that he was moving into one of the dark areas with his back to her.

She sighed and quickened her pace slightly. Any faster and she would be running.

As she moved back into a spray of lamplight, she saw a man and woman come out of an apartment house several doors ahead and climb into a waiting buggy. The simple sound of horses' hooves echoing along the street comforted her. Then the buggy turned the corner and the clip-clop of the hooves died out.

Suddenly she heard the sound of steady, measured footsteps keeping pace with her own. She imagined whoever it was to be about forty feet behind. *Where did he come from?*

Stefanie's mouth had gone dry and her legs ached. But she kept her pace and soon reached the corner. She crossed the street, hoping…praying that the footsteps would begin to fade as the man took another direction.

No…he was following her across the street.

Turn around and stare him in the face! Stefanie told herself. But she couldn't bring herself to do it.

When she reached the opposite corner, the footsteps seemed to quicken.

Why doesn't he slow down? Doesn't he know he's frightening me?

Maybe…maybe it's that young man I saw back there. Maybe he decided to offer to escort me to my destination. Certainly he isn't the Strangler. He was so polite.

She *must* turn and look! She had to see him! She gulped a deep, shaky breath and prepared to look over her shoulder. Suddenly the man's footsteps slowed and quickly faded.

She licked her dry lips and looked back without breaking stride. He must have slipped between two buildings. No doubt he lived in one of the apartment buildings. The entrance to his apartment must be on the alley.

Relief washed over her as she continued to walk. She could see the outline of the boarding house at the other end of the block. Just a minute more and she would be home.

Her nerves were just beginning to settle down when the same measured footsteps sounded behind her.

Stefanie's head whipped around. The man had stepped into shadow between street lamps, but she could tell he was stocky and not much taller than herself.

She felt the hair rise on the nape of her neck. She broke into a run and glanced back again. When the man came under the next street lamp, she could tell he was not the young man she had seen earlier. He wore no cap, and he was older—maybe in his forties.

Then she saw a length of rope in his right hand.

Raw terror rose in her throat, but she couldn't scream. She felt as though she was dreaming the kind of nightmare where someone chases you and your legs are so heavy you can hardly lift them.

Only this was not a dream.

Her pursuer drew up just as she looked back again. He lunged, but she dodged to one side, avoiding his hands.

He ejected an animal-like growl and she could see cold madness in his eyes.

When she finally did scream, the sound came out in a shrill, piercing wail that echoed down the dark street. She was at the iron picketed fence in front of her boarding house. She could see the lantern burning above the door.

She rounded the corner of the fence, and her pursuer touched her back. She screamed with all her might as she struggled toward the porch. She could see lantern and candle-light from a few windows. Someone was still up!

Halfway up the steps she felt the Strangler's hot breath on her neck as he tried to bring the rope over her head.

She clawed at his eyes, causing him to stumble back slightly, and started up the steps again. He grabbed her ankle. She dropped to a sitting position on the steps and kicked at his face, raking it with her heel.

He howled and let go of her ankle, throwing his hands to his face.

She scrambled to her feet and stepped up to the porch. He reached for her again.

In desperation, she lunged at him. Her head struck his chest and staggered him backward. One foot slipped over the porch's edge, and he fell at an angle toward the iron fence.

There was a strange, sodden sound as he impaled himself on a picket. The picket protruded from his left shoulder, dangling him a few feet from the ground.

Alex Baker was one of the first men out the door, and he rushed to comfort a gasping, disheveled Stefanie. Then he spotted the length of rope lying halfway down the stairs and hurried to pick it up.

STEFANIE STOOD FROZEN to the spot as people came out of the boarding house, and doors and windows opened all along the street. People gathered, many in their robes and some carrying lanterns.

Stefanie's pulse pounded in her ears. It was not loud enough, however, to drown out the screams of the Strangler, who was writhing and kicking frantically, his protruding eyes gaping through pain-widened lids.

"Somebody get the police!" someone yelled.

Two teenage boys took off at a run.

The Strangler's ear-piercing screams suddenly stopped as he lost consciousness. All eyes turned toward the fence.

Stefanie rushed to the limp form and said, "Alex, come help me lift him off the picket! He's going to bleed to death if I don't get it stopped!"

Alex stared at Stefanie as if she had lost her mind. "Why do you want to save his life? I say let him die!"

A man shouted, "Leave him be, Stefanie! He's murdered eight women and tried to murder two others, includin' yourself! Why would you want to save him?"

"Yeah!" called a woman in hair curlers and robe. "Let 'im die! It'll save the county the trouble of hangin' 'im!"

Stefanie scanned their shadowed faces and said, "I'm a nurse! It's my duty to preserve human life, not *take* it!"

"You're not taking it, honey. Just let nature take its course. He'll die all by himself!"

Stefanie wheeled about. "Please!" she begged. "Somebody help me!"

Another female voice cut the night air. "Hey! Even if you save his rotten hide, he'll die at the end of a rope!"

"I know that! But I must do all I can to save this man's life right now!"

When no one came forward to help, Stefanie tried to lift the heavy body off the picket by herself. She soon realized the impossibility of her task. She pushed back her hair with bloodied hands and faced the crowd with blazing eyes. "It's up to the law to execute this man, not us! If you won't help me save his life, you are murderers, too!"

Alex tucked the length of hemp rope under his belt and turned to the crowd. "C'mon, men! Help me get him off the picket! Stefanie's right. If we have it in our power to save this man's life, as worthless as it is, and we don't do it, we *are* guilty of murder. We're no better than he is."

Suddenly Alex Baker had more help than he needed, and the unconscious Strangler was lifted by strong hands and laid on the ground.

Stefanie knelt beside him and tried to compress his wound. She glanced toward the porch, looking for her landlady. "Myrtle, I need towels to help stay the flow of blood!"

"It'll ruin my towels!"

"I'll buy you new ones. Please don't argue with me! I'm trying to save a human life, here!"

"I'll get the towels," Myrtle called, heading for the door, "but I still say you should let the dirty scum die! If he'd had his way, you'd be lyin' dead on this porch right now!"

Stefanie did not reply. She was too engrossed in doing all she could to keep the unconscious man from bleeding to death.

Alex took the towels from Myrtle and knelt beside Stefanie, who began to make compresses.

"Nurse Andrews," Alex said, "I'd bet there wouldn't be one nurse out of a thousand who would have your attitude toward a man who'd tried to kill her."

"You remember all those talks I've had with you when you've walked me home?"

"You mean...about being saved?"

"Yes. Well, Alex, being a born-again Christian is more than just being saved from hell and the wrath of God; it's taking on the mind of Christ. As a nurse, but even more as a Christian, I must do everything in my power to save this man's life because that's what Jesus would have me to do."

Alex shook his head in wonderment. "I'll say this, Stefanie. If there's such a thing as a real Christian, you are it."

Clattering hooves pounded the cobblestones as a police wagon charged down the street. A pair of officers leaped from the vehicle before the puffing and snorting animals came to a full stop. When they reached the spot where Stefanie and Alex knelt beside the unconscious man, one of them recognized Stefanie. "Miss Andrews, these boys told us this is the Bay Area Strangler, and that he tried to kill you!"

"He's the Strangler, all right," Alex said, pulling the rope from under his belt. "Here's the rope he tried to kill her with!"

"Is he still alive?"

"Yes," Stefanie said. "Let's get him to the hospital!"

The other officer looked at the Strangler's features in the dim light of a lantern. Bending closer, he said, "Give me some more light here." Several people crowded in with their lanterns.

"Sure enough, I *do* know him," the officer said. "His name's Burton Meade. He's caretaker for that rich banker who lives up on Telegraph Hill. The one from Europe. Uh... Wilhelm Von Brunner."

"Oh, yeah? So Von Brunner's caretaker is the Strangler. Wait till Von Brunner finds out!"

"Please!" Stefanie said. "Let's get him to the hospital!"

Dr. Patterson and the hospital staff on duty were stunned to know they were treating the Bay Area Strangler, and that he had tried to kill Stefanie. Their admiration for her grew when Alex explained how she had fought back and caused the Strangler to fall and impale himself on the iron picket.

Meade was taken to surgery immediately, accompanied by a police officer who would stay close. The other officer told Stefanie he would return to headquarters and make a report. The chief of police would want to talk to her first thing in the morning.

Stefanie rubbed her tired eyes. "What time is 'first thing', sir?"

"Chief Harrigan is in his office by eight o'clock. Would that be too early?"

"Not if I can get to bed within another hour or so," she said. "Right now I'm pretty tired...and I've got to take a bath."

"How about we send a taxi by the boarding house at 7:45?"

"That will be fine," she said.

"And another thing..."

"Yes?"

"There will be reporters at the police station in the morning. They'll be wanting an interview, and they'll have a photographer with them."

"Oh. I hadn't thought about the newspapers."

"You can see why, though, can't you? This Strangler is San Francisco's most notorious criminal. You brought his killing career to an end tonight. You'll be a celebrity, ma'am."

Stefanie shook her head and sighed.

"I know they'll want you dressed in your nurse's outfit and your cap for the pictures."

"All right," she said, wearily. "I'll come properly attired."

The usual morning fog hung over San Francisco as the taxi rolled to a halt in front of police headquarters. The fog was thinning already, however, and the sun's rays were starting to shine through the mists.

Stefanie had slept well, and except for a slight nervousness she felt fine.

There were four men waiting on the curb next to two uniformed police officers—a reporter from each of San Francisco's newspapers. A man with camera and flash equipment stood a few steps behind them.

As promised, Stefanie was clad in a pink dress with starched white pinafore and white cap. The pink and white combination made her silky black hair look even darker.

While the taxi driver helped Stefanie from the vehicle, a well-dressed man emerged from the police building, wearing a badge on his vest. "Miss Andrews?"

"Yes…"

"I'm Captain Fallone. I'm to escort you to Chief Harrigan's office."

The reporters moved close, forming a semicircle. The man with the camera followed.

"Ma'am," said the tallest of the four, touching the brim of his hat, "Chief Harrigan has granted us permission to interview you and take a few pictures, if you will allow us the time."

"Only after the chief has finished talking to her," cut in Fallone.

"We understand that, Captain," the reporter said. "I just wanted to ask Miss Andrews if she will give us the interview."

"I'll be glad to."

"Thank you, ma'am. We'll be waiting outside the chief's office. There's a room where we can meet, just down the hall."

Police Chief Harvey Harrigan rose to his feet when Captain Fallone led Stefanie into his office. He was a big, beefy Irishman with rosy cheeks and eyelids that drooped at the corners.

After Fallone had introduced the two, Stefanie was offered a chair. A young police officer in plain clothes came in to take down her statement.

Then she told the story of how the Strangler had stalked her and finally made his attack, and how she had managed to fight him off. All three men commended her for her courage and quick thinking.

Chief Harrigan's face beamed. "Miss Andrews, all of us here in the department had envisioned catching the Strangler on Telegraph Hill or Russian Hill. Whichever of our men finally captured him would be a hero. Little did we know that a little lady like yourself would render him helpless. You are a genuine heroine, Miss Andrews, and I hope the newspapers write it up that way. You will be a celebrity in this city! It's rather embarrassing, but you did what our police failed to do."

Stefanie blushed. "Chief Harrigan, I have no desire to be a

celebrity. I just want to be known as a nurse who loves her God and loves people."

Captain Fallone leaned toward her. "Well, you certainly proved that last night. People all over your neighborhood are talking about how you were so intent on saving the life of the man who tried to kill you. Only the love of God in a woman's heart and a love for her fellowman could bring about what you did."

"We did some investigating of Burton Meade, ma'am," Harrigan said. "As you already know, he's caretaker for the Von Brunner family on Telegraph Hill."

"Yes."

"The Von Brunners also have a mansion in Switzerland, and have been there for almost a year. They're not expected to return to San Francisco for several more months. Meade has had complete access to the mansion and grounds, so there was no one to observe his wanderings. Thanks to you, Meade has laid hands on his last victim. He'll go to the gallows as soon as he can face a judge and jury."

Stefanie nodded solemnly.

Captain Harrigan rose to his feet. "Well! I guess it's time to turn those reporters loose!"

At 1:40 that afternoon, Stefanie turned off the cobblestone sidewalk and headed for the front doors of City Hospital. She had already seen copies of all four newspapers, which had published special editions late that morning. Her picture was on the front page of each, along with bold headlines declaring that the Bay Area Strangler had been foiled by his intended victim, a nurse from City Hospital. Included in the story was the heart-wrenching account of her effort to save the life of Burton Meade.

Stefanie thought it strange that there were no other hospital employees on the street. Ordinarily, they would be stringing along from both directions, arriving for the early evening shift. The only sign of life was a taxi waiting in front.

When she passed through the door, doctors, nurses, and employees from all three shifts broke into applause and cheered.

Someone else was there, too. Lucy Campbell broke from the group, threw her arms around her friend, and wept. "Oh, Stefanie, I'm so glad you're all right. And I'm so glad he's in custody and will never kill again."

The entire group converged on Stefanie, lauding her for the stand she took to save Meade's life when bystanders would have let him die. Embarrassed by all the acclaim, Stefanie ran her gaze over their faces and said, "Thank you for your kind words. I appreciate how all of you feel. But, please, I'm nobody special. As I told the reporters, I just want to be known as a nurse who loves her God and loves people."

At that moment, Dr. Matthew Carroll came through the lobby door, out of breath. "Sorry I'm late, Stefanie. I...knew about this welcoming party, but...I got delayed...at the asylum. Congratulations on your display of courage. And...let me say that I'm...grateful to our Lord that you're still here with us today!"

More cheers and applause, then those who were coming on duty for the early evening shift had to get to work. Stefanie thanked everyone, then she and Lucy talked privately for a few moments and agreed to meet at church the next day.

When Lucy was gone, Dr. Carroll drew Stefanie aside and said in a low tone, "Since you've endeared yourself even more to the hospital administrator, it's going to be harder than ever to tell him I'm taking you to Denver with me. He'll probably offer to double your salary here."

Stefanie muffled a giggle. "Dr. Carroll, I'm still just Stefanie Andrews, plain and common nurse. It won't be hard to replace me."

"I'm glad you feel that way. I'd hate to go home and tell Dottie and those children you've decided to stay."

"Not a chance! I'm Denver-bound!"

"Whew! Well, I've got to go. The Carrolls will pick you up for church at the regular time."

"I'll be ready. I'm really looking forward to hearing Mr. Moody speak."

"Yes, me too!"

Dr. Carroll hurried away, and Stefanie made for the nurse's station, hoping Isabel Grady would be there. She breathed a sigh of relief to see the head nurse. Sometimes Isabel was hard to track down.

"Well, there's our brave girl!" Isabel said, smiling from ear to ear.

"Yes. I was so brave I almost fainted when the ordeal was over. Nobody but the Lord and I knew that my head was spinning and my heart was about to jump through my chest."

"Well, honey, the main thing is, you're all right."

"I'm fine. Which room is Meade in?"

"I really don't think you ought to subject yourself to that monster's presence yet."

"I appreciate your concern," Stefanie said with a smile, "but seeing him isn't going to bother me."

"Well, that's all you'll be able to do. We're keeping him heavily dosed with laudanum for his pain. He's pretty well comatose most of the time. It'll be a while before he's able to talk. But then, you don't want to talk to him, do you?"

Stefanie hesitated a moment. "Yes, I do."

"Well, I doubt he'll be able to talk until Monday."

"Monday?"

"Mm-hmm. And besides, you won't be working till then, anyway."

"Pardon me?"

"Oh, did I forget to tell you amid all the excitement? Sylvia Henderson came in and volunteered to relieve you for this evening, free of charge. And tomorrow's your day off. So, scoot your little self out the door and go home. After what you've been through, you need a rest. Go on, now."

On Sunday morning, Stefanie sat between James and Molly Kate in church with Lucy and Dr. Carroll. Dottie was in the choir. Everyone was thrilled to see the bearded evangelist on the platform beside Pastor Dorsey Hall. The building was packed to capacity, and chairs had been added down the aisles to seat all who had come to hear Dwight L. Moody.

At announcement time, Pastor Hall reminded the congregation of Stefanie Andrews's ordeal on Friday night. He asked Stefanie to stand, and the crowd gave her a rousing ovation.

There were two more congregational songs, then Pastor Hall gave a glowing introduction of the famous evangelist and brought him to the pulpit.

Moody greeted the crowd then said, "Before we go into the Word, I want to make a personal comment to Miss Andrews." He looked down at Stefanie, who sat three rows from the front. "Young lady, I read the account of your ordeal with the Bay Area Strangler. We've been reading about him for several weeks in our Chicago papers. And then to read that you bucked the crowd who wanted to let the man die, and you saved his life. God bless your compassion, young lady!

"The newspaper, of course, did not say you were a Christian," proceeded Moody, "but I was not surprised when I arrived at the railroad station last night and learned from your pastor that you indeed are a born-again, blood-washed child of God. What a testimony! You are a tremendous example of what a Christian should be. May the Lord always shower His blessing upon you!"

Thoroughly humbled, Stefanie sat in silence and smiled back at the man of God.

Moody opened his Bible and preached. The power of God came down, and a great number of men, women, and young people walked the aisles to receive Jesus Christ. Stefanie walked the aisle with Lucy Campbell, who went to make her public profession of faith.

After church, Stefanie rode in the Carroll surrey toward their home on Nob Hill for Sunday dinner. James took hold of her hand and said, "Miss Stefanie, I sure am glad you're going to Denver with us!"

"Me, too!" Molly Kate said, grabbing Stefanie's other hand. "And you're gonna live with *us*, aren't you?"

Stefanie smiled. "Well, honey, I hope I can live close to you, but I'll have to get a place of my own like I have here."

"But, Mommy and Daddy said—"

"Molly Kate!" Dottie whirled around on the seat. "Didn't Daddy and I tell you and James that we had to talk to Miss Stefanie about it, first?"

The little blonde, who so strongly resembled her mother, stuck out her lower lip and looked down. "Yes, ma'am."

Dottie looked at Stefanie and said, "Well, I guess I'd better go ahead and tell you."

"Tell me what?"

Matt Carroll glanced over his shoulder and grinned. "We've just cooked up a little something. Go ahead, honey. Tell her."

Dottie explained that through Dr. Lyle Goodwin, they had put money on a fairly new house in Denver and would complete the purchase upon arrival. There would be a room for Stefanie in the house if she wanted it. She could stay until she wanted to get a place of her own, or until she got married.

Stefanie laughed and said it looked as if she was going to be an old maid. Here she was, twenty-five, and still not married. She didn't even have a steady beau.

"I've dreamed about meeting the right man and falling in love...but up until now it's been an elusive dream."

James squeezed her hand. "If you'll wait till I grow up, Miss Stefanie, I'll marry you!"

Molly Kate leaned toward her brother. "Oh, James! Miss Stefanie wouldn't want to marry you!"

"Yeah? Why not?"

"Because you belch at the table!"

The adults laughed while James gave his sister an I'll-get-you-for-that look.

"Well, how about it, Stefanie?" Dottie said. "Will you come and live with us until your dream is fulfilled?"

"I'd love it!"

✦

On Monday afternoon, Stefanie entered the hospital and reported to Isabel Grady. She learned that Burton Meade was awake and feeling stronger.

"Since I know you're bent on talking to him," Isabel said, "I've included Meade as one of your assigned patients tonight."

"Thank you. I'll see that the others are taken care of before I go to his room. Once I'm there, I want some uninterrupted time."

Nearly an hour had passed when Stefanie pushed the door of room twenty-two open, carrying a Bible. Two uniformed policemen sat on either side of the Strangler's bed. They both rose to their feet when they saw her.

"There she is, Rex," the older one said. "Just as pretty as her picture in the paper. Miss Andrews, I'm Officer Clete Millard, and this is Officer Rex Johnson."

"Gentlemen." She nodded and smiled, then looked at the man in the bed.

Burton Meade stared at her with cold eyes. One arm was in a sling, and a bandage covered his left cheek where Stefanie's heel had gashed it on Friday night. The claw marks left by Lucy Campbell were still quite visible.

"Do you remember me?"

Meade held her gaze for a moment. "Yeah."

"I'm your nurse for this shift."

"So what?"

Officer Millard moved closer. "Mister, I was here when Dr. Patterson told you how this woman saved your life the other night. After what you tried to do to her, nobody would've blamed her if she'd let you hang on the fence and bleed to death. Now treat her with some decency."

Meade flashed a hot look at the officer, then set his eyes on the Bible in Stefanie's hand. "I don't wanna hear no religious stuff. So you and me ain't got nothin' to talk about. You got some nursin' to do in here, get it done and leave me be."

"What I want to talk to you about, Mr. Meade, is not religion. I want to tell you about the Lord Jesus Christ and the salvation He provided for sinners when He died on the cross."

"I don't wanna hear it."

"Mr. Meade, you're going to be executed within a few days after you're released from the hospital. If you die without letting Jesus save your soul and cleanse you of your sins, you'll go to hell. He loves you. He died for you so you could be saved if—"

"Get her outta here!" Meade shouted, his whole body trembling.

"Settle down, pal!" Officer Johnson laid a hand on Meade's good shoulder. "The lady is trying to help you."

"I don't want any help. Especially *hers!* Make her do her job and get outta here!"

Stefanie quietly placed her Bible on a small table and went about her normal work. She filled his water pitcher with fresh water, got him a clean glass, and fluffed up his pillow. She then checked his chart and saw that it was time to give him powders for pain and swelling. When she had administered those, she said in a friendly tone, "If you need anything else, Mr. Meade, just ring the bell beside your bed. I'll be back in a couple of hours to look in on you."

"All I need is for you to get that Bible outta here."

Stefanie looked at him with compassion as she picked up her Bible. "You have only days to live, Mr. Meade. You've got to go into eternity and face God, having rejected His Son, and with all those murders on your record. Won't you let me read some Scripture to you? I want to show you how Jesus loves you and—"

"Get out! I don't wanna hear it!"

"But you'll go to hell if you die without Jesus."

"So what? I *want* to go to hell! Get outta here!"

The two policemen watched the nurse back toward the door. With tears in her eyes, she said, "Then you'll get your wish, Mr. Meade. God's Word says that murderers have their part in the lake of fire. Jesus can save you and forgive you for the murders and all your other sins if you will let him. But if not, you definitely will get your wish."

Meade unleashed a string of profanity, screaming for her to get out of his room.

When Stefanie was gone, Clete Millard stood over the Strangler and said, "You cold-hearted ingrate. That little lady saved your life in spite of the fact you tried to kill her."

Meade looked up dully and mumbled, "Savin' me was a waste of her time. I'm gonna die on the gallows anyway."

"Yeah. And you deserve it, too, pal. Nobody in this city is going to weep when you hit the bottom of the rope."

8

IT WAS LATE AFTERNOON in Denver as Russ Cullen showed
Dr. Goodwin the bookshelves and cabinet he had built in the
new chief administrator's office.

"Looks great, Russ. Dr. Carroll will love them."

Cullen measured the office with an experienced eye and
pointed. "His desk will sit right here. It will give him a good
view of the street outside, and he'll face the door while sitting
at the desk."

The crash of breaking glass came from down the hall. Then
a loud voice bawled, "Meldrum, you drunken fool! Look what
you did!"

"Aw, shuddup! I ain't drunk. I just stumbled."

"Don't you tell me to shut up. You broke that window, and
Mr. Cullen's gonna make you pay for it!"

"You just keep your big mouth shut, Fender!"

"Sorry, Doctor," Cullen said, heading for the office door.
"Sounds like I've got to handle a problem. See you later."

Russ Cullen hurried in the direction of the angry voices.
Both men were still bickering when he stepped through the
door and shouted above their harsh words, "Hey! What's going
on?"

The room smelled of fresh paint. There was a ladder in

Clay Meldrum's hands and an open bucket of white paint on the floor.

Bob Fender gestured toward the window. "Take a look, Mr. Cullen. This drunken sot can hardly stand up. He was carrying the ladder from one side of the room to the other and knocked out the window. If the paint odor wasn't so strong in here, you'd be able to smell the whiskey on his breath."

Meldrum started to defend himself when Cullen said, "I've told you before, Clay, don't come to work with liquor on your breath. You'd been drinking the other day when you dropped the hammer, hadn't you?"

Meldrum only stared at his employer.

"The only reason I didn't fire you then was that Nurse Baylor asked me not to. I've had all I can stand of you. This time you're fired. Now, get out of my sight!"

Tears filled Meldrum's bloodshot eyes. "Please, boss, don't fire me. My wife and kids—"

"You should've thought of your wife and kids before you put that bottle to your lips, Clay. Now get out!"

Clay's mouth drew into a hard line. He jutted his jaw stubbornly, let the ladder fall to the floor, and walked away.

Cullen and Fender moved to the broken window and looked toward the street. Within seconds, an unsteady Clay Meldrum was making his way down the street, anger showing in every stiff-legged step.

"Which saloon do you think he'll go to?"

"The closest one, I imagine," Cullen said.

Nurses Letha Phillips, Missy O'Day, and Breanna Baylor were cleaning up the clinic and office at the end of the day. They had been busy all day and had hardly spoken to one another.

As Missy swept the floor she said, "Breanna, I didn't mention it this morning, but you were talking in your sleep last night."

"What? Me?" Breanna smoothed out a fresh cloth on the examining table.

"Yes, you."

"What was I talking about?"

"Well, I kept hearing the names 'Dottie' and 'Molly Kate.'"

Breanna paused in her work and rubbed her injured arm. "I'm not surprised. I'm so excited about Dottie and her brood coming to Denver."

Missy smiled. "You and Dottie must love each other very much."

"That's for sure. And I love those precious children. And I'm sure the better I get to know my new brother-in-law, the more I'll love him, too. I wrote the whole family a letter day before yesterday to say how happy I am they're moving to Denver."

"Dr. Carroll must be a wonderful man to take on the responsibility of those children," put in Letha.

"That he is. They suffered so much when their real father was going through the stress disorder. It's going to be great to have Dr. Carroll as chief administrator of the hospital, too. You'll see what I mean, Missy. I can just imagine how the directors of the asylum hate to lose him."

Letha noticed Breanna rubbing her arm again. "Honey, if you're tired of all that traveling, I'm sure Dr. Carroll would hire you in the blink of an eye if you wanted a steady job at the hospital. There's no question Dr. Goodwin would put his stamp of approval on it."

"I'm sure you're right, but there's a certain satisfaction in working as a visiting nurse that working in the hospital wouldn't give me. Maybe someday..."

"Maybe someday you and John will get married, and you'll settle down and be a housewife and mother," Letha said.

"Mmm. That sounds good. All in God's own time, Letha."

Outside the clinic, Dr. Goodwin pulled up in his buggy with a newspaper in hand. As he alighted, a teenage boy wearing a Western Union cap dashed up. "Dr. Goodwin!"

The gentle physician turned and nodded warmly. "Hello, Willy. That telegram for me?"

"Yes, sir. I thought I might have to take it to your house like I did this morning, since it's closing time for the clinic."

Goodwin placed a shiny quarter in Willy's hand and thanked him. Before entering the clinic, he opened the envelope and read its contents, then placed it in his coat pocket.

The office was already dusted, swept, and straightened when he entered. He smiled to himself as he passed through and entered the back room.

The three nurses were just about to leave for the day. They greeted their boss, and Missy asked, "How are things at the hospital today? Everything going well, Doctor?"

"Not everything," Goodwin said. "That Meldrum fella seems to be in trouble again. But other than that, it's looking good. I'm sure we're going to make our opening date."

Goodwin unrolled the afternoon edition of the *Denver Sentinel* as he said, "Something interesting in here, ladies."

The nurses waited for him to go on.

"You recall that we've been reading about that Bay Area Strangler out in San Francisco."

"Yes," Breanna said. "I've prayed daily that he would be caught."

"Well, your prayers are answered," he said, and opened the paper to page three. "It says here that last Friday night—"

He was interrupted by gunshots from some distance up the street. Then all went quiet.

When there were no more shots after a few seconds, Dr. Goodwin said, "Last Friday the Strangler was foiled in an attempt to kill a nurse who works at San Francisco's City Hospital. According to this, she fought the Strangler on the steps of her home. Somehow she knocked him off balance, and he fell several feet before impaling himself on an iron picket fence."

"What's her name, Doctor?" Breanna said. "Since I was there only a couple of months ago, I might have met her."

"Stefanie Andrews."

"Oh! Stefanie! Yes, I met her. I watched her work in the hospital when Dottie was a patient there. Sweet girl. Good at what she does. A fine Christian, too. Dr. Carroll was the one who led her to the Lord."

"'Sweet girl' is a mild way of putting it," Goodwin said, waving the newspaper at Breanna. "After the Strangler was impaled on the picket, a large crowd gathered, and this Stefanie Andrews asked some of the men to help her get him off the fence so she could stop the bleeding and save his life. The crowd wanted to let him hang there and die."

Missy frowned. "But they *did* take him down?"

"Mm-hmm. And Nurse Andrews indeed saved his life. The law will hang him, but she did the humane thing, even though he'll die shortly, anyhow."

Letha clucked her tongue. "She must be a nurse from the bones out to have done that. The man tries to kill her, and she saves his life. I'd like to meet that little miss!"

The doctor's eyes twinkled. "Well, I'll make sure you do."

"Pardon me?"

"Miss Andrews is coming to Denver to work at the hospital. I received a telegram from Dr. Carroll this morning before I left the house. He wanted me to know that the nurse who was his first choice to bring with him had eagerly accepted the job. It was Stefanie Andrews."

Breanna smiled her approval, saying, "Stefanie really impressed me. She's warm, intelligent, and has a way with her patients. Dr. Carroll has made an excellent choice. Stefanie will be a real asset to the hospital staff."

"Well, if you like her that much, Breanna, that makes me feel confident."

Suddenly the rumble of heavy footsteps came from the outer office. Dr. Goodwin spun around to find Sheriff Curt Langan and Deputy Steve Ridgway carrying an unconscious Clay Meldrum. Blood streamed from a gash on Meldrum's temple.

"What happened?" Breanna asked.

"Apparently this guy showed up half-drunk on the job today," Langan said. "Russ Cullen fired him a little while ago. Madder than a wet hornet, he went into the Gun Barrel Saloon, belted down several shots of whiskey, then yanked a gun from a man's holster. He backed his way out of the saloon, holding the gun on its occupants, then ran up the street and started shooting the windows out of the new hospital building. It just so happened that I was riding down Wynkoop Street when he opened fire. He put all six shots into the windows just as I came along. I put him under arrest, but when he resisted I had to clobber him with my gun barrel."

"Let's get him on the examining table," Dr. Goodwin said, leading the way to the back room. "That cut looks pretty bad. I'll have to take stitches."

"I'll help you, Doctor," Breanna said. "Letha, honey, you go on home."

"Can't do it, Breanna. Your arm is giving you pain. You go sit down till we're done here, then Dr. Goodwin can take you and Missy home."

"Do what Letha says, Breanna," the physician said as he moved toward the cupboard to wash his hands. "Missy, I want you to observe what we do here."

Missy nodded and moved up close.

When the unconscious man had been stretched out on the examining table, Sheriff Langan turned to his deputy. "Steve, you go on back to the office. I'll stay here. When Meldrum comes to, he's going to pay for the broken windows. If he balks, I'll jail him."

"All right, Curt. See you later," Ridgway said.

Letha placed a sterile needle and thread on a tray, then began washing the blood from Meldrum's face.

Dr. Goodwin glanced at Breanna. "I want you to go to the waiting room and sit down. Sheriff, you can keep her company. This shouldn't take long. Meldrum will be conscious shortly, and then you can talk to him."

"All right," Langan said, and gestured for Breanna to head for the door. "After you, Miss."

Breanna moved past him into the waiting room, and they both sat down.

Curt eyed the purple mark on her arm. "Is it getting any better?"

"Oh, yes. But it bruised the arm to the bone, and it's going to take a few more days to stop hurting." She paused, then looked into Langan's eyes. "Speaking of hurt, is your heart healing from Sally Jayne—I mean, Morgan Montgomery?"

Curt bent his head and looked at the floor. "I...ah...I still have dreams about Sally. Dreams that seem so real. In them, she's the sweet, lovable person I thought she was until…until that horrible day when I learned how underhanded and devious she'd been all along. Then I wake up and the awful truth hits me like a sledgehammer. Sally is gone…dead. And the Sally I thought I knew never existed at all. She was unreal, Breanna. Just a dream. But the love I held for her in my heart was real. It still is."

"I'm sorry you've been hurt so deeply, Curt."

He raised his head and met her gaze. "I don't know how I would have stood it if you hadn't led me to Jesus, Breanna. Thank you for caring enough about me to keep pressing the gospel home to my heart."

"You don't have to thank me for that. Now you know that when a person is saved, he or she wants to see everyone else saved, especially friends and loved ones."

Curt nodded. "You're right about that. And…and though I'm having a hard time getting over Sally, the Lord is giving me strength to handle it."

"The Sally who never existed, Curt—the one you were in love with—may be only a dream right now. But one day, in the Lord's time, your dream will become a reality. You have such a big heart; I just know the Lord has a special Christian woman for you to love the way you loved Sally. When He brings her into your life, you'll fall so deeply in love with her, you'll forget there was ever anyone else."

Curt nodded and smiled. "I hope you're right. So where's John?"

"Somewhere in western Kansas or eastern Colorado."

"On a mission for Chief Duvall, I presume."

"Yes. A manhunt. There's a killer on the loose."

"Well, if I know John, he'll get him."

They were still discussing John Stranger when Missy O'Day opened the clinic door. "Sheriff, Mr. Meldrum is conscious. Dr. Goodwin says you may come in."

Langan waited for Breanna to precede him through the door, then came alongside the examining table where Meldrum was sitting up.

Meldrum started to speak. "Sheriff, I'm sorry. You clonked me a good one, and I had it coming. It was the whiskey in me. I—"

"That's a big part of your problem, Clay. The whiskey. Now it's cost you your job. And it's going to cost you for the windows you shot out, too."

"Yes, sir. I don't have much money. I have a wife and three children to feed, clothe, and house. I'll have to find another job, but when I do, I'll pay the hospital for the broken windows."

"If that's a promise, I won't put you in jail."

"I swear I'll pay them whatever they say I owe."

"All right," Langan said. "So you're low on money?"

"Uh-huh. My wife and kids need things, but we can't afford to buy them."

"But you can afford whiskey?"

Meldrum's face blanched. "I've been a no-good scoundrel, Sheriff."

"You won't get any argument from me on that. Pay the doctor and go on home."

"I...uh...can't pay him right now, Sheriff. I haven't got a cent on me."

"If you'll promise to lay off the whiskey and take better care of your family, I'll call your bill paid," Dr. Goodwin said.

Relief flooded Clay's features. He grinned slightly. "I promise, Doctor."

"Then go on home, like the sheriff said."

Moments later the clinic was locked up, and Breanna and Missy were in the buggy with Dr. Goodwin.

"Breanna," Dr. Goodwin said, "I need to discuss something with you."

"Yes, sir?"

Missy was sitting between them. "Would you like for me to walk the rest of the way home, Dr. Goodwin? So you can talk to Breanna, I mean."

Goodwin chuckled. "Oh, no, Missy. This doesn't have to be private. You'll be interested in this, too. It involves you indirectly."

"Oh. All right."

"I received a telegram just as I was returning to the office a while ago. It was from Mary Donelson."

"Oh, the head nurse at Philadelphia Hospital."

"Yes. She says she may have to delay her departure from the hospital more than a month until they find her replacement. She'll probably not arrive in Denver until mid-October."

"Well, I can certainly understand that. Mrs. Donelson has been head nurse there for a long time. It won't be easy to replace her."

"Well, I...ah...I want to know, my dear, if you will take the job as head nurse at Mile High Hospital on an interim basis until Mary Donelson can get here. You have plenty of hospital experience, especially in getting one started. How about it?"

Breanna winked at Missy and said, "I don't want the job."

People seldom fooled Dr. Lyle Goodwin. But this time Breanna and Missy burst out laughing at his expression. Then he started to laugh too. "Breanna Baylor, one of these days I'm going to take you over my knee and give you a good spanking!"

"You may actually do that, Doctor, if I don't do a good job as interim head nurse."

"And who's worried about that?" he said. "I'd have offered you the job permanently if I didn't know your heart is in your visiting nurse work. I have the utmost confidence in you."

"Thank you, Dr. Goodwin. I'm honored you feel that way about me."

"We both do, Breanna," Missy said.

9

DOTTIE CARROLL WAS IN THE KITCHEN when she heard James and Molly Kate welcome her husband. It thrilled her to hear them call him "Daddy."

With Molly Kate in one arm and James holding his hand, Matt entered the kitchen. "Mm-mm-mm, Mrs. Carroll! It sure smells good in here!"

"It's fried chicken, mashed potatoes, cream gravy, hot bread, and spinach, Daddy!" Molly Kate almost chirped her delight.

"Spinach?" James said, grabbing his throat. "Yu-u-u-k!"

Dottie pointed a finger between his eyes. "You'll eat your spinach like the rest of us, young man. It's good for you!"

"How could anything that tastes that bad be good for me, Mama?"

"Well, it is. Ask the doctor."

James looked up at the man who would soon adopt him. "Daddy, spinach isn't really good for us, is it?"

"It sure is, son," Matt said, roughing up the boy's hair. "And we'll all obey the cook and eat our share."

Defeat was evident as James gave his mother a sad look.

"You two go wash your hands while I kiss Daddy hello."

Matt eased Molly Kate down. As the children hurried to

the wash room, he folded his wife into his arms, kissed her soundly, and held her close. "I love you, Mrs. Carroll."

"I love you, too, Dr. Carroll," she whispered, hugging him tighter.

"Something else I love."

"What's that?"

"Those kids calling me Daddy."

"Oh, I love it, too!"

Later, after James had led the family in a prayer of thanks—though he felt like a hypocrite for thanking the Lord for spinach—Matt looked across the table at Dottie and said, "Honey, we're going to be delayed somewhat in getting to Denver."

Dottie set down her coffee cup. "What do you mean?"

"I went to the railroad station at noon to buy the tickets and was told there won't be any trains running east from San Francisco for at least three months."

"Why?"

"Four of the trestles between San Francisco and the Nevada border have been burned and destroyed."

"Oh, no! Who would do such a thing?"

"The agent said the authorities think Indians did it. Some of the Mojaves have been on the prowl lately."

"This is awful! We have to wait until November...or longer?"

"The agent said the California Stagelines are running special stagecoaches from Placerville up over Luther Pass and down the east side of the Sierras to Reno, where travelers can catch the eastbound trains. They'll do so until the snow flies, then the service will cease."

"Well, since we're leaving our furniture with the house and buying new furniture in Denver, I guess we can carry our clothing and personal things on a stagecoach as well as we could have carried it on a train. The boot and rack can hold quite a bit. Of course if the other passengers have much in the way of luggage, we might have a problem."

"Well, let me tell you about that. I went directly from the railroad station to the stage office to sign up. The agent told me I could charter a stage to Reno so that besides the driver and shotgunner, only Stefanie and the four of us would be on it. When I explained what we were bringing, he said there should be no problem getting everything on the stage. Of course we have to board the stage at Placerville. That's where it turns around."

"So did you charter one?"

"Mm-hmm. There was nothing available until the twenty-fourth…three days after we were supposed to leave here for Denver on the train. Of course, we'll have to hire a wagon and driver to take us to Placerville, which is a hundred and forty-five miles. That'll take us three days, so we'll still leave here on the twenty-first."

"How long will it take us to get to Denver?"

"If all goes according to schedule, five days from the day we board the stage at Placerville—three days from Placerville to Reno, and two days from Reno to Denver, since the train travels day and night."

"Well, that's not too bad. I know you and Dr. Goodwin wanted a good five weeks with you on the job before the hospital opens. But we'll still be in Denver more than four weeks before opening time."

"Oh, goody!" Molly Kate said, waving her fork. "We're still going to see Aunt Breanna real soon! For a minute I was afraid we might not get to go till the trustles got fixed."

"Trestles," James corrected her.

"Huh-uh," argued his little sister. "It's *trustles,* isn't it, Daddy?"

"Tell her, Daddy. Show her how dumb little girls are!"

Matthew Carroll gazed steadily at James. "You haven't eaten your spinach yet, son."

James glared at Molly Kate, who grinned and lifted her plate. "See, James? My spinach is all gone already. I really like it!"

"Speaking of Aunt Breanna," Dottie said, "we got a letter from her today. It's in the bedroom. I'll go get it."

"No need to do that, honey," Matt said. "Just tell us what she said."

"Well, she wants us to know how happy she is that we're moving there…and how glad she is that her brother-in-law is going to be chief administrator of Mile High Hospital. Dr. Goodwin has scheduled her to work at the hospital for three months to help get it running smoothly."

"Hey, that's great! I figured she'd be traveling as usual, popping in and out of Denver. That'll give me a good chance to get to know her better."

"Yeah, and we'll get to see her more!" Molly Kate said.

James frowned at his sister. "Aunt Breanna doesn't wanna see a girl who calls trestles *trustles,* Molly Kate."

Molly Kate glanced at her brother's plate and said, "You haven't cleaned up your spinach yet."

"Anyway, Aunt Breanna says to tell her favorite niece and nephew that she loves them and can't wait to put hugs on them."

"I can't wait either," Molly Kate said, glorying in the look on her brother's face as he chewed his spinach. "I really love Aunt Breanna, don't you, James?" Since James couldn't answer, Molly Kate smiled and said, "You love Aunt Breanna more than you love spinach, don't you?"

"Molly Kate, that's enough," Dottie said.

"I'll be at the hospital tomorrow afternoon, Dottie. I'll tell Stefanie about the change in travel plans and then wire Dr. Goodwin about when to expect us."

Dottie went to the kitchen to get more coffee. As she poured a fresh cup for Matt, she remembered something Breanna had told her. "Since we're going over Luther Pass, will we be staying a night at the way station up there?"

"Yes. The agent said the way station is run by a tough old woman named—"

"Judy Charley," cut in Dottie.

"How did you know?"

"When Breanna came to California with that wagon train, they came over Luther Pass and stayed at the way station. She told me all about the woman."

"Yeah? Well, the agent said the old girl is a delight to be around."

"Mm-hmm. Breanna said she's a joyful old soul. She runs the California Stagelines way station—which has several rooms like a hotel—and she also owns and runs a general store."

"Yes, that's what the agent said. Supposedly, she wears overalls and packs a Colt .45 on hips so skinny they'll hardly hold the gunbelt up. She wears men's work shoes and chews tobacco."

"Not any more, she doesn't."

"What? Wear men's work shoes or chew tobacco?"

"Chew tobacco. Breanna rode in a wagon driven by a man name of Curly Wesson—all the way from South Pass, Wyoming. Bald as an egg."

Matt laughed. "That's a good one!"

"On the trip from South Pass, Breanna said Curly was always spitting tobacco. She kept witnessing to him about the Lord, and when he finally got saved, he threw the tobacco away. And when the wagon train stopped at the way station, Curly and Judy became instant friends. Curly used what Bible Breanna had taught him to lead Judy to the Lord. Breanna said that when she left the wagon train on level ground on this side of the Sierras, Curly told her he was going back up to the way station and 'do a little courtin', as he put it."

"Did Breanna say how old these two are?"

"She guessed they were somewhere between seventy and eighty. I hope they're both at the way station when we get there. I'd sure like to meet them."

The Carrolls and Stefanie Andrews bid their church good-bye at the midweek service on August 19. On Thursday, August 20, Dr. Carroll and Stefanie told all their friends at the hospital and asylum good-bye. Late in the afternoon on August 23, Stefanie and the Carrolls arrived by wagon at Placerville. The sweet aroma of fresh-cut wood filled the air, for there were several logging mills near the town.

Matt entered the California Stagelines office to confirm their departure on the stage to Reno. The agent behind the desk was a short, chubby man in his late fifties, with only a gray fringe above his ears for hair. His handlebar mustache was the same shade of gray. He looked up at the sound of their entry and smiled at James and Molly Kate, then looked at the tall, handsome man. "Howdy, sir. I'm Wally Beemer. What can I do for you?"

"I'm Dr. Matthew Carroll, sir. This is my—my son and daughter, James and Molly Kate."

"Oh, sure! You're the one who's chartered one of our stages to Reno."

"Yes. My wife and a young lady who's traveling with us are outside. I assume we're to unload our luggage and boxes here so they can be loaded on the stage."

"That'll be fine, Doctor. I'll help you unload the wagon. We'll put your stuff in the storeroom over here. The stage you chartered is on its way down from the way station atop Luther Pass right now. Oughtta be in here about dark. We'll load your stuff on the stage at dawn, and you'll move out after breakfast."

That evening the Carrolls and Stefanie enjoyed a good meal at the café across the street from the Placerville Hotel, then walked to the nearest sawmill so the children could get a look close up. James was enthralled with the massive stacks of logs.

Twilight was on the land as they returned to the hotel. When they entered the lobby, Wally Beemer and a short, wiry little man were coming down the stairs.

"Ah, there you are!" Beemer said. "We've been looking for you!"

The little man with him wore a tattered old hat, but it was evident that he was bald. There was not even a fringe above his ears. He had sparkling blue eyes, rosy cheeks, and a built-in grin on his lips. He was clean shaven, and looked to be somewhere in his seventies. There was a thoughtful expression on his face as he studied Dottie.

"Dr. Carroll," Beemer said, "this is Curly Wesson, the stage driver who'll be taking you over the mountains to Reno. He wanted to meet you before morning and talk to you a little about the trip."

At the mention of the driver's name, Dottie and Matt exchanged glances and smiled. Before either of them could speak, Curly stepped up to Dottie, cracked a nearly toothless smile, and said, "Pardon me, ma'am, but you shore do look a whole lot like a lady what rode my wagon with me a few months ago…all the way from South Pass, Wyomin' right here to ol' Californy! You look too much like her not to be her sister. You *are* Miss Breanna Baylor's sister, ain'tcha?"

Dottie laughed. "I sure am, Mr. Wesson! And I feel like I know you. Breanna told me so much about you!"

"Well, that sister o' yours talked a whole lot about you on the trip, Miss Dottie. I feel like I know you, too!" His gaze shifted to the children. "An' I know who these two are, sure as shootin'! This here perdy little gal is Molly Kate, an' this here handsome boy is James, right?"

Both children nodded, a little subdued.

The old gent cackled and dug in his pocket. Pinching two quarters between gnarled fingers, he handed one to Molly Kate and the other to James. "There's some money so's you two can buy some candy!"

"What do you say?" Dottie asked them.

"Thank you," brother and sister said in chorus.

"You're mighty welcome." Then Curly looked at Matt. "Let's see, here…you gotta be Jerrod."

"Ah…no. Jerrod Harper was Dottie's first husband. He died several months ago. We just married the first of this month."

The old man's cheeks darkened. "Oh. Please forgive me. I…I didn't know. Breanna talked a lot about her brother-in-law, Jerrod, sayin' she'd never seen him, and was lookin' forward to meetin' 'im. I…uh…didn't think about it when Wally here tol' me your name was Carroll. Please forgive me."

"There's nothing to forgive, Mr. Wesson," Matt said, extending his hand. "I'm Dr. Matthew Carroll."

Curley smiled a fetching grin and gripped Matt's hand. "Glad to meet you, Doctor." Then, catching sight of Stefanie, he said, "An' who might this perdy little thing be?"

"This is Stefanie Andrews, Mr. Wesson. She's a Certified Medical Nurse. You know...like Breanna. You see, my family and I are moving to Denver where I'm going to be chief administrator of Denver's new hospital, and Miss Andrews is going with us. She'll be working at the hospital."

"Well, now ain't that great! Denver's where Breanna makes her home, ain't it?"

"It sure is," Dottie said.

"Well, I sure cain't blame you. That Breanna is a wonderful little gal. Since she tol' you about me, Missus Carroll, did she tell you 'bout punchin' Bible into my heart mile after mile till she finally won me to Jesus?"

"Yes, she did. Quite convincing, isn't she?"

"You might put it that way! I tol' her if'n she was a man, she'd prob'ly be one o' these 'vanglists."

"Look, folks," Wally Beemer interjected, "my wife's expecting me home for supper. So I'll just excuse myself and see you at dawn."

They all bid him goodnight as he headed out the door.

"Mr. Wesson, if you need to talk to us about the trip, why don't you come up to our room for a while?" Dottie suggested.

"Well, now, guess I could do that."

When they entered the hotel room, Curly saw that it was actually a suite. The ladies, he was told, would be sleeping in one room, and the gentlemen in the other.

"Curly," Dottie said, "before we talk about the trip, I would like to ask you about Judy Charley. Breanna told me so much about her. Is she still running the way station and general store on top of the pass?"

The mention of Judy put a wide smile on the old man's cherubic face. "She shore does. Only now she's Judy Charley *Wesson*. We done got hitched 'bout six weeks ago."

"Hey, that's great!" Matt said. "I understand that you led Judy to the Lord while the wagon train was stopped at the pass."

"Yep. Weren't hard. She'd heard a lot 'bout Jesus an' the gospel. All I had to do was show her some Scriptures Breanna showed me, an' she got saved!"

"I'm sure that having the Lord in your lives has made a big difference, hasn't it?"

"You can say that again! I used to cuss some before I got saved. The Lord did with me like you doctors do with a appendix."

"Pardon me?"

"You know...an appendectomy."

"I'm not sure I follow you."

"Well, when Jesus saved me, He took my cusser out. You know, He did a cusserectomy on me! An' me an' Judy both used to chew an' spit that nasty ol' terbaccy. But the Lord done cleaned us up there, I'll tell you."

"He has a way of doing that," Matt agreed.

"Me an' Judy are now co-owners of the way station and the general store, an' we're co-agents for the Californy Stagelines there."

"So you're not traveling with the wagon train anymore?"

"Nope. I done settled down since I married my perdy little gal. I do miss the wagon train business and travelin' like I done for so many years, but bein' married to Judy and settlin' down is a real joy."

"Curly," Matt said, "I assume you're driving the stage because of the trestle problem, since you're an agent for the California Stagelines."

"You got it. I'm drivin' only chartered stages. Will do so until the trestles are rebuilt and the railroad can once't again run their trains as usual. 'Course if the trestles ain't rebuilt by the time the snow flies in these mountains, the whole shebang will have to wait till spring."

James leaned close to his sister and whispered, "See? Even he knows it's trestles, not *trustles!*"

"Anyway, main thing I wanted to talk to you about was if *you*, Doctor, would mind ridin' shotgun on the trip to Reno. My reg'lar shotgunner is ailin' right now. The shotgunner is needed jist in case there's any trouble from robbers or hostile Injuns on the trip. But, then, you already know that, I'm sure."

Carroll grinned. "Yes, sir."

"Y'ever use a shotgun?"

"Mm-hmm. Not on a human being, but when hunting pheasants."

"Well, hopefully, you won't hafta use it on nobody on the trip. But...ah...bein' a doctor an' all, would you use it if you *had* to, to protect your family?"

"Without hesitation."

"Good. You're my kinda man. Well, that was my big question. And since it's been answered, I'll be leavin' you be till mornin'."

Curly turned back at the door and said, "I cain't wait for you to meet Judy, Miss Dottie. The two of us have often talked about Breanna and that tall, dark man o' hers, John Stranger. Quite some feller, that one."

"That's what I'm told," Dottie said. "I'm looking forward to meeting John. *And* I'm looking forward to meeting Judy."

"Oh, you'll love 'er, ma'am. *All* of you will. She's the sweetest and most bee-yoo-ti-ful woman in captivity!"

↑

The next morning Matt bought a copy of the *San Francisco Chronicle* at the drugstore next door to the stage office.

Curly had just finished loading and was battening down the lid of the boot while the rest of the Carrolls and Stefanie stood around talking. Dottie noticed Matt intently reading the paper as he walked toward them.

"What's in the news, darling?"

Matt hesitated a moment and then said, "Headlines say today is the Strangler's day to be hanged…at sunrise."

Stefanie looked eastward. The sun was up, and at that moment it detached itself from the earth's edge. Burton Meade had already taken the drop to the end of the rope.

She thought about how close she had come to being murdered and silently thanked the Lord for sparing her life. She remembered the day at the hospital when she had tried to press the gospel home to Burton Meade's heart, and how he had cursed her, saying he wanted to go to hell. She knew at that very moment, he was wishing he had listened to her and opened his heart to the Saviour.

Now it was forever too late.

10

DAWN BROKE OVER THE TOWERING Sierra Nevada Range and over Luther Pass, sending night shadows into oblivion. Soon the sky turned red, then gold, and it wasn't long before it became a canopy of blue without hint of a cloud.

A wagon train bound for Sacramento had pulled in at dusk the evening before, and the travelers were buying food and supplies at the general store for the remainder of the journey. There were many children in the train, which had nineteen wagons. Some of them were in the store with their parents, while others were playing happily around the buildings and among the canvas-covered vehicles.

Wagon master Webb Rice had worked late into the night with three other men to repair an axle by lantern light. He had not slipped into his bedroll until nearly two o'clock in the morning and didn't rise until the sun's rays woke him.

As Rice climbed down from the rear of his wagon, he smiled at the children, who seemed glad to be able to run around and burn up some energy.

Rice had been leading wagon trains to California from the Missouri River for nearly twenty years. Even the Civil War hadn't kept people from migrating west. He yawned and stretched his arms, then headed toward the general store where he knew Judy

Charley would have a pot of coffee brewing. At least she always had before when he brought his trains over the pass.

It was then that the wagon master noticed a new sign above the door.

Wesson's General Store
Curly and Judy Charley Wesson, Proprietors
California Stagelines

He read the sign slowly a second time before entering the store. Inside, the place was alive with activity. He smelled hot coffee and headed for the stove in a rear corner, unnoticed as yet by Judy. He let his eyes drift to the old woman. He had seen her countless times before, but each time it was a fresh experience.

Judy had a slight hump to her back, and she stood just about an even five feet tall. She wore an old drover's hat that looked to be almost as ancient as she was. From beneath its tattered brim, coarse gray hair stuck out in strands of varying lengths. Her face was deeply lined, and she had a pointed, jutting chin.

Her large eyes seemed to look right and left at the same time, and Webb Rice was never sure which one was looking at him when he talked with her face-to-face. Judy was so skinny that the man's shirt and overalls she wore looked as if they were hanging on a scarecrow. She wore number 10 men's work shoes, and on her narrow hips hung a Colt .45 in a black leather gunbelt.

Rice picked up a tin cup from the stack Judy kept nearby and poured himself a steaming cup of coffee. Just as he lifted it to his lips, Judy caught sight of him and grinned widely. All of her teeth were missing except one snaggletooth that protruded from her upper gum in front.

"Howdy, Webb. Ain't seen you in a month o' Sundays. I expected to see you las' night when I learned it was your train."

"I was busy till real late fixing an axle, Judy. Slept in a little this mornin'. As soon as you have a minute, I'd like to talk to you."

"Just a second." Judy pointed her face toward the rear and called, "Davey Dean! I need you!"

Seconds later, a young man with a peg leg limped out of the back room. He had a haircut that looked as though somebody had placed a bowl on his head and chopped away.

"Yes'm," Davey Dean said, limping toward the counter. "What can I do for you, Miss Judy?"

"Take over for me here, okay?"

She hurried toward the wagon master. "Webb, it shore is good to see you! What's it been? Four months?"

"Five," Rice said, blowing on the hot coffee. "I was through here in April when there was still some snow on the pass. Went back another way, so I missed you on the return trip." He gestured toward the counter. "Who's the kid?"

"Davey Dean Domire. Lives 'bout a mile west o' here, an' a little lower. Takes care of his widowed mother. Lost his leg in the War. Gettysburg. He really ain't no kid. He's twenty-five. Helps me out here when things is busy. Only been doin' it for 'bout a month."

"I see."

"Well, what was it you wanted to see me about?"

"*Wesson's General Store,* that's what. Who's this Curly?"

Judy threw back her head and guffawed. "That's my husban'! I done got myself all hitched up since you was here last!"

"Well, tell me about it."

The old woman blushed. "Well, Curly showed up here a couple months ago in a wagon train an', uh…well, we fell all over ourselves. He's such a handsome dog, and he talks right."

"*Talks* right?"

"Yep, shore does. Just like me. We hit it off real quick like."

Webb took a swig of the strong black coffee. "Well, Judy, I'd like to meet this man of your dreams. Is he around?"

"Not at the moment. Have you heerd 'bout them railroad trustles bein' burnt by the Injuns?"

"It's the talk of the territory."

"Well, then, you must know 'bout Californy Stagelines providin' coaches for Union Specific Railroad customers, 'cause the trains cain't travel 'tween the coast an' Reno without no trustles to cross."

"Yes."

"Well, my sweetie is a-drivin' one o' them coaches. Fact, he's pullin' outta Placerville this mornin' on his way to Reno. You'll meet him on the way down the mountain. When you see a stage, that'll be Curly at the reins. Just hail 'im down an' interduce yourself."

The way station and general store compound was built under towering pines, which grew thick and heavy on top of the pass, along with white-barked birch and scraggly piñon. It was alive with squirrels, chipmunks, and chattering birds. Where the high country slanted downward, steep natural trails cut through the broken cliffs that were heaped with stones and boulders.

Some of the smaller children were amusing themselves by gathering pine cones, while a few of the families walked the edges of the surrounding forest, enjoying the view of the cliffs and trails below.

Twelve-year-old Everett Nelson and ten-year-old Timmy Reynolds were standing under one of the towering pines near the road as their mothers passed by, heading toward the store.

The older boy gazed upward, marveling at the height of the tree, and said, "Hey, Timmy. Let's climb it. I bet we could see all the way to the Pacific Ocean from up there."

Olive Nelson stopped and pointed a stiff finger. "Everett, you stay on the ground, you hear me? You boys could fall and get seriously hurt."

Melba Reynolds set stern eyes on her son and said, "Timmy, do I have to remind you that you've gotten hurt many times before when you disobeyed me? No tree climbing. Understand?"

"Yes, Mama."

"Same goes for you, Everett. Understand?"

Everett set his jaw. "Aw, Ma, we wouldn't go very high."

"You listen to me, boy. If you so much as start up that tree, your dad will blister your britches. Now, if you think the temptation is too much, you can just come into the store with me right now."

Everett shook his head. "I won't climb it, Ma."

"Is that a promise?"

"Yes, ma'am."

"All right. Why don't you boys collect some pine cones like the other children?"

When their mothers had entered the store, Everett bent to the other boy's height. "We'll have to do it quick, Timmy, before our parents come out of the store. C'mon!"

Timmy stiffened his legs as Everett pulled him toward the trunk of the pine. "No! We're not supposed to!"

"What are you, a sissy?"

"No, I'm not a sissy! But our mothers told us not to climb it!"

127

Everett cuffed him on the chest. "You *are* a sissy if you don't climb the tree with me!"

"I am not!"

"Prove it!"

Timmy glanced toward the store. He paused for a long moment under the pressure of his friend's scathing glare. "Oh, all right. But we won't go very high, okay?"

"Okay!"

Quickly, Everett boosted his small friend up so he could reach the bottom limb. Everett scurried up behind him. When Timmy was some fifteen feet above the ground, he fixed his feet on a limb, gripping a higher one tightly, and said, "This is far enough."

"Aw, c'mon, Timmy! We ain't near high enough to see the ocean. Keep goin'!"

"No! If you want to climb higher, go ahead. I'm goin' back down before my ma and pa come out of the store."

"They ain't comin' out yet," Everett said. "C'mon, keep climbin'! Hurry up! If you don't, you're a sissy!"

Timmy reached for the next branch. He was barely able to curl his fingers over it. He gave a little jump and lost his footing. He brushed Everett on the way down and landed with a sickening thud.

Gardner Helms and J. D. Cassidy were crossing the road from their wagons when they saw Timmy fall. Gardner got there first and knelt over the boy. "Hold him still, J. D., while I pull up his pants leg."

Timmy's leg was broken between the ankle and the knee, the bone protruding through the skin.

"J. D., you stay with him. I'll go get his parents."

↑

Darrell and Melba Reynolds were standing near the counter, talking with the Nelsons when Gardner Helms burst through the door.

"Darrell! Melba! Timmy just fell out of a tree! His leg's broken!"

Timmy's parents and several others bolted for the door. Judy told Davey Dean to stay at the counter and hurried after them.

Seconds later, the Reynolds were kneeling beside the wailing boy. J. D. Cassidy had used his bandanna to help stay the bleeding.

Melba Reynolds lifted panicky eyes to her husband. "Oh, Darrell! What are we going to do?"

"Folks," Judy said, "I've had some 'sperience with broke bones. I'll do what I kin fer the leg if'n you want me to."

Webb Rice had joined the growing crowd. He took one look at the leg and said, "My advice is to let Judy do what she can, Darrell. She's got more experience with broken bones than anybody in the wagon train."

A silent question floated between husband and wife, then Darrell turned to Judy and said, "All right, Mrs. Wesson."

Judy laid a hand on Melba's shoulder. "Let's git him inside. I'll work on him in one o' the way station rooms."

Darrell picked up his son, speaking words of comfort to him, and headed for the store with the crowd following. Melba walked close beside her husband, stroking her son's hair.

Judy clucked her tongue as she examined the leg closely. "All I can do is try to set the bone in place, stitch up the tore skin, an' splint it. The stitchin' I can do real good. It's the settin' of the bone that I'm worried 'bout. I ain't never seen a break as bad as this. I'll set it the best I can, but it won't be done like a doctor would do it. You'll need to git him to the doctor in Placerville as soon as you git down there."

Melba gripped her husband's hand and tried to blink back the tears. "It'll take the wagon train two days to get to Placerville. By that time, the bone will begin to fuse itself, and the doctor in Placerville will have to break it again."

"You're right, honey, but there ain't no other choice. You gotta let the doctor break it again, 'cause if'n it don't git set properly, Timmy'll limp the rest o' his life. But I gotta set it the best I can right now, or he won't quit hurtin'."

"Judy's right, Melba," Darrell said. "There's nothing else we can do."

The worried mother nodded, placed a loving palm on her son's brow, and said, "All right. Let's get it done so we can start down the mountain. Do you have anything to ease his pain, Judy?"

"I've got some headache powders in the store. Nothin' else. They'll help a little."

When the headache powders had been given time to take effect, Judy went to work. The boy screamed and passed out when she set the bone. Judy made the stitches as quickly as possible, bandaged the leg, and splinted it.

She was in the hall with the rest of the people, explaining Timmy's condition, when Darrell opened the door and said, "Mrs. Wesson, Timmy's awake now, but he's hurting pretty bad. Do you have some more headache powders? They would at least take the edge off the pain."

"Shore do. Be right back."

Chester and Olive Nelson waited in the crowd, looking

grim. Everett stood beside his father, eyes toward the floor.

Judy returned with a cup containing powders mixed with water and stood by while Melba gave it to Timmy a sip at a time.

Darrell watched his son grimace in pain, though Timmy tried not to cry out. After a while, Darrell said, "Melba, he's not going to be able to stand the bumps and jarring of the wagon. We'll have to give it at least a day before we head down the pass. I'll talk to Webb. He needs to get the train rolling. They'll just have to go on without us. If the doctor in Placerville is going to have to rebreak the leg to set it right, another day or so won't make that much difference. We can't put Timmy through any more pain right now."

Webb Rice's deep voice came from the open door. "Darrell, we aren't going without you. Everybody out here in the hall agrees. The whole train will wait till Timmy's able to travel."

The voices in the hall confirmed Rice's words.

"Mr. Rice, are you sure?" Darrell asked. "That's a lot to ask—"

"Save your breath, Darrell. It's settled, and that's it."

"Well...please go out there and make sure they all know how much we appreciate this."

"I'll do that," the wagon master said.

Chester Nelson stood back to let Rice out, then moved forward. "Darrell, could Everett come in and say something to Timmy? It'll only take a minute."

"Sure. Bring him in."

Chester and Olive accompanied their twelve-year-old as he approached the bed. "I...I just wanted to tell you that I'm sorry, Timmy. This whole thing is my fault. It was me callin' you a sissy that made you climb the tree. I shouldn't have done that. I disobeyed my ma and I caused you to disobey yours. I wish it was me with the broken leg."

Timmy licked dry lips. "It's my fault, too. I shouldn't have let you talk me into it. I guess we've both learned a good lesson."

"Yeah. Are we still friends?"

Timmy nodded slowly. "Sure."

The Nelsons stayed with Timmy the rest of the day, glad to see him sleeping most of the time.

When the sun was setting, Judy and a small group who were standing around talking heard the pounding of hooves and the rattle of harness. The old woman looked toward the open door. "That'll be my husban'!"

Judy waved at Curly from the porch, then focused for a moment on the young man who sat beside him holding the shotgun. She looked back at her husband and said, "Howdy, you mighty hunk o' manhood!"

Curly slid to the ground while Dr. Carroll climbed down and opened the coach door for his family and Stefanie.

Curly grinned from ear to ear and wrapped an arm around his wife, saying, "Howdy, yourself, you sweet thing!" He took off his hat and covered their faces on the crowd's side while they kissed with a big smack.

As Curly replaced the hat on his bald head, Judy eyed the passengers. "Well, I'll be a bowlegged mule, if it ain't Miss Breanna Baylor! Honey, I don' know what your doin' on that there stagecoach, but we got a boy inside that can shore use a good nurse!"

"Uh...sweet potato," Curly said, "that ain't Breanna. But your close. It's her younger sister, Dottie Carroll. And this here is her husban', Dr. Matthew Carroll. An' these children are their son and daughter, James 'n Molly Kate…an' this here cutie is Miss Stefanie Andrews, who is one o' them certificated nurses like Breanna!"

Judy looked back at the tall, handsome man. "You a *medical* type doctor, Dr. Carroll?"

"Yes, ma'am. You say you have a boy who's sick?"

"Well, sick ain't really the word for it, Doctor…he's got a broke leg. I set it for him, but I ain't no M.D., so he's gonna need it set again. Can you take care o' him an' mebbe let this here cute little nurse help you if need be?"

"We'll get right on it. Curly, my medical bag is up there on the rack in that big wooden box of medical supplies. Stefanie and I'll go on in. Will you bring it to me?"

"With pleasure."

Timmy's parents were elated when they were introduced to the doctor and nurse, and stood by as Matt removed the splint, unwrapped the bandage, and examined the broken leg. He told Judy she had done an excellent job of stitching the leg, but that the broken bone would need to be reset.

Curly came in with the medical bag, and Stefanie gave Timmy a child's dose of laudanum while Dr. Carroll explained to the parents what he would have to do. When the laudanum had taken effect, Dr. Carroll ran experienced fingers over the break and began his task.

An hour later, Timmy's leg had been reset and resplinted. Carroll assured his parents that the break would heal properly if the leg was taken care of, and Timmy would walk normally within a few months.

The Reynolds embraced and said, "Dr. Carroll, thank you so much. Our money box is out in the wagon. How much do we owe you?"

"Well, let's see," Carroll said, rubbing his chin and looking toward the ceiling. "My fee for services like this is two million dollars...however, a mother's tears are worth at least that much, so let's call it even."

The next morning at sunrise, the stagecoach passengers got ready to board.

When Judy hugged Dottie good-bye, she said, "Honey, you tell your sister and that tall drink o' water she's in love with howdy for me."

"I sure will." Dottie hugged her a second time and wondered how Judy held together with so little on her bones. When she released her, Dottie said, "Matt and I sure would love to have you and Curly come to Denver and visit us if you could ever get away from here."

"Well, that ain't so furfetched," Judy said. "Davey Dean could run the place for a while. We might just do that little thing."

11

ON MONDAY MORNING, August 31, Drs. Lyle Goodwin, Glen Wakeman, and Newt Stratton stood with the newly arrived Dr. Eldon Moon on the boardwalk in front of the new hospital, watching workmen come and go.

Dr. Goodwin pointed to the unfinished section on the south side. "Dr. Moon, you will recall that in one of my letters I explained we would finish the north end first, so we could get in and do business."

"Yes, and I think that's a good idea, even though it will mean some noise and inconvenience until the whole thing is finished. But at least this bustling town will have a hospital."

"Good, I'm glad you concur with our wisdom," Goodwin said with a smile. "Let's go on inside."

Dr. Stratton hurried ahead and pulled open one of the double doors, allowing the others to pass through. Dr. Goodwin was up ahead and saw Russ Cullen come out of one of the offices.

"Russ!"

Cullen had started in the opposite direction, but turned and smiled.

"Russ, I want you to meet Denver's newest physician. I've told you about Dr. Moon."

"Yes."

Dr. Goodwin introduced everyone and then said, "Russ, I received confirmation by wire that the trainload of equipment will be arriving from Chicago on September 15. Think you'll be ready?"

"We'll be ready, Doctor. Installation of all your equipment can begin the moment it's delivered. Right now we're just about two days ahead of schedule, and we're working hard to keep it that way."

"My kind of contractor," Dr. Moon said. "I like a man who works hard to deliver the goods."

At the close of the day, Cullen Construction men were leaving the job site to head home or to a café for supper. Near the front door of the hospital, Herb Louis and Jim Varner, who had been hired by Cullen just the week before, were talking to long-time employees.

"Jim and I were just talkin' about the boss," Louis said. "We haven't heard him mention a wife or family. Is he married?"

"He's a widower," Mack Tilley said. "If he's got children or grandchildren anywhere, he's never said."

Louis elbowed Varner. "Well, at least our plan won't be foiled by a naggin' wife, Jimbo."

"Yeah. Oughtta work just great."

"Plan?" Tilley said.

"Yeah. Jim and I have worked construction together in Kansas, Nebraska, and Texas. We've found that if we take the boss out for a few drinks and some poker now and then, he'll treat us better. It's worked real good so far."

"We're gonna invite him to go to the Golden Slipper Casino for an evenin' of poker and drinkin'," Varner said.

"The Golden Slipper, eh? You been there yet?"

"Nope, but a professional gambler friend of ours by the name of Lowell Jessup arrived in town last night from Dodge City. We met him on our way to work this mornin'. He's been in Denver a few times and told us about the Golden Slipper. Sounds like a real fun spot."

"Well, you can forget invitin' Russ," Tilley said.

"How come?"

"Well, for some unexplained reason, the boss shies away from gamblin' places."

"Well, Herb and I will get him over that!"

Russ Cullen was renting a small house near Broadway on Colfax Avenue, close to Denver's business district and just a few minutes' walk from the saloons and gambling houses.

He had just eaten supper at a nearby café and returned home to read the paper when someone knocked. As he opened the door, the lantern light from the parlor revealed the smiling faces of Jim Varner and Herb Louis. "Well, to what do I owe a visit from my employees?" Cullen then noticed a third man standing in the shadows.

"We got to thinkin' that maybe you were bored and lonely here all by yourself, boss," Louis said. "We'd like to invite you to spend the evenin' playin' poker at the Golden Slipper with us and a friend of ours."

Cullen's eyes flicked to the man in the shadows, then he said politely, "Fellas, I appreciate the invitation, but I'm not a gambler. That's one thing I won't do."

The third man stepped forward, letting light flood his angular features. A slow smile spread across his face as he said, "Aw, c'mon, Mr. Cullen. Be a sport. Let's play a little poker together. Be good for you. Your boys here just want to show you a good time!"

Louis and Varner noticed Cullen's face turn pale as he stared at the man.

"Hey, you two know each other?" Varner asked.

Cullen continued to stare. The well-dressed stranger held Cullen's gaze and said in a low tone, "I've never met Mr. Russ Cullen before."

Russ flicked his tongue across dry lips.

The man extended a hand and said, "Mr. Cullen, my name's Lowell Jessup. Your boys seem to think a lot of you."

Cullen met Jessup's grip solidly but did not reply.

Jessup chuckled hollowly. "I'd really like to play poker with a big construction mogul. How about it, Mr. Cullen?"

"Well, if you insist, Mister...Jessup, is it?"

"Yes. Jessup. J-E-S-S-U-P. I'm sure we'll be good friends before this night is over."

"Great, boss!" Herb Louis said. "Jim and I want you to know that tonight the drinks are on us!"

It was nearly midnight when Russ Cullen came home. He had left one lantern burning low. He turned up the flame and lighted two more lanterns, turning their wicks high. He paced the floor, seething with wrath and cursing the name of Lowell Jessup. He could still hear the gambler's ironic tone as he said, "I've never met Mr. Russ Cullen before."

Cullen's eyes caught his reflection in the mirror above the

fireplace—a face raw with anger. He stopped and was about to speak to his reflection when he heard a knock at the front door. He crossed the room and threw open the door. There stood Jessup with bright mocking eyes.

"I didn't give you away, pal," Jessup said. "Want to talk now?"

At the Goodwin home, Breanna Baylor and Missy O'Day were eating their breakfast as usual with the doctor and his wife. "I have a special assignment for you this morning, Breanna," Dr. Goodwin said.

"All right, boss-man. And what might that be? If you have some medical problem you can't handle, I'll be glad to do it for you. And I promise never to tell your colleagues unless they come up with a sizable bribe."

Martha Goodwin snorted and covered her mouth.

"Tell you what, young lady. I wouldn't doubt that there *are* some medical problems you can handle that I can't. You'd make a good doctor. I've thought many times that you should go to medical school and get your M.D. degree."

"Sure. A female doctor in a man's world? They'd run me off the campus after they tarred and feathered me, *if* I had the audacity to walk in and ask to enroll."

"Well, now, I don't know about that. I heard of two women who enrolled in the Boston School of Medicine and received their degrees."

"I know about them," Breanna said. "And I also happen to know they put up with a lot of harassment from the male students. Not only that, but they're both trying to establish practices in eastern cities and having a hard time of it. There was an article about it in the paper a few months ago."

"Well, if you ever need backing and want to give it a go, let me know."

"I appreciate that, sir," Breanna said softly. "Now what assignment do you have for me?"

"It's actually a co-assignment."

"Oh? With whom?"

"The most beautiful woman in the world."

Martha touched her face. "You're very kind, dear husband, but I'm afraid these wrinkles have stolen away any beauty I might have had once."

Lyle Goodwin shook his head. "Never. Those lovely time lines are a part of you, and that makes them beautiful."

Martha's eyes misted as Breanna said, "Doctor, I hope John feels that way about me after we've been married forty years. Now, what is it Martha and I are going to do for you this morning?"

"Well, I've already told Martha about it. Three of our new nurses are arriving on the ten o'clock train from Chicago this morning. I can't get away from the clinic, and I'm going to be doing some skin work on Mrs. Shrewsberry where she scalded her hands. I want Missy to work with me. So, I'd like for you and Martha to be the welcoming committee. I'll arrange for a carriage to pick up their luggage and take it to the hotel."

Breanna grinned at Martha. "It will be my pleasure to be half of the welcoming committee."

At 9:45, Martha and Breanna alighted from their buggy and mounted the steps at Denver's Union Station. The platform was crowded with people waiting for the Chicago train. Soon they could see black billows of smoke as the big engine came into view.

About half the passengers had left the train when Breanna spotted two young women who stepped off the platform of the third coach, looking around expectantly.

"I think these may be our gals," Breanna said to Martha. "They have that special 'nurse' look, don't you think?" Breanna walked toward them with Martha close behind. "Good morning, ladies. Do you happen to be Alicia Fortune and Betty Olson?"

The young women's faces brightened.

"Yes, we are," the brunette said. "I'm Alicia and this is Betty."

"My name is Breanna Baylor. I'm acting head nurse for Mile High Hospital, and this is Dr. Goodwin's wife, Martha. Dr. Goodwin sent us to pick you up and take you to your hotel. There'll be a carriage here to transport your luggage."

Breanna explained they were waiting for another nurse on the train, coming from Philadelphia. Her name was Veronica Clyburn. Veronica was to have traveled with Nurse Mary Donelson, who had been delayed in coming. It was Mrs. Donelson who would be head nurse upon her arrival a couple of weeks after the hospital opened.

At that moment, Breanna saw another young woman looking around in the same manner as Alicia and Betty.

"Pardon me," Breanna said with a smile. "Are you Veronica Clyburn?"

"Yes."

"I'm Breanna Baylor, acting head nurse at Mile High Hospital."

Then Breanna introduced Martha and the other two nurses, explaining that they had come from Women's Hospital in New York.

Veronica greeted them warmly, then said to Martha, "I have a message for Dr. Goodwin from Mary Donelson, ma'am."

"Good news, I hope."

"Yes. Things are moving better than expected in finding her replacement. It's looking like she'll be able to leave Philadelphia within three weeks."

"Oh, wonderful!" Breanna said. "She'll be here just before the hospital opens."

"Lyle will be happy about that!" Martha said. "It will help considerably if Mrs. Donelson can be here a little early to set up the nursing staff the way she wants it."

The new nurses were eager to tour the hospital, so Martha and Breanna agreed to take them immediately.

When the Goodwin buggy pulled up in front of the impressive building, Veronica said, "Oh! It's so...*new!* The Philadelphia hospital is a hundred and nineteen years old, and it's really starting to show it."

"I'm so happy to be here!" Alicia said.

"Me, too," Betty said. "I'm going to love living in this wonderful Mile High City."

"Well, come on, ladies," Breanna said. "Let's start the tour."

As Breanna and Martha guided the new nurses through the building amid carpenters and painters, they came upon Russ Cullen, who was putting the finishing touches to the counter and cabinets at the first-floor nurse's station.

"Russ, you look a little peaked," Breanna said. "Are you all right?"

"I'm awfully sick, ma'am," Cullen said, rubbing his stomach. "Do you know where I can find a good nurse?"

"Real funny," Breanna said. "Now, what is it, Russ? I can tell you're not up to par."

"I'm just a little tired, Breanna. I had an upset stomach during the night and didn't sleep well. But I'm okay now. I'll catch up on my sleep tonight."

At that moment, Sheriff Curt Langan walked through the door and looked straight at Russ Cullen.

"Morning, Sheriff," the contractor said.

"Good morning...good morning, ladies."

"Sheriff," Breanna said, "I'd like you to meet three of our new nurses."

When the introductions had been made, Langan said, "Russ, I'm sorry to keep you from your work, but I need to talk to you."

"No problem, Sheriff," Cullen said. "Mrs. Goodwin and Breanna were giving these ladies a tour of their new place of employment. They don't need me."

As Martha and Breanna led the women away, Langan looked at Cullen and said, "You have two new carpenters, I believe. A Herb Louis and a Jim Varner."

"Yes. Why?"

"I need to talk to them, too. The three of you together."

"Sure. They're upstairs."

"Jim Varner...Herb Louis...shake hands with Sheriff Curt Langan," Cullen said.

"What's this about, boss?" Louis asked.

"The sheriff hasn't told me. But I guess we're about to find out."

The sheriff looked from one face to another and then said, "Were you gentlemen in the Golden Slipper Casino last night?"

Cullen spoke for all of them. "Yeah. Why?"

"Playing poker for about four hours?"

"Yeah. Guess it was about four hours, wasn't it, guys?"

Varner and Louis nodded.

"It was a foursome, right? Fourth man was a professional gambler named Lowell Jessup?"

"Yeah. What's this all about?"

"When did you last see Jessup?"

The trio exchanged glances, then Louis said, "We left him on the boardwalk in front of the Slipper about...uh...what was it? Close to midnight, I suppose."

"Left him?"

"Yeah," Cullen said. "Jessup was going to his hotel, and we were heading home. Herb and Jim live in a boarding house over on Glenarm Street. I live in a small house on Colfax Avenue near Broadway."

"Did you see Jessup head for his hotel?"

Cullen looked at the other two. "Well...I guess we did. I really didn't pay any attention to him after we separated. You guys?"

"Not me," Varner said. "Why all these questions, Sheriff?"

Langan hooked a thumb in his gun belt. "A man who was playing poker last night next to your table came into my office about an hour ago. He found Jessup's body floating in the Platte River. Identification on the body shows it's Lowell Jessup, without a doubt. He was stabbed six times before his body was dumped."

144

12

"I WAS HOPING maybe you fellas could help me," Sheriff Langan said.

"In what way?" Russ Cullen asked.

"By answering some questions at my office. I'd like to talk to each of you, one at a time."

"You don't think we had anything to do with it, do you, Sheriff?" Jim Varner said.

"I didn't say that, sir. I just have some routine questions to ask each of you. Maybe you can give me something to go on to bring in the killer."

"Sure, Sheriff," Herb Louis said. "But, uh…who's this guy that sat close to us in the Slipper and pulled Jessup's body from the Platte?"

"He wishes to remain anonymous. He fears the killer might come after him if he knows who he is. Shall we head for the office then?"

As they walked toward Tremont Street, Langan said, "One thing I'd like to know from you fellas right now."

"What's that?" Cullen asked.

"How did you happen to get into a game with a professional gambler?"

"Jim and I know him from Dodge City, Sheriff," Louis

said. "He was a close friend to the owner of a saloon we redecorated. Jessup was in there a lot, and we got to know him. Played poker with him a few times."

"We saw him on the street yesterday morning on our way to work," Varner said. "We figured to get to know our boss better, so we stopped by his house, introduced him to Jessup, and asked him to spend the evening playing poker with us."

"I see. Okay, I'll save the rest of my questions for our individual sessions at the office."

Russ Cullen and Herb Louis sat outside the sheriff's office while Jim Varner was interviewed. It took only ten minutes for Varner to appear and tell Louis he was next.

Louis came out in just under ten minutes and sent his boss in.

Russ Cullen sat down in front of the desk. Deputy Steve Ridgway sat on a hardbacked chair on one side of the desk, leaning against the wall. He looked at Cullen with interest, but sat quietly.

"I have only one question to ask you that isn't routine, Russ," Langan said. "I've been told that you've flat refused other men who've asked you to go gambling with them. Most everyone in town knows that you shy away from it. That's a proper assessment of you, isn't it?"

"Well, Sheriff, getting good men to work for my company isn't easy. I've had to fire a few since starting this job because they either don't do quality work or they're just plain lazy. Herb and Jim are excellent carpenters, and they give me an honest day's work. I don't want to lose them. So, I went against my normal course and gave in when they asked me to play poker at the Slipper with them."

Langan nodded. "All right. Now, the routine stuff."

Some twenty minutes after he entered the sheriff's office, Russ Cullen emerged and looked down at his two employees. "Okay, men. Let's get back on the job."

As they walked toward the hospital, Louis said, "Boss, I have to tell you it got my attention last night when I saw the look on your face—you know, on your porch, when Jessup moved into the light."

"Oh?"

"I'd have sworn you knew him. But when Jim asked Jessup if you two knew each other, and he said he had never met you before, I didn't think any more about it."

Varner turned to catch Cullen's eye. "Boss, you really did look like you'd seen a ghost when you saw Lowell's face. What was wrong?"

"Well, I'll tell you, Jim. Jessup strongly resembled an old friend of mine who died several years ago. His name was Clarence Boatman. When Jessup stepped out of those shadows, it jolted me. I thought for a moment that Clarence had come back from the dead. So it really was like seeing a ghost."

"Well, it's a crying shame about Jessup. Somebody must've had it in for him."

"Wasn't robbery," Louis said. "From what the sheriff said, his identification was still on him, which means his wallet was. If the money had been taken, I'm sure Langan would have said so. It was just cold-blooded murder."

"Well, I hope the sheriff catches the dirty snake," Cullen said.

⚓

"I don't know, Sheriff," Steve Ridgway said. "The other two guys seemed quite calm during the questioning, but Cullen was awfully nervous. Notice that?"

"Mm-hmm. I noticed," Langan said.

"And he was working hard at covering it up."

"Yeah. I noticed that, too."

"Doesn't that mean something? Like maybe he knows more than he's telling us? Or worse?"

"Not necessarily, Steve."

"No?"

"Cullen's being nervous doesn't make him guilty of any-thing. Some people just naturally get nervous when confronted by the law." Langan scratched behind his ear. "But I'll be honest with you, my friend. Mr. Russ Cullen does leave me a bit on edge, though I can't say why. It's more than the fact that he was nervous during questioning, but I can't quite name what it is."

"Same here. And then there's that business of him giving in to those two guys and playing poker for four hours at the Slipper. I don't know, Sheriff. Something smells fishy. The man has been adamant about staying away from the gaming tables ever since he hit town. Nobody would have thought anything about it except that several sources say he spoke out sternly against gambling. Not the way Pastor Larrabee would, like it's against the Bible, but like a man who's been burned and shies away because he's afraid it might happen again. Understand what I'm saying?"

"I do. But even though it doesn't add up in our thinking, that doesn't mean Cullen killed Jessup."

"I agree, boss, but I still smell rotten fish."

↟

Late in the afternoon, Russ Cullen was working with two of his men on the hospital reception desk.

"Boss," Jock Elam said, "Damon and I were really surprised to learn you'd played poker at the Golden Slipper. How many times have *we* asked you to go? And you've always turned us down. How come you'd go with the new guys but not with us?"

"Herb and Jim just caught me in a weak moment, that's all. We all have those now and then, don't we?"

Jock nodded, flicking a glance at Damon Barber. "Yeah, guess we do."

"I'm sorry now that I gave in. I've been upset ever since Sheriff Langan told me about Mr. Jessup being found stabbed to death, especially after I just spent the evening playing poker with the man."

"So what kind of questions did the sheriff ask you?" Barber said.

"Just routine stuff. You know…did we notice Jessup being upset or showing fear like maybe he knew there was somebody after him. That kind of thing."

"So, had you noticed anything?"

"Nope. He seemed as normal as a man could be."

"From what I've heard," Elam said, "the motive wasn't robbery."

"Apparently not. I guess whoever killed him was either a maniac or had it in for him. Gamblers do tend to make enemies."

Cullen then excused himself, saying he had to check on some other men.

↑

Undertaker Noel Crawley heard the tiny bell that signaled someone had entered the front door. He was in the back, building a coffin. He laid down the hammer and pushed dark purple curtains aside.

"Oh, hello, Sheriff...Steve. I did exactly as you told me. Mr. Jessup's body hasn't been touched since I brought it in this morning. I have it here in the back room."

Curt Langan and his deputy followed Crawley into the work room. They could see the undertaker was making a cheap coffin out of knotty pine. In a shadowed corner lay a body under a white sheet.

As Crawley led them toward the body, Langan glanced at the partially finished coffin. "That Jessup's?"

"Yes, sir. Tain't much, but since you said to keep it cheap, that's what I'm doing."

"No embalming either, I suppose," Ridgway said.

"Nope. Unless the sheriff wants to take twenty dollars out of the dead man's funds to cover it. But as far as I can tell, Mr. Jessup won't care whether he's embalmed or not."

Crawley pulled the sheet down to Jessup's waist, then stepped aside. Langan and Ridgway could easily see the six stab wounds in the gambler's expensive suit coat and vest.

"Sheriff, we didn't have time to talk when I picked the body up this morning," Crawley said. "Do you think the stabbing was done at the river or somewhere else?"

"Somewhere else. Steve and I walked both banks for quite a distance upstream. There was no blood anywhere on the ground. There had to have been blood at the scene of the murder. When the body was found it was snagged in some brush near the bank. There's no telling just where the body was thrown in the river, nor how far it floated until it got caught in the brush. But I'm sure Jessup was killed elsewhere."

"It's not going to be easy to catch the guilty party, is it?"

"No, but we're working on it. And of course there's always self-incrimination."

"Pardon me?"

"Sometimes a killer unwittingly gives himself away."

Russ Cullen sat in his overstuffed horsehide chair, reading the *Denver Sentinel.* The front page carried a photograph of Lowell Jessup's body lying on a table at Crawley Undertaking Parlor. Sheriff Curt Langan had been interviewed by a *Sentinel* reporter, and the full story nearly filled the page.

Cullen laid down the paper, and his attention was drawn to the sound of plodding hooves and a horse blowing out front. He went to a window and peered past the edge of the curtain. Though it was past twilight, Cullen could make out the form of Sheriff Langan dismounting. He stepped back from the window and took a deep breath.

He heard the sound of a boot scraping the porch, then came a knock. He waited until the sheriff had knocked a second time, then he shook back his shoulders and forced a smile to his lips before pulling open the door. "Well, howdy, Sheriff. What can I do for you?"

"Just need to ask you something," Langan said.

"Sure. Come on in."

Langan stepped inside, then turned to Cullen. "I didn't give a thought to asking you about this when I questioned you today, Russ."

"What's that?"

"Well, I had occasion this evening to spend some time with the man who found Jessup's body in the river. You know, the fellow who observed the four of you from a nearby table during the evening. He said he noticed you and Jessup eyeing each other as if you had something going between you—as if you knew each other. You *were* sitting with him at your elbow, weren't you? Not across from each other."

"Yes. That's right. But—"

"Let me just ask you point-blank, Russ. Did you know Lowell Jessup before last night?"

"No, I didn't. I never laid eyes on him until last night." He slid his sweaty hands into his pockets.

"Then what my man says was familiarity was something else?"

"Had to be. In fact, you can ask Herb and Jim. Jim thought he saw something between Jessup and me that looked like we might have been acquainted. He asked Jessup if we were, and Jessup clearly told him we'd never met before. And that's the truth."

"Okay." Sheriff Langan turned toward the door. "I won't bother you anymore tonight."

When Langan opened the door, Cullen said, "Sheriff, am I a suspect?"

"No, I just have to follow up all the facts. You understand."

"Oh, sure. Well, if I can help you in any way, please let me know."

"Will do." Langan nodded and closed the door behind him.

Cullen walked to the kitchen, dipped his hands in the water bucket, and splashed cool water on his face. He picked up a towel and blotted water from his face and beard.

Again he heard a knock at the front door. He steeled himself for whatever Langan had forgotten to ask him and went once more to open the door.

Cullen's smile faded when he found himself looking at a skinny little man who was somewhere in his fifties or sixties. His slender face was well weathered, and his hair was almost totally white.

He glowered at the man. "Yeah? What is it?"

"Mr. Cullen, I'm Lenny Pinder. May I come in and talk to you?"

"Do I know you?"

"No, sir, but *I* know *you.*"

"Whattaya want?"

"I have a little business deal I want to discuss with you."

Cullen stepped back and swung open the door. "Well, come on in. But make it snappy. I've got better things to do than to talk some silly business with a stranger."

"Oh, this is anything but silly business, Mr. Cullen."

"Okay, let's have it. I'm a busy man."

Lenny Pinder wasted no time. "I saw you. I know you murdered that Jessup fellow and dumped him in the Platte."

13

"I WAS VISITIN' A FRIEND of mine last night, Mr. Cullen, a few doors down the block from you. I was headin' home 'bout midnight when I almost run into you a-carryin' the limp form of that there gambler over your shoulder."

The urge to reach out and destroy the little man welled up in Cullen. "You got cat's eyes or something? It's plenty dark at midnight in the alley."

"Don't need cat's eyes when you see a man's face under a street lamp. I follered you all the way to the river and watched you dump that body in right where the Platte bends just after it passes under the Colfax bridge. That's where you dumped it, so you can't say I didn't see you. I waited for you to head back for your house. You stayed away from the street lamp when you were carryin' Jessup to the river, but you got a little careless when headin' home. I saw you, plain and clear."

Cullen's slightly reddened face was the only sign of the rage within him.

"Y'see, Mr. Cullen, I recognized you right off as the contractor who's buildin' the new hospital. You know where the Rocky Mountain Mercantile Company is, don't you?"

"Yes."

"Well, I work there. Janitor. I've seen you plenty of times."

"That so?"

"Uh-huh. The news of that gambler's murder was spread all over town by ten o'clock this mornin'. And I guess you know it's in the *Denver Sentinel* all over the front page."

"So what do you want?"

"Well, I could have gone right to Sheriff Langan and told him what I saw last night, couldn't I? But you know I didn't, 'cause if I had, you'd be locked up in his jail right now. Am I right, or am I right?"

"I asked you what you want."

"I'm a businessman, Mr. Cullen, even though I make my livin' pushin' a broom. There was a time when I ran my own shoe and boot repair shop. St. Louis. Did right well, if I do say so myself."

"You did so well you're pushing a broom now?"

Pinder dipped his head and looked at Cullen out of the tops of his eyes. "Well, I run into some problems. But I didn't come here to talk about Lenny Pinder. I come here to talk about Russ Cullen and his future. For five thousand dollars I'll forget what I saw, and my mouth will be shut about it forever. How's that? Good business, I'd say. You pay me five thousand and keep your neck outta the noose. I'll be happy and rich, and you can go on makin' big money in your contractin' business."

"Be a lot cheaper for me to just dump you in the river, too!"

"Wait a minute!" Pinder threw his hands up, palms toward Cullen. "You better listen to me. It'd be a whole lot better for you to pay me the money. I wrote down what I saw, namin' you as the man I saw carry Mr. Jessup's body to the river. I sealed what I wrote in an envelope, Mr. Cullen, and left it with a friend of mine. He won't open it unless somethin' happens to me."

Cullen stared hard at Pinder, then sighed and said, "Look, I don't keep that kind of money in the house. Meet me in front of the Rocky Mountain Bank at ten-fifteen tomorrow morning. I'll give you the money then."

Lenny Pinder smiled and moved toward the door. "I thought you'd see it my way, Mr. Cullen. Well, goodnight then. I'll see you in the morning."

Cullen closed the door. He waited a moment, then moved out onto the porch. He could see Pinder moving down the street at a good clip.

Cullen hurried to the kitchen, opened a drawer, and pulled out a knife. Then he rushed outside and followed Pinder at a safe distance. He saw Pinder bound onto the porch of a house some ten doors down.

Cullen stood behind a big cottonwood and watched Lenny slip inside. He knew that an old bachelor named Hector Thompson lived there. He eased up beside the house and peered through a parlor window. The night was warm, and the window was open about two inches. Cullen watched as Lenny paced the floor in front of Thompson.

"I'm tellin' you, I had him eatin' outta my hand, Hec! I've got him, and he can't do a thing about it!"

"So lemme see the money," Thompson said.

"Well, I don't have it yet. I'm s'posed to meet him at the Rocky Mountain Bank in the mornin'. And for keepin' that envelope for me, Hec, I'm gonna give you a cut! How's five hunnerd sound?"

"Five hundred! I've never seen that much money all at once in my whole life!"

"Well, sleep good tonight, ol' buddy, 'cause you'll see it tomorrow!"

Both men heard a noise at the front door and whirled to see a flashing knife with a fourteen-inch blade.

↑

The next day was Saturday, September 3. At 10:00 A.M., the Goodwin buggy swung into the parking area of Denver's Union Station, carrying the Goodwins and two excited young ladies.

Clint Byers was on the 10:05 from Pueblo. He had Saturday and Sunday off from his job laying track for the Union Pacific, and he wanted to spend it with Missy.

The 10:15 from Cheyenne City would bring the Carrolls. Dottie had wired Breanna from Reno that they would be two days later than scheduled because of sabotaged track east of Reno.

The 10:05 was already chugging into view when Missy broke from the others and ran to meet it. She had barely reached the edge of the platform when she saw Clint standing on the bottom step of the third car, waving at her. He hit the platform on the run.

Breanna and the Goodwins looked on as Clint and Missy embraced, holding onto each other for a long moment. Then Clint greeted Breanna and the Goodwins.

"Clint," Missy said, "there's another train coming in shortly from Cheyenne City. Breanna's sister, Dottie, and her family are on it. Dottie's husband is Dr. Matthew Carroll, chief administrator of the new hospital."

"Hey, that's great, Breanna!" Clint said. "I remember you telling me that Dottie was engaged to a doctor. I'm looking forward to meeting your family, Breanna, but right now, I'd like to be alone with my little gal. So, Missy, how about the two of us taking a walk by the river?"

"Sounds good to me," Missy said.

"I suppose your sister and her family will be at church tomorrow?" Clint said.

"Oh, I'm sure they will," Breanna said.

"Well then, Missy and I will meet them then."

The 10:15 from Cheyenne City rolled in moments after the happy couple had left the depot. Breanna smoothed her dress and patted her hair as the big engine chugged to a hissing stop.

The Goodwins stayed close to Breanna as she moved slowly through the crowd, scanning the coaches with anticipation.

"Aunt Breanna! Aunt Breanna!"

Breanna looked back and forth along the platform, then she spotted the bright face of little Molly Kate through an open window in the second coach. James's face soon appeared beside hers.

"Aunt Breanna!" he shouted. "We'll be off in a minute. Don't go away!"

Breanna laughed. "Don't you worry about that!"

The children's faces vanished, and Breanna and the Goodwins threaded through the crowd and stood a few feet from the coach's front platform. Soon they saw James and Molly Kate emerge through the door, followed by Matt Carroll. Behind him came Dottie and a beautiful young woman.

Dr. Carroll offered his hand to Dottie and then Stefanie while the children leaped onto the depot platform and ran to their aunt's open arms. Breanna kissed their bright faces, and then she and Dottie were in each other's arms. Dr. Goodwin introduced Martha and himself to Matt, the children, and Stefanie Andrews.

When the sisters finally let go, Matt introduced Dottie to the Goodwins, and Breanna embraced Stefanie and welcomed her to Denver and Mile High Hospital.

"Thank you, Breanna," Stefanie said. "I've really looked forward to seeing you."

Breanna released her with a final squeeze and then turned to Matt. "Hello, brother-in-law!"

Matt opened his arms. "Hello, sister-in-law!"

Stefanie leaned toward Dottie and whispered, "You weren't kidding. You and your sister do look a lot alike!"

"It just looks better on Dottie!" Breanna said.

The group laughed, then Lyle Goodwin said, "Dr. Carroll, since you'll be staying at the Great Western Hotel until we get your house sale completed, you can store what you brought with you at our place."

"Thank you. I appreciate that."

"Stefanie," Breanna said, "in Dottie's last letter she said you would be living with them in their house, at least for a while."

"Yes. They've been very kind."

"Well, rather than you having to stay at the hotel until the house is available, how about staying with me?"

"Well...sure! All right!"

"I live in a small cottage at the rear of the Goodwins' house. Right now another nurse, Missy O'Day, is living with me, but there's room for you too. The couch in the parlor makes into a bed. You'll be comfortable, I promise."

The men went to hire a carriage and wagon to carry them and their luggage, while the women and children strolled slowly toward the Goodwin buggy. James and Molly Kate clung to their aunt.

"Oh, Breanna," Dottie said, "I'm so anxious to meet John. Is he in town?"

"Not right now, I'm sorry to say. He's on a mission for Marshal Duvall, tracking down a cold-blooded killer known to be in western Kansas or eastern Colorado."

"John should have been a lawman," Dottie said. "From what you've told me, he's so often chasing outlaws and the like."

"Well, John's calling in life takes him so far beyond the limits of a man who wears a badge. When you hear John preach, you'll say he should be pastoring a church or preaching as an evangelist instead of chasing down bad guys. Of course, some folks don't like his preaching because he steps on their toes."

"I like a preacher who's not afraid to tell it like it is," Stefanie said. "Just preaches the Bible straight from the shoulder and lets its truth cut a swath wherever it goes. That's how our pastor at First Congregational Church in San Francisco is."

"Our pastor here at First Baptist is like that too," Breanna said. "You can all hear him tomorrow."

"We'll look forward to it," Dottie said.

"Oh, Breanna," Stefanie said. "We got to hear Dwight Moody at our church a few weeks ago."

"You did? Really? I've heard so much about him. I hope some day I get to hear him preach."

"You've heard his sage words about being sold out to God, haven't you, Breanna?" Dottie said.

"Yes. I read them in our church paper one time. When Mr. Moody surrendered to preach, he said, 'The world has yet to see what God can do with one man who will totally surrender to Him...and by His grace, I will be that man.' A model goal for all of us, I'd say."

"Aunt Breanna?"

"Yes, James?"

"When will Mr. John Stranger be back? I really wanna meet him."

"Well, honey, that's hard to say. It probably won't be too

long, though. He brings in the bad guys quite handily."

"Yeah! That's what I wanna talk to him about! I want him to tell me about all the outlaws he's shot and captured, and…and about fightin' the Indians, and…I *really* wanna hear about those fast-draws when he killed those smart-aleck gun-fighters who thought they were faster'n him!"

"Oh, James!" Molly Kate said with a sigh. "That's crazy! How come you don't want to hear Mr. Stranger preach? Why do you want to hear about guns and arrows, and people bleeding. You—"

"Just because you're a girl, M. K., and you like dolls and teacups and that kind of stuff don't mean what I like to hear is crazy. And just because I want to hear Mr. Stranger tell about his gunfights and stuff don't mean I don't want to hear him preach! Girls are so dumb!"

"Children!" Dottie said. "That's enough!"

When everyone was in the parking area and all the luggage and boxes were loaded in a hired wagon, Martha Goodwin said, "All of you are invited to dinner at our house tonight. Seven o'clock. Breanna and I will cook you up a nice meal."

"I'll be glad to help with the cooking," Stefanie said.

"Well, you're more than welcome to pitch in, dearie."

Molly Kate gave her brother an impish look. "Mrs. Goodwin…"

"Yes, honey?"

"My brother likes spinach. Could you fix him some for supper?"

"Why, of course. We sure will!"

James opened his mouth to speak, but Dottie touched his lips with the tip of her forefinger and said, "Let it go."

The boy scowled at his sister, who gave him a mockingly sweet smile.

Matt turned to his colleague. "Dr. Goodwin, I'm really eager to get a look at the hospital. How soon could I do so?"

Goodwin smiled. "How about just as soon as we get everything in place, including the Carrolls checked into the hotel?"

The sun reflected off the surface of the lazy Platte as Clint and Missy found a grassy spot on the bank and sat down.

"Missy," Clint said, kissing her hand, "I sure have missed you."

"I've missed you, too…more than you'll ever know."

She then asked how work on the railroad track was going. Clint told her the track was almost to the Colorado-New Mexico border.

"The way it's looking, we'll have the track laid to Santa Fe within another year. And since Union Pacific has promised me a job right here in Denver when the project is done, our wedding should be in September of next year."

"Oh, I can hardly wait to become Mrs. Clint Byers! *Missy Byers.* Has a nice sound, doesn't it?"

"Sure does." Clint cupped her face in his hands and kissed her, then asked if Dr. Goodwin was satisfied with her progress toward becoming a certified medical nurse. She was happy to tell him the doctor had remarked just yesterday how well she was doing.

"Great!" he said. "I pray every day the Lord will help you. I'm so proud of you. I know you'll be a wonderful nurse. You have such a sweet way about you, and you have such a love for people."

"Speaking of having a love for people…I'm really looking forward to meeting this Stefanie Andrews—she's a nurse the

Carrolls are bringing with them to work in the new hospital."

"Why are you so eager to meet her?"

"Do you ever get a newspaper down there working on the track?"

"No. We just have to wonder what's going on in the world."

"Well, remind me to tell you about the Bay Area Strangler attacking Stefanie on her very doorstep. It's quite the story, but I'd rather not talk about it just now."

Clint thought about pursuing it, but decided instead to ask how things were going at the church.

"Things are going great," Missy said. "We've seen people come to the Lord week after week, and we've seen Christians get their lives right with God and begin to really serve Him."

"Sounds like I've been missing out on a lot," Clint said, letting his gaze roam over the sunlit surface of the river. "Sure am glad I can be in church tomo—"

"What is it, Clint?" Then Missy saw it too.

"Wait here," Clint said, leaping to his feet.

Missy watched him as he scrambled to the river's edge some twenty yards from where she sat. Clint's eyes were riveted on a body bobbing face-down under a clump of bushes. He knelt at the water's edge and closed his fingers on the dead man's shirt collar. He heard rapid footsteps behind him and looked up and saw Missy. "I don't think you'll want to see this, Missy."

"I'm working to become a nurse, Clint. I'll see a lot of dead bodies. Here, let me help you pull him out."

They had the body almost out of the water when Missy looked down and said, "Oh, Clint, there's another body down there!"

The second corpse was totally submerged in the shallow

water, facing the surface. The water was clear, and they could tell it was a man. Cords were tied to him and wrapped around a large rock. The first body had been weighted down also, but the cord had slipped and allowed the body to surface.

Clint glanced over his shoulder. There were plenty of people on the street. Some were on foot, others were in wagons and buggies. When he saw two teenage boys riding double on a horse, he stood up and called to them.

The boys' eyes bulged as they drew up and saw the lifeless form lying on the bank.

"I need you boys to ride fast and bring the sheriff. Would you do that?"

"Yes, sir!" said the youth who held the reins. "Bobby, you stay here. I'll go get the sheriff lickety-split!"

One boy slid off the horse's back, and the rider galloped away. People were starting to gawk, and some were heading toward the river bank.

"Bobby," Clint said, "would you go stop those people? Tell them we've found two dead men down here, and the sheriff's on his way. He won't want people tromping all over this area."

Bobby dashed to do as Clint had requested.

In order to remove the second body from the river, Clint had to take off his boots, wade in, and use his pocket knife to cut the cord. He was just pulling the body toward the bank when Missy said, "The sheriff's coming, Clint."

Curt Langan and Steve Ridgway drew their horses to a skidding halt and slid from their saddles.

"What've we got here, Clint?" Langan asked.

"Two men who were stabbed to death. Both of them have several knife wounds. Missy and I were just sitting on the bank up there when I caught sight of this little man. As you can see, they were both weighted down with rocks."

Langan was kneeling over the bodies as Steve came up beside him. "Lenny Pinder and Hec Thompson!"

"So you know them?" Clint said.

"Yeah. Both bachelors. Been in this town since before I came here."

"Killer has to be the same guy who stabbed Lowell Jessup, Sheriff," Ridgway said. "Maybe I should make that *killers*. Be pretty hard for one man to have stabbed both of these men unless he did it at separate times. Multiple knife wounds just like Jessup, though."

"Somebody else been killed like this lately?" Clint asked.

Langan nodded and looked more closely at the bodies. "One man could have done this, Steve."

"Why do you say that, Sheriff?"

"Well, for one thing, Hec was getting along in years. He wouldn't have been able to fight off a strong man. And Lenny's quite small, so he wouldn't have been too much of a problem either. Steve, you go get Noel Crawley so he can pick up the bodies. I want to check for footprints on the bank. We know the killer walked right here because he weighted the bodies and put them in the water by this bush."

14

JUST BEFORE SEVEN O'CLOCK that evening, Dr. Matthew Carroll and his family pulled up in front of the Goodwin house in a rented carriage. Matt hopped out, tied the reins to one of the fancy hitching posts with a horse's head on it, then helped Dottie alight.

James dropped from the carriage where he had been sitting beside his sister and bounded for the porch steps. Matt cleared his throat loudly, giving James the eye.

The boy stopped and said, "Oh. I forgot."

He dashed back to the carriage where his sister was waiting at the edge of the rear seat. James raised a hand toward her. "May I help you down, Miss?"

"You may, sir," Molly Kate said with a giggle.

Just before they knocked, Dottie warned, "Now you two mind your manners."

"Yes, ma'am," they said in chorus.

Molly Kate giggled. "James, I hope you like the spinach Mrs. Goodwin is fixing for you!"

"James," Dottie said, "since your sister found it necessary to set you up, you don't have to eat any spinach tonight."

"Thanks Mom! Tell you what, M. K., you can have my share!"

The door opened, and Dr. Goodwin greeted them warmly, then led them toward the dining room.

"Anything I can do to help?" Dottie asked.

"It's all done, except for getting the bread out of the oven," Martha said, heading for the kitchen. "The rest of you sit down. Lyle, would you show everybody their places?"

The aroma of fresh-baked bread topped off the many pleasant smells that already filled the dining room as Martha set the loaf on the table.

Dottie looked around. "Missy and Clint aren't eating with us?"

"After their ordeal today, they just wanted to be alone," Martha said. "They're eating out somewhere."

"Ordeal?"

"Oh, you haven't heard? It's all over town, but I guess it could have missed folks in the hotels."

"Are they all right?" Dottie said.

"They're fine," Lyle said. "Let's pray, then I'll tell you about it. Dr. Carroll, would you voice our thanks to the Lord for His bounties?"

After the "Amen" and while the food was being passed, Dr. Goodwin said, "Before I tell you about Clint and Missy's adventure today, let me first explain that we had a man murdered here in town a couple of nights ago."

He told them about Lowell Jessup, and how his body was found floating in the Platte River. Then he explained that Clint and Missy had found two more bodies in the river that afternoon.

"So, I hate to hit you with it when you've just arrived in Denver, but you'd hear it pretty soon anyhow. We've got a killer on the loose."

"Looks like we can't escape it," Matt said.

"Ah! You must be referring to the Bay Area Strangler," Goodwin said.

Matt glanced at Stefanie, then turned to his host. "I know I said it four or five times when we were touring the hospital, but I'll say it again. I've never seen one I like so well."

Goodwin smiled broadly. "I'm glad you're pleased with it. We owe a lot to Russ Cullen for doing such a great job. He's very meticulous about his company's quality of work, and he's come up with so many novel ideas that have made the hospital more efficient."

"I especially like the way he's designed the operating room," Matt said. "The offices are laid out well, too."

"This all sounds intriguing to me," Stefanie said. "I'm looking forward to the tour on Monday."

Conversation dwindled for a few moments, then Dr. Goodwin said, "Breanna, if Mary Donelson doesn't make it before opening time, I still want you to be head nurse until she does arrive. You understand that, don't you?"

"I thought I should be ready, just in case," Breanna said. "If she's not here within two days of opening, I'll go ahead and have a meeting with the nurses. I'll teach them my philosophy on hospital nursing, then Mrs. Donelson can add or subtract anything she wants after she's here."

"She certainly comes to us with a high recommendation," Goodwin said. "The woman is like our Breanna, here. She could easily become an M.D. if given the opportunity to enter medical school."

"What age is Mrs. Donelson, Dr. Goodwin?" Stefanie asked.

"If I remember correctly, she's in her late forties."

"Oh. Well, at that age, she probably wouldn't be interested in becoming a doctor."

Breanna chuckled. "I'm quite a bit younger than her, but with all due respect to Dr. Goodwin's appraisal of me, I'm not interested, either."

Dottie smiled at her sister. "But you *are* interested in getting your MRS. degree, aren't you, big sister?"

"I won't deny that. I love nursing, and I'll do it as long as the Lord wants me to. But it would be the most wonderful thing in life to meet my John at the altar and become 'bone of his bone and flesh of his flesh.'"

"Do you plan to give up nursing when you and John marry?" Martha asked.

"No plan. I'll just have to see how the Lord leads. Of course, I'm hoping that when it's time for John and me to marry, the Lord will settle him in one spot."

"You've told us a great deal about John in your letters," Dottie said, "but you've left so much out, too. The silver medallion he leaves with people he's helped…you said it's inscribed with words from Deuteronomy."

"Yes. Deuteronomy 29:22. 'The stranger that shall come from a far land.'"

"What exactly does that mean?"

"It means that the man who has just helped you through a crisis, or even saved your life, is from a country a long way from the United States and its territories."

"Well, where is he from?"

"I can't tell you that, honey. John wants it kept a secret."

"Let me ask you this," Matt said. "You've told us about so many people he's helped financially. Is he independently wealthy?"

Breanna smiled. "Again, a question I'm not allowed to answer."

"Mysterious man," Stefanie said.

"That he is. But the most wonderful man I've ever met."

Molly Kate spoke up. "Aunt Breanna, when James and I meet Mr. John Stranger, can we call him Uncle John? I mean, since you're Aunt Breanna?"

"You and James will call him Mr. Stranger, honey," Dottie said.

Breanna looked at her sister. "Dottie...if you and Matt don't object, I think John would be pleased if they address him as Uncle John, even though he's not my husband yet. He's often mentioned how eager he is to meet all of you."

"Well, as long as you say it's all right, Breanna, it's all right with Dottie and me," Matt said.

"Aunt Breanna..."

"Yes, Molly Kate?"

"When James and I meet Uncle John, is it all right if we give him a hug?"

Breanna smiled. "Yes, sweetie. Your Uncle John is a very kind and loving man. He would like that."

"But he isn't kind and loving to bad guys, is he, Aunt Breanna?" James said.

"No, he's not. He's known to be pretty rough on lawbreakers and on men who mistreat or beat up on women. He's every inch a gentleman."

"God give us more like him," Martha said.

"Amen to that," Stefanie said. "And God give *me* a Christian man like him!"

Everybody laughed.

"How long have you been a Christian, Stefanie?" Martha asked.

"Just over two years, ma'am. It was Dr. Carroll who witnessed to me and finally led me to the Lord. I'll be eternally grateful that he cared about where I would spend eternity."

Martha was about to ask of Stefanie's family when her husband said, "Stefanie, I read about your encounter with the Bay Area Strangler. You are a remarkable young lady. Would you mind sharing the experience with us? I, for one, would like to hear it from your lips."

"Lyle," Martha said, "you're asking a lot. It may be difficult for Stefanie to talk about it."

"It's all right, Mrs. Goodwin. I'll admit that once in a while the thought comes to me how very close I came to being strangled, but the Lord has given me a deep, settled peace about it. What would you like to know, Dr. Goodwin?"

"The whole thing."

Everyone had finished eating, and Breanna and the Goodwins sat spellbound as Stefanie told the story. She wept when she told them of trying to lead Burton Meade to Christ, and how he had cursed her and rejected the Lord. "The man died without being saved. And now, according to the Word of God, he's burning in hell."

Martha Goodwin began to cry. "Oh, you precious dear. It takes the real love of God in a person's heart to feel that way about such an awful man."

"Jesus loved Burton Meade enough to die on the cross for him, ma'am," Stefanie said. "I can feel no different about him, even though but for the hand of God, he would have killed me."

Breanna reached across the table and took hold of Stefanie's hand.

"Well," Dottie said, "we'd best help Martha get these dishes done and clean up the kitchen. It'll soon be bedtime for a certain boy and girl I know."

Before anyone could shove back a chair, there was a knock at the front door.

"That will probably be Clint and Missy," Martha said, "unless somebody's got a medical emergency."

Dr. Goodwin returned with the couple, and Breanna introduced them to her family and Stefanie. Then everyone plied them with questions about the two bodies they'd found that morning.

Martha told everyone to go into the parlor, the dishes could wait.

When Clint and Missy had finished their story, Dr. Goodwin said, "Well, I'll say this about it—the murderer won't be on the loose for long. Curt Langan may be the youngest man to wear a sheriff's badge in Colorado, but he's a sharp cookie. He'll nail the killer."

"This Sheriff Langan sounds like quite a man," Stefanie said.

"You may get to meet him tomorrow," Breanna said. "He and his deputy, Steve Ridgway, trade off coming to church, since outlaws and other types of no-goods don't take Sundays off."

Stefanie's eyes widened. "You mean both your sheriff and his deputy are Christians?"

"They sure are."

"Breanna won't boast about it, Stefanie," Martha said, "but it was she who led the sheriff to the Lord."

"I haven't heard of many lawmen becoming Christians, Breanna. I'd like to hear how you did it."

"I'll tell you sometime."

Stefanie felt emotionally full as she thought of her newfound friends and the way God had led her to them. She left her chair and bent over to hug Breanna's neck. "You and I are going to be good friends."

Breanna hugged her back, sensing that Stefanie was right.

✦

That night, when Breanna, Missy, and Stefanie were preparing for bed, Stefanie asked how the other two had become interested in nursing. Stefanie found Breanna's story intriguing, but her heart leaped when she heard about Breanna and Missy's captivity in an illicit gold mine. It was there Missy decided to become a nurse. Breanna had so impressed her that she wanted to be just like her.

Missy pressed Breanna to tell Stefanie how the mine incident had led to Sheriff Langan's conversion.

Stefanie was deeply touched to learn what devastation Sally Jayne had inflicted on Curt Langan's heart, but she praised the Lord He had used Sally's deception to convince Curt that Satan had deceived him, too—and that he needed to trust Christ.

The three young women were thoroughly awake now and decided to talk until they were sleepy again. As they sat around the small kitchen table, Breanna said, "Tell us about yourself, Stefanie. Your family...where you're from...how you chose nursing as a career."

Stefanie told them about her mother dying when she was two years old...her vague memories of Mexico...the years of moving from place to place in California until she and her father ended up in San Francisco. She told them of her father's strange disappearance, resulting in the Hazletts taking her into their home and how living there influenced her to become a certified medical nurse.

Breanna said it was odd Stefanie's father never told her where her mother was buried so she could at least visit the grave.

"I agree it's odd, Breanna. But then my father did so many

odd things. I loved him dearly, but his strange behavior often puzzled me. He's left me with a life full of unanswered questions."

"It's good that you know the Lord," Breanna said. "He gives us peace, even when life is puzzling."

"Oh, yes. He's certainly done that for me. What a wonderful God we have!"

"You said something this evening, Stefanie, about wishing God would bring a man like John into your life. You left no young man in San Francisco, I take it."

"No. The Lord must want me to be an old maid. I've met some nice young men, but I've never found one I was interested in romantically. Somehow that man has been like an unfulfilled dream."

Breanna left her chair and wrapped Stefanie in her arms. "Stefanie, I'd be surprised if the Lord wants you to be an old maid. I suspect He has the right man picked out for you, and when it's His time, He'll bring the two of you together in His own wonderful way."

"You'd make a great mother, Breanna. Thank you for those encouraging words."

"Tell you what, Stefanie. Missy and I always have prayer together at bedtime. Let's pray and ask the Lord to guide all three of our lives day by day and step by step."

Thirty minutes later, lying in her couch-turned-bed, Stefanie Andrews wept silently, thanking God for her two new friends.

15

THE NEXT DAY, at Denver's First Baptist Church, Breanna proudly introduced the Carrolls and Stefanie Andrews to Reverend Lin Larribee and his family. They took an instant liking to each other. The pastor showed special interest in James and Molly Kate, and had his son and daughter take them to their Sunday school classes.

When the Sunday morning service was over, the Carrolls and Stefanie and Breanna slowly followed the crowd toward the foyer.

"Well, sister-in-law," Matt said, "you certainly didn't oversell your pastor to us. The man can preach. And his Sunday school lesson was really inspiring."

Breanna bent down to her niece and nephew. "Did you two like your Sunday school classes?"

"Yes, and I liked the pastor's preachin', too," James said. "Molly Kate didn't understand it, but I did."

Molly Kate flashed him a pouty look. "Boys! They think they're so smart! I understood everything Pastor Larribee said, James! *Everything!*"

"Yeah? How about—"

"James," Matt said, "that's enough."

Breanna looked at Dottie. "You and I never had a dispute.

I wonder how it would have been if we'd had a brother. Do you suppose we would've fussed with him?"

"I can guarantee it," Dottie said with a smile. "The brother-sister combination is like mixing glycerol with nitric acid."

Breanna laughed. "Nitroglycerin!"

When they reached the door where the pastor and his wife were shaking hands with people, Matt commended Larribee for the good sermon and Sunday school lesson.

"I know only one man who can out-preach him," Breanna said.

"Oh, is that so?" Pastor Larribee said. Then he put a hand to his brow and looked heavenward. "Oh, of course. The stranger from a far land."

Dottie hugged her sister. "Why aren't the pastor and I surprised you feel that way?"

Larribee leaned down to Breanna's height, placed an open hand beside his mouth, and said loud enough for everyone close by to hear, "I agree with you one hundred percent!"

The others laughed and stepped out into the warm September sunshine.

The next morning, Breanna, Missy, and Stefanie sat down for breakfast with the Goodwins.

As soon as they started eating, Dr. Goodwin said, "Okay, ladies, here's the agenda for the day. Missy, as usual, will be working all day at the office so she can continue learning and working toward her certificate. Breanna and Stefanie will go with us to the office. When the Carrolls arrive at 7:45, Breanna will take Stefanie and Dottie on a tour of the hospital, which should take no more than an hour."

"Then you want me back at the office to work the rest of the day," Breanna said.

"No. I'll let Stefanie work in the office…for which she will be paid, of course." He glanced at Stefanie. "That all right with you, my dear?"

"Of course. I'm not used to being idle."

"So what have you planned for *me*, Doctor?" Breanna said.

"Last night before going to sleep, I was thinking this situation over with Mary Donelson barely arriving in time for the hospital to begin operation. Since all of our new nurses except Mrs. Donelson are here, I'd like you to meet with them. We need to organize the work shifts and set up who will be working what shifts. That's something we'll have to take care of, no doubt, before Mrs. Donelson arrives. The nurses need to know how to plan their days."

"I agree," Breanna said. "And I need to learn just what experience each nurse has so I can blend experience with inexperience in all fields. Each shift must be covered for any and all kinds of emergencies."

"Good thinking," Dr. Goodwin said. "See why I lined you up for interim head nurse?"

"I'm sure there are others in the group who could've done as well or better, Doctor," Breanna said. "But it will be good to get all the nurses together so they can become acquainted before it gets too close to opening time."

"That's *very* good thinking," Goodwin said, chuckling. "No doubt they'll work better together if they all know each other. Breanna, you're a genius."

"You really think so, Doctor?"

"Absolutely!"

"Well, I understand that acting head nurses who are geniuses get paid *double* what non-genius acting head nurses do. I hope Mrs. Donelson gets delayed for a few weeks! Yours truly will be able to fatten up her bank account!"

Dr. Goodwin shook his head in mock exasperation, then looked at Martha. "Now what do I do?"

"Don't ask me, dear! You dug the hole, now figure out how to fill it back in without going bankrupt!"

Everyone had a good laugh, then Breanna said, "Any particular time you want me to meet with the nurses, Doctor?"

"Why not early afternoon? I'll send a messenger to the hotel where the nurses are staying. You can meet in one of the hotel's conference rooms. I've got a meeting set up with Drs. Wakeman, Stratton, and Moon this morning from eight till ten. We need to meet with Dr. Carroll and discuss hospital business."

"Sounds like everybody is going to have a busy day," Martha said, and then sighed. "Guess I'll lock myself up in my sewing room and produce Mrs. Goodwin a new dress!"

At seven-thirty that morning, Sheriff Langan and his deputy arrived at the office from opposite directions on Tremont Street. There was a brisk wind, and what had started out as a sunny day was quickly becoming cloudy.

"Good morning, boss," Steve Ridgway said.

"And top o' the mornin' to yourself. Think it'll rain?"

"Good possibility."

Langan turned the key and opened the door. "First things first," he said.

"Yeah, I know. 'Sweep the place out, Slave Ridgway.'"

"Just be glad we don't have any prisoners right now. At least you don't have to cart their breakfasts from the café across the street this morning."

"Life does have its small blessings, doesn't it?"

Langan sat down at his desk and began sifting idly through a stack of papers. From the corner of his eye, he saw Steve pull a broom out of a small closet. "I heard the preaching was red-hot yesterday. Quite a few people got saved," Curt said.

"You heard right. By the way, I met the new chief administrator of the hospital and his family—the Carrolls—and one of the new nurses. It looked like they all hit it off with Pastor Larribee." Steve paused with the broom in hand. "How'd you sleep last night, boss? Any bad dreams?"

"No bad dream about Sally Jayne last night, praise the Lord. But Saturday night—that was probably the most vivid dream I've had in a couple of weeks. But Steve, when I woke up, the hurt in my heart wasn't so bad. I think my subconscious is beginning to accept the fact that Sally's gone and I really never meant a thing to her. You understand what I'm saying?"

"Sure," Steve said, sweeping the dirt and dust into a small pile in the middle of the floor. "And I'm glad to hear it."

Langan rose from his chair. "Something else, Steve."

"Yes, sir?"

"Last night I had a different kind of dream."

"Oh? You mean that you were as handsome, rugged, broad-shouldered, and fast on the draw as me?"

"No, better than that. I met the one true love of my life. Steve, the dream was so real. She was a committed Christian, and more beautiful than any woman I've ever seen."

Steve looked at the ceiling and rolled his eyes. "Now we're getting somewhere!"

Heavy footsteps came from the boardwalk outside and the door opened. Two federal deputy marshals entered with a handcuffed man between them.

Langan and Ridgway knew the deputies, Spencer and Kurtz, who worked out of the Denver office under Chief U.S. Marshal Solomon Duvall.

"Howdy, fellas," said Langan. "Who you got here?"

"You ever heard of Reid Shelby, Sheriff?" Kurtz asked.

"Yep. He's on a wanted poster in my file."

"Well, this is him. We've been chasin' him for three weeks. Finally out-foxed him and got him in a trap. He'll be stayin' here in your jail till he can be tried in court."

"Trial won't help him any," Spencer said. "He's guilty of just about every crime you can name. He's gonna hang, for sure."

Shelby looked at the lawmen with hateful eyes.

"Put him in number one back there. Steve, lead them back, will you?"

Langan turned around to see a tall figure in the doorway. "Oh, hi, Chief," he said. "Come on in. Your boys just brought in Reid Shelby."

"So I heard. I'd like to talk to him."

Langan opened the door that led to the cell block. "He's the only prisoner back there, Chief. Can't miss him."

Duvall thanked him and moved through the door.

Sheriff and deputy stepped outside for a look at the clearing sky. They were discussing the next step in the murder investigation when a familiar sound met their ears. From the north end of town came the bawling of cattle mixed with the rumble of hooves and the yipping of cowboys. A cloud of dust could be seen above Denver's stockyards.

"I wonder if this bunch will give us any trouble," Ridgway said.

"Tell you what," Langan said. "Why don't you ride up there? Maybe they'll see your badge glistening in the sun, and they'll give another thought to acting like fools."

"Will do. Ol' 'Dirty Job' Ridgway will obey the master."

Langan gave him a swift kick on the posterior and laughed. "Now git!"

Langan watched his deputy ride north, then stepped back into the office. He had been at his desk for about five minutes when Chief Duvall returned from the cell block.

Duvall sat down with a sigh. "Well, Curt, I wish all the outlaws in the west were behind bars like that one. He's as tight-lipped as they come, though. He knows where a whole gang of outlaws are holed up, but he'll die before he tells me. So, what've you uncovered about this stabbing business. Any leads?"

"Nothing concrete to go on. But I've got it settled in my mind that I'm dealing with one man. Confirmed it when I did a footprint check. Other than the prints of myself and the young couple who found them, there was only one other set of prints. Had to be the killer the way they led down the bank into the water."

"What do you know from the prints?"

"Only that the killer wears a size ten boot, and by comparing the imprint with my own and doing a little calculating, he weighs about a hundred and sixty pounds when he's not carrying a dead body in his arms."

"I see what you mean, 'nothing really to go on.' There must be five hundred men in this town who wear a size ten boot. And if you're right about the weight, half of them will weigh somewhere between a hundred-fifty and a hundred-seventy pounds. You've got your work cut out for you, Curt. I'd put some men on the case to help, but I just don't have them to spare. Spencer and Kurtz don't know it, but they have exactly one day to rest before I send them out again."

"I appreciate that you'd like to help me, Chief, but I'm going to work on this case till I solve it. I want to see that knife-wielder hang. I just hope I can catch him before he kills again."

"I do too. Problem is, when you put this guy on the gallows, there'll be two more to take his place."

"We really need more lawmen west of the wide Missouri, don't we, Chief?"

"Yeah. About five times as many as we have. If I had a hundred like John Stranger, we could make a dent in these parts, I can guarantee you."

"He's a good one, that's for sure. Any word from him about his pursuit of Bill Gregg?"

"Not yet, but John has never failed to get his man. If the reports that Gregg is in these parts are true, John'll get him."

The loud sounds of bawling cattle and the whistling, yipping cowboys continued to drift from the north end of town.

"Say, speaking of this Bill Gregg, Chief, I just had a thought."

Langan pulled open a drawer and rifled through it for a few seconds, then pulled out a wanted poster. "Just as I remembered!"

"What?"

"Bill Gregg. I wish we had a picture of him, but anyway, it says here that most of his killings have been with a knife. Only a few were done with a gun. He seems to like to do his work the quiet way."

"Yes. That's him, all right."

"Well, Chief, what just hit me was this knife thing. Maybe the reports are absolutely correct. Maybe Gregg's in Denver!"

Langan read the small print on the poster. "Chief, right here it says he's killed more gamblers than any other kind of victim. Lowell Jessup was a gambler."

"But the other two weren't. Besides, we don't know what size boot Gregg wears. But even if it turned out to be number tens, you said the killer would weigh around a hundred and sixty pounds. Look at Gregg's weight on there."

Langan studied the poster. "It says Gregg weighs well over two hundred pounds."

"Something like two-thirty the last I knew."

Curt rubbed his ear and grinned at the federal man. "Oh, well, it was a thought."

16

AT 7:45 THAT MORNING, the five doctors of Mile High Hospital met together while Breanna loaded her sister, the children, and Stefanie into Dr. Goodwin's buggy and headed up Tremont Street. Dottie needed to pick up a few things at the general store, then they would go to the hospital for the tour.

As they rode along the dusty street, Dottie said, "Now, James and Molly Kate, if you'll be real good, I'll buy you some candy at the store."

Breanna looked over her shoulder. "Dottie, dear, are you insinuating that my niece and nephew are ever anything but good?"

"What should I tell your aunt, kids?"

James leaned up close behind Breanna and half-whispered, "Don't believe it, whatever she tells you!"

"Just tell her 'bout James being bad, Mommy," Molly Kate said. "He's bad a whole lot more than I am."

James whipped around and was about to defend himself when Dottie said, "Ah-ah-ah! No candy if a fight starts!"

"Well, she—"

"James!"

"I'm sorry, Mommy," Molly Kate said. "I didn't mean to

start a fight. I was just being truthful. James gets more lickings than I do."

James wanted to blurt out, "Yeah, because girls get away with being naughty more than boys do!" Instead he said, "I hope this store has lots of candy."

When Breanna pulled rein in front of the general store, James said, "All you ladies will have to wait your turns as this gentleman helps you from the buggy."

While James was giving his hand to each of the ladies—including his sister—the sound of bawling cattle and hollering cowboys met their ears.

"Sounds like we're on the Chisholm Trail," Stefanie said.

"Not quite," Breanna said, "but Denver is running a close second to Abilene, Kansas, when it comes to cattle drives. The railroad is handling them by the thousands. The cattle have been driven down from the Rockies, where there are hundreds of cattle ranches."

"Does this go on year round?" Dottie asked.

"The drives start in late spring and run through early fall. Nobody wants to drive cattle in winter. Too much snow in this country."

"Living here is going to take a little getting used to," Stefanie said. "Far back as I can remember, I've never lived where it snows. I know I'll love it."

"Well, children," Breanna said, "let's help your mother find what she needs in the store and then scout out that candy."

Stefanie had noticed a ladies' ready-to-wear shop across the street. As the group started toward the general store, she said, "Breanna...I just noticed Darlene's over there."

"Oh, the ready-to-wear shop."

"Yes. Do you see that green-and-white dress hanging in the window?"

"It's beautiful."

"I want to take a look at it. You go on, and I'll meet you in the store in a few minutes."

"Okay."

Stefanie left the boardwalk for the soft dust of the sunlit street. She had to wait for some buggies and wagons to pass and thought she heard thunder above the rattle of wheels. Funny, there were only a few drifting clouds.

When she was about a third of the way across, the sound of thunder grew. Suddenly, several dozen head of cattle rounded the nearest corner to the north, their fear-maddened eyes bulging, their horns glistening in the sun.

People ran for cover, and frightened saddle horses whinnied and darted away, carrying their riders from the wild-eyed, charging herd. Horses hitched to vehicles whizzed by Stefanie, who now stood almost directly in the middle of the street.

For a moment her legs refused to move. A scream finally escaped her lips, and she bolted toward the boardwalk. In her panic, she neglected to hoist her skirts and fell face-first in the dusty, wagon-rutted street.

Just moments before the stampeding steers rounded the corner at Sixteenth and Tremont, Sheriff Langan sat at his desk, listening to the sounds of the cattle drive ending at the stockyards. His deputy had been gone for almost half an hour.

Something wasn't right. Suddenly he realized the usual sounds had been replaced by a much louder roar of hooves.

Curt picked up his hat and hurried to the door to see people and horses scattering. To his horror, he saw a young woman in the middle of the street, frozen in terror as the herd bore down on her. Then she bolted. Three steps and she fell.

Curt ran into the street as fast as he could and gauged the distance to the front line of steers. He knew he would never be able to whisk her to safety in time.

The herd was coming in a V shape, led by one huge steer. If he could bring the leader down, there was a possibility the others would veer around the woman.

Curt planted his feet just behind the woman, held his Colt .45 with both hands, took careful aim, and fired.

The forelegs of the lead steer buckled, and it went down in a heap no more than twenty feet in front of Curt and Stefanie, its huge body blocking the way of the steers charging behind it.

Curt pushed Stefanie down and threw himself on top of her. She could feel the earth trembling beneath her, and the bellowing of the frightened beasts vibrated through her. It seemed to go on forever.

Finally, the last of the thundering hooves faded away, and the next sound was of shouting cowboys as they chased the runaway herd.

"You all right, ma'am?" Curt said as he helped Stefanie to her feet.

Dust was in her hair, on her clothing, in her mouth. She could feel the grit of it in her teeth. Stefanie blinked against the dust in her eyes and nodded.

People had come out of the stores and were lining the boardwalks, looking on. Curt saw Breanna Baylor leave the crowd and dash toward them as he took hold of Stefanie's trembling hand. Her entire body was quaking.

Curt folded her in his arms, saying, "It's all right now, miss. The danger's over."

Stefanie gripped his shoulders and looked at the dead steer.

The crowd lifted a cheer for their sheriff and shouted words of acclamation.

Breanna drew up, gasping. "Are you okay?"

"Yes'm." Langan nodded, keeping Stefanie in his grasp to prevent her knees from buckling. "The little lady here was crossing the street when the cattle bore down on her. She started to run for safety but got her feet tangled in her skirts and fell. There was no time to get her out of the way. The only chance was to drop the lead steer and hope the others would make paths around it. Thank God it worked!"

Breanna caressed Stefanie's dust-filled hair. "Thank the Lord you're all right, honey. You too, Curt. God certainly had His mighty hand on both of you."

"You know her, Breanna?" Curt asked.

"Yes, and I think you're about to squeeze the breath out of her."

"Oh, I'm sorry, Miss—"

"Andrews—Stefanie Andrews," she said with a smile. "Sheriff, I don't know how to thank you. You could have been killed!"

"It didn't matter about me, Miss Andrews. I was just concerned about saving you."

"Curt, Stefanie is one of the nurses who'll be working in the new hospital," Breanna said. "She came here from San Francisco with Dottie and Dr. Carroll. She's a C.M.N. Not only that, but she's a dedicated Christian."

"Oh, really?" he said, meeting Stefanie's brown-eyed gaze for the first time. "Welcome to Denver, Miss Andrews."

"I've told Stefanie about you, Curt," Breanna said. "She's been looking forward to meeting you."

"I doubt she thought she'd meet me under these circumstances."

"Not quite," Stefanie said.

"Curt," Breanna said, "I want you to meet my sister and her children."

When Dottie, James, and Molly Kate were introduced to Sheriff Langan, Dottie commended him for his courage.

"I just did what any other red-blooded man would do, Mrs. Carroll. A life was at stake, and it was my responsibility to save that life if possible."

"A bit modest, aren't you, Sheriff? I doubt there would be one man in a hundred who would have hazarded his life against such odds."

Curt cocked his head to one side and said, "Mrs. Carroll, I'm really amazed at how much you and Breanna resemble each other."

"You can call me Dottie, Sheriff. And I'm glad you see the close resemblance. To me, that's quite a compliment."

"I was about to take Stefanie, Dottie, and the children on a tour of the hospital, Curt," Breanna said.

Curt saw Steve Ridgway riding toward them and said, "I'd like to go along, if that's all right. I see my deputy heading this way. I'll have him watch the office."

Suddenly Stefanie began brushing dust from her dress. "I must look a fright! Maybe I shouldn't be seen like this."

"You look just fine," Breanna said, brushing at her dress.

"Here, honey," Dottie said, "let me get the dust out of your hair."

Steve Ridgway saw the sheriff with the women and children, and veered toward them. His eye caught the crumpled form of the dead steer in the middle of the street. "Looks like all the cattle that are coming in today are in, boss. None of the cowhands are acting like they're going to cause trouble."

"That's good."

"I see you've met Miss Andrews," Steve said. He glanced back at the dead steer. "Looks like somebody put a slug into that one's brain."

"You might say that," the sheriff said.

"We'll need to get it hauled away."

"Go on back to the stockyards and get somebody to do it."

"Okay. Any damage when that bunch stampeded?"

"None that I know of," Curt said.

"There almost was, Steve." Breanna then told the deputy how Curt had risked his life to save Stefanie.

Steve was shaken to learn how close he'd come to losing his boss. "I'm sure glad both of you are all right."

"Thank you," Curt said with a grin. "Steve, I'm going over to the hospital with the ladies. Breanna is going to give Stefanie, Dottie, and the children a tour. After you go to the stockyards, hold the fort at the office, will you? I'll be there in an hour or so."

"Sure, boss." Steve tipped his hat to the ladies and rode away, staring long and hard at the dead steer.

"Sheriff," Dottie said, "I didn't get my shopping finished. It'll take a few more minutes."

"That's all right. I'll stay here with Miss Stefanie. Take your time."

Dottie and Breanna smiled at each other and returned to the store with James and Molly Kate on their heels.

"Thank you, again, Sheriff, for saving my life. Words seem so frail at a time like this, but they're all I have."

"Just seeing you alive and unharmed is thanks enough."

Stefanie looked at the dress shop. "I didn't finish my shopping either, but it'll have to wait."

He followed her glance. "Darlene's?"

"Yes. See that green-and-white dress in the window?"

"It's a pretty one."

"Well, I was crossing the street to look at it when the cattle stampeded."

"We can go over there now."

"Thank you, but I'll look at it later. Dottie will be finished with her shopping in a few minutes."

Curt nodded. "I assume you worked with Dr. Carroll at the asylum out in San Francisco."

"On my off days, yes. My regular job was at City Hospital."

"I recall someone telling me that Dr. Carroll was going to bring a nurse with him. They just didn't tell me she was going to be so…beautiful."

Stefanie had never felt as nervous yet happy.

"So are you from San Francisco originally?" Curt asked.

"No."

"Back east?"

"Well, I'm really not sure. It's a long story. If you want to hear it, I'll tell it to you sometime."

"I'd like that. Are your parents living?"

"My mother died when I was two. My father and I traveled northern Mexico and southern California when I was small. We ended up in San Francisco when I was twelve. I became quite ill and my father put me in City Hospital. He…he never came back. I have to assume he's dead."

"How terrible! What did you do?"

"It's all part of that long story. Here they come. Looks like they're finished shopping."

James and Molly Kate were happily rolling hard candy around in their mouths as the group piled into the Goodwin buggy. Moments later they hauled up in front of the glistening white hospital.

With Curt beside her, Stefanie followed Breanna and the others on the tour. She loved the way the building was laid out. Soon they climbed the stairs to the second floor, and as they neared the nurses' station, Breanna saw Russ Cullen working alone on the counter.

"Good morning, Russ."

"Good morning." He smiled and glanced at the faces of the newcomers. "Good morning, Sheriff."

Langan returned the greeting. Then Breanna said, "Russ Cullen, I want you to meet my sister, Dottie."

"Ma'am."

"And these are her children, James and Molly Kate."

"Hi, kids."

"And this is Stefanie Andrews. She's a C.M.N. Came here from San Francisco with Dottie and Dr. Carroll. She'll be working in the hospital."

Cullen nodded at Stefanie. "Hope you enjoy the tour. Please excuse me. I have to go check on some work at the end of the hall." He left his tools and quickly walked away.

Stefanie tilted her head quizzically, and she started to say something. Then she hurried after Russ Cullen.

"I think those two know each other," Curt said.

Cullen reached the last room on the left and entered without looking back.

Stefanie ran faster, then slowed as she came to the open door. Cullen's back was toward her as he faced two men who were painting the walls.

She stepped up behind him and said, "Daddy..."

17

CULLEN BIT DOWN HARD and turned slowly to meet Stefanie's gaze. "Excuse me, young lady. Were you speaking to me?"

Tears misted Stefanie's eyes. "Daddy, why are you going by the name of Russ Cullen?"

The contractor took a step toward her and said, "Young lady, I am not your father. He and I must strongly resemble each other, but—"

"It's been thirteen years, Daddy. You've lost considerable weight, your hair has grayed up, and you've grown that beard, but I know my own father. What happened in San Francisco? Why didn't you ever come back for me? I didn't know whether you were dead or alive."

Sweat trickled down Cullen's back when he saw Sheriff Langan ease up behind Stefanie. No doubt Langan had heard every word.

"Boss, if she's botherin' you—"

Cullen raised a palm toward the painter. To Stefanie, he said in a low, even tone, "Miss, I don't know what your purpose is in making me out to be your father, but I've got work to do. Now please, leave me alone."

Stefanie began to weep. Curt put an arm around her shoulder and said, "Russ, Stefanie told me that when she was twelve years old, her father put her in San Francisco's City Hospital because she was very ill…and he never came back. She didn't know whether he had deserted her, been killed, or what."

"I'm sorry about that, Sheriff," Cullen replied. "But I'm not her father. I've never seen this young woman before, and I've never had a daughter. Now, if you'll please escort her away from here, I've got a building to finish before October first."

Stefanie's body quaked as she sobbed, "Daddy, why are you doing this?"

"Sheriff, please," Cullen said.

Curt pulled Stefanie closer to him and turned her toward the door. "Come on. Let's go."

Cullen had never seen such pain in the eyes of a human being as when Stefanie looked at him over her shoulder as the sheriff ushered her out. He turned to his men and said, "Poor little mixed-up gal. Hope Langan can help her."

"You must really look like her father, boss."

"Yeah, I guess so. Well, how's the painting going?"

When Breanna and Dottie saw the sheriff with his arm around Stefanie, they hurried toward them.

"What's going on?" Breanna said, running her gaze from Curt to Stefanie.

Before the sheriff could reply, Stefanie said, "That man who calls himself Russ Cullen is my father, Will Andrews! He says he's not, Breanna! But I know my own father when I see him!"

Dottie took her hand and squeezed it tight. "Stefanie, honey, it's been thirteen years since you last saw your father. That's a long time. Mr. Cullen no doubt resembles him, but if he says you're not his daughter—"

"No, Dottie! That man is my father! I know it!"

"Let's get you out of here, Stefanie," Curt said.

Dottie and the children followed as Curt guided Stefanie to the Goodwin buggy with Breanna by her side.

James took his mother's hand. "Is she gonna be all right, Mom?"

"Yes, honey. She's very upset right now, but she'll be okay."

When they reached the buggy, Curt said, "James and Molly Kate, how about you riding in the front seat with me? We'll let Miss Stefanie sit in the back between your mother and Aunt Breanna."

"I think it would be best if we go to our cottage, Curt," Breanna said.

"All right."

"Too much company is not good at a time like this," Dottie said. "Would you take the children and me to the hotel, please, Sheriff?"

"Yes'm."

Dottie turned to Stefanie. "If there's anything I can do for you, all you have to do is say the word."

Stefanie patted Dottie's hand. "Thank you, I appreciate that. I'll let you know if there's anything you can do." Then to Breanna, "I just need to get my nerves settled down. You're having the meeting with the nurses this afternoon, and I want to be there."

"Well, if you're up to it," Breanna said. "But if not, I can fill you in later."

"I'll be all right."

Shortly after Dottie and the children got off at the hotel, Langan pulled behind the Goodwin house. He kept his arm around Stefanie as he and Breanna walked her to the cottage.

Before Breanna could open the cottage door, Martha Goodwin emerged from her house and hurried toward them. "Is something the matter? Stefanie, you've been crying."

Curt helped Stefanie to the couch, and Breanna told Martha about the cattle stampede and Stefanie's brush with death. Then she explained what had happened with Russ Cullen.

Stefanie turned to Curt. "Sheriff, I want to see my father alone, and I want to do it tonight. Do you know where he lives?"

"Yes, I do. But maybe you should wait a little longer."

"No. Please, I must talk to him alone as soon as possible."

"All right. I'll take you to his house this evening. But I'm going with you."

"He'll be just like he was at the hospital if you come in with me," she said. "I must talk to him by myself."

Curt took a deep breath and let it out slowly. "Okay, but I'll be just outside the door."

"I appreciate your concern for my safety, Sheriff," she said, "but my father isn't going to harm me."

Curt rose from the couch. "I've got some business to tend to. What time do you want me to pick you up this evening?"

"Right after supper."

"That'll be about seven-thirty, Sheriff," Martha said.

"Fine. See you then, Stefanie."

Stefanie stood and walked him to the door. "Sheriff Langan, thank you once again for saving my life. And thank you for being so kind."

"The pleasure is mine, little lady. I'll pick you up at seven-thirty."

Breanna moved up beside Stefanie and called to Curt.

"Would you like me to drive you to your office in the buggy?"

"No, that's all right. The walk will do me good." He started forward, then paused and said, "I would like to ask your advice about something though, Breanna. In private?"

"Sure."

Stefanie and Martha watched as Breanna hurried to the sheriff. Langan guided her a little farther from the cottage to make sure they were out of earshot. He said a few words, then Breanna smiled and nodded as she answered him. They conversed for another few seconds, then Breanna turned back to the cottage and Langan left.

Breanna entered the cottage and saw the two women studying her. "Don't either of you ask a thing, because I won't tell you."

Martha shrugged. "Well, I guess we're going to stay in the dark on this one."

"Not for long," Breanna said with a smile. Then she took Stefanie by the hand. "Now, as your private nurse, young lady, I want you to come over here to the bed and lie down. Your morning has been a harrowing one, and you need to rest."

"Martha, could you stay with her for a little while?" Breanna asked as Stefanie headed for the bed. "It's almost eleven o'clock. I need to go to the hotel and make sure all my nurses are planning to be at the meeting, and set an exact time with the hotel manager to use the conference room. Think I'll make it for around 2:30."

"I'll be glad to stay with her. After all she's been through this morning, she shouldn't be left alone."

"I'll be all right, Martha. The Lord is with me."

"I know He is, honey, but He knows we sometimes need people too."

Breanna told them she would be back in an hour or so, and left.

Martha sat down in an overstuffed chair near the bed after picking up Breanna's Bible, which lay on a small table nearby. She opened it and started to read silently.

Stefanie closed her eyes and struggled with the turmoil that stirred within her. She wrestled with it for several minutes, then prayed in her heart: Lord, please make Daddy be home when Curt—when Sheriff Langan—takes me there. Please make everything all right between Daddy and me. And Lord…I want Daddy to be saved. Help me to be a witness to him.

Soon Stefanie's thoughts veered in another direction. Something strange had happened in her heart out there on the street after Curt Langan had saved her life. And it wasn't just on her part. She saw something in his eyes when he looked at her.

"Martha…"

"Yes?"

"Since Sheriff Langan went through that horrible ordeal with Sally Jayne…has he been seeing anyone?"

"Oh, a little, I guess. He's taken three or four of the young ladies in the church to dinner, but as far as I know, there's nothing serious with any of them."

Stefanie nodded and laid her head back on the pillow.

Sheriff Langan bypassed the office and went straight to the hospital. Upon entering the reception area, he came upon two workers who were hanging lanterns above the desk and counter. From them he learned that Russ Cullen was on the second floor, finishing the counter at the nurse's station.

He took the stairs two at a time and entered the second-floor hall. Cullen was working alone and looked up as the lawman approached him.

"Howdy, Sheriff," the contractor said.

"Russ, I need to talk to you."

"Sure."

Langan noted the workmen at the end of the hall. "I mean in private."

"Okay. Let's take a walk."

The two men said nothing to each other until they had left the building and were moving along the boardwalk.

Cullen spoke first. "What is it, Sheriff?"

"I won't beat around the bush with you, Russ. I'm asking you straight out. Are you Stefanie's father?"

"No."

"Well, she's absolutely sure you're Will Andrews—that was her father's name."

"She's mistaken, Sheriff. Has the poor girl ever had mental problems?"

"Not that I'm aware of."

"Well, something's wrong. Somehow she's mistaking me for her father, and it just isn't so."

"She said something to you this morning about your losing a considerable amount of weight. Were you heavier in the past?"

"I've weighed the same since I was in my twenties."

"Okay. That's all. I just wanted to hear it from you man-to-man that you're not Will Andrews."

"Well, now you've heard it."

"Sorry to take up your time, Russ," Langan said.

"Hey, it's all right. Far be it from me not to cooperate with the law." He paused, then added, "I guess you'll tell the young lady not to bother me any more?"

"I'll let you get back to work now."

The sheriff made his way to Tremont Street and headed for Darlene's Ladies' Ready-to-Wear Shop.

↑

Russ Cullen told his men he had some errands to run. He had a headache by the time he reached his house. As soon as he was inside, he went to the kitchen and took down a bottle of whiskey. He twisted the cork, tilted it to his lips, and took a long pull. His eyes watered as he smacked his lips and took another pull.

Russ thought of all the bad luck he had experienced in his life and counted Stefanie's appearance among the worst. He swung his fists as if punching an unseen opponent and cursed, half-screaming, "Why did she have to show up here? Big as this country is…why did she have to come to Denver? Stefanie, why? Now, you've got the law breathing down my neck!"

He wanted to run—get out of Denver. But he knew if he did, the sheriff would be on his trail like a hound after a fox. It was best to stay put. If Stefanie bothered him again, he would demand that Langan make her leave him alone.

Besides, she couldn't prove a thing. It was her word against his. In time, he was sure, she would give it up. He would just have to be more stubborn than his daughter.

At 2:30 that afternoon, Breanna Baylor stood before Alicia Fortune, Betty Olson, Veronica Clyburn, Donna Wygant, Flora Richards, Stefanie Andrews, and prospective C.M.N., Missy O'Day. Since Missy was going to work part-time in the hospital to enhance her nursing experience, Dr. Goodwin had sent her to the meeting.

The seven young women sat at tables with pencils and

paper for taking notes. They had introduced themselves to each other, so there was nothing else to do but get started.

"To begin with, ladies," Breanna said, "let me say that I am aware that some of you are more experienced than others, though all of you except Missy have your certified medical nurse certificates. Dr. Goodwin knows that I've done hospital work in many parts of the country, both during my training period and after. So even though my main work is as a visiting nurse, he asked me to talk to you about the 'glamorous' work of hospital nursing.

"When your head nurse, Mary Donelson, arrives, she no doubt will want to meet with you and instruct on how she wants the job done. But Dr. Goodwin felt this meeting would sort of get us all on the same level of thinking. I want you to ask questions at any time I am speaking. Just raise your hand and I'll acknowledge you."

Betty Olson raised her hand.

"Yes, Betty?"

"I want to ask the *big* question. 'Hey, nursie, you're so cute. Why are you still single? When you going to quit this job and get married?'"

Everyone laughed, for all but Missy had heard those words from patients countless times.

"People are the same everywhere, aren't they?" Breanna said. "So you've probably heard: 'Nursie, nursie, I need an angel of mercy!' And: 'Nurse, nurse, it's getting worse!'"

They laughed again, nodding and exchanging glances.

When the laughter died out, Breanna said, "All right, let's deal with the basic question: What is a nurse? As you know, that has been debated for a long time. Most nurses consider nursing a profession. Some doctors do not. Those are the doctors who consider a nurse the doctor's handmaiden. They even expect them to stand and give up their chairs when doctors enter the nurses' stations."

"I can speak for Dr. Carroll," Stefanie said. "He's a gentleman first and a doctor second."

"Good for him," Flora Richards said. "I can say the same for Dr. Moon."

"And I can speak for Drs. Goodwin, Wakeman, and Stratton," Breanna said. "They look on us as professionals, not handmaidens. I'm glad to know it's the same with Dr. Moon. We'll have one happy family, here."

"Unless we get a new one some day with a different outlook," Veronica Clyburn said.

"Then we'll gang up on him and straighten him out."

More laughter.

"Anyway," proceeded Breanna, "though we must always remember that doctors are better educated than we are, we are not to consider ourselves their puppets. We nurses have a right to bring our own intelligence to the job, and a good doctor wants the nurses he works with to be aggressive enough to question his decisions when they feel it necessary. In the mind of a good doctor, questioning is considered good nursing judgment. So is making suggestions to doctors about things that might help patients."

Stefanie Andrews's hand went up.

"Yes, Stefanie?"

"What is your opinion about a nurse refusing to carry out a doctor's order when she is in disagreement with it?"

"I'll give you a direct answer in a moment, but let me point out that we nurses are with our patients day in and day out. The doctor comes in and sees them for a matter of a few minutes, maybe once a day, maybe less. He doesn't know the patient like the nurse does, and sometimes he will give an order that the nurse knows is wrong for that patient. She must then make a decision that affects her own personal work with that patient. My direct answer is, it is not wrong for a nurse to refuse to carry out an order given by a doctor, as long as what she does is within the bounds of established procedures."

"That's good," Veronica said, making notes.

"But let's face it, a nurse's job is not glamorous. A nurse's role tends to be whatever other people decide it should be. Maybe someday they'll come up with some kind of aide for nurses, but until they do, we have to empty the bedpans, and strip, wash, and make the beds…do whatever doctors and janitors won't do."

All nodded, writing their notes.

"Hospital nursing is a restrictive profession; we're confined to the floor. If a patient's heart stops, the resident doctor arrives, handles the situation, and leaves. You take part in one emergency, and you can be in on another one right behind it. That's true whether the patient lives or dies. When each emergency is over, it's the nurse who's left behind to clean up whatever mess there is, and to try to pull together what was interrupted. If a nurse is upset, she just has to handle it and go on. She can't leave."

Missy's hand went up.

"Yes, Missy?"

"Can't a nurse leave the floor if she gets sick? I mean, when I've had to help somebody who's vomiting at Dr. Goodwin's office, it's made me do the same thing."

The others laughed.

"Well, honey, in a case like that, the nurse would have to leave the scene, do what she had to do, then come back and take up where she left off."

"How well we all know," Flora said.

"And then there's the patient who is combative or depressed. That one person can take a great deal of the nurse's time and drain her strength. The consulting doctor comes in for a few minutes and is gone, but the nurse is stuck there for her entire shift. This is our lot, ladies. If we're going to be good nurses, we will live with it and do our job cheerfully.

"Nurses are visible at all times. We're the largest group in the hospital. We have to answer to a lot of people—doctors, attendants, patients, and patients' families. Nurses are go-betweens. Everybody expects the nurse to do everything. It seems that everything filters through her hands at one point or another. We're more responsible for the patients than anyone else. We deal more closely with the business of the hospital, which is to care for the sick and dying, than anybody else.

"More often than not, nurses bear the blame for everything that goes wrong. That's rough on the nerves, and so are all the demands put on us. Every patient, almost without exception, considers himself or herself the most important one you are caring for. So we get the brunt of it when we don't pay them as much attention as they think we ought. You know in your hearts, ladies, that the patient who's sickest needs you the most. Naturally, you'll go to that patient first. But sometimes you go to the one who hollers the loudest."

"Don't we ever!" Veronica said.

"And yet, as demanding as our job is, we love it."

All nodded.

"Nursing is demanding physically. It's hard work to get a three-hundred-pound patient out of bed. Or even a two-hundred-pounder! It's hard work to be on your feet for eight hours.

"Nursing is demanding emotionally. It's hard to watch a patient suffer...or die. Yes, Alicia?"

"Miss Baylor, on that subject—watching your patient die—what is your opinion about how close we ought to let ourselves get to the patients? I've heard some older nurses say we shouldn't get too involved with them. It hurts too much when they die."

Breanna was silent for a moment, closing her eyes with her fingertips pressed to her temples. She chose her words carefully. "The original idea of professionalism in nursing was that you didn't get close to your patients. You remained aloof, not allowing yourself to invest in this human being who was your patient. I...I recall an older nurse I met when I worked in a Kansas City hospital for a while right after I received my C.M.N. She had the 'stay-aloof-and-don't-get-hurt' philosophy.

"I happened to be in the room, delivering some medicine, when a very sick man said to her, 'Hattie, I really like you. Why can't you take care of me every day?' And Hattie answered, 'Because we don't want to become attached to our patients. If something happens to you, it upsets us terribly.'"

Flora lifted her hand.

"Yes, Flora?"

"Is this type of attitude what causes many people to get the idea that nurses are uncaring? I've heard it many times: 'Nurses are harsh. Nurses don't care if their patients are in pain.'"

"I'm sure much of that thinking stems from nurses who take the attitude that they're not going to get close to their patients so it won't hurt so much when they die. I've met some hospital nurses who avoid working with dying patients for that reason."

"So give us your opinion," Flora said.

"All right. Sure it hurts when you've cared for a patient long enough to really get to know them and then they die. But you get over the hurt. Personally, I think hurt makes you grow as a

209

person. If you don't hurt a little bit now and then, you don't grow. To me the idea of cold professionalism is wrong. If you're not going to care enough about your patients to get involved with them—invest a certain amount of emotion in them and try to make them as comfortable as possible during the time they are under your care—why be a nurse?"

"That's right," Stefanie said.

All the others agreed.

"Another thing," Breanna said. "I mentioned the families of the patients a while ago. From what I've observed, I believe most hospital nurses want to give emotional support to the families of their patients. And they should. It's part of our job. We need to work at doing it better all the time. We can learn from experience and from observing nurses who are more experienced than we are. We must do all we can to help the families."

For the next hour, Breanna answered questions as best she could. Finally, she discussed their work shifts and set up proposed schedules to combine the more experienced nurses on the same shifts with those less experienced. It would all be finalized when Mary Donelson was on the scene.

18

IT WAS ALMOST 7:30 THAT EVENING when Sheriff Langan pulled up in front of the Goodwin house, parked his rented buggy, and walked around back with a package in hand.

He knocked softly on the door of the cottage and Breanna quickly answered. By the light of the porch lantern, Breanna saw the package and whispered, "She's fixing her hair in the back bedroom. Come on in."

He stepped inside and was greeted by Missy O'Day. "Breanna told me what you did, Sheriff. She's going to love it!"

They heard footsteps coming from the back of the house, and Curt flipped the package behind his back and was grinning broadly when Stefanie entered the room.

"Oh, Sheriff! I didn't know you were here yet."

"Man would be a fool to be late for a date with you," he said.

Stefanie blushed and tried to cover the fact that her heart was pounding. Curt brought the package from behind his back and extended it to Stefanie. "A little present for you," he said softly.

"For me?"

"Yes'm, and I'd like for you to open it right now."

Her fingers trembled slightly as she took the package,

untied the bow, and pulled away the wrapping. She slowly lifted the lid. "Oh! It's the dress I saw in the window this morning!"

As she held it next to her, Curt said, "I think it will fit okay. Since you and Breanna are just about the same size, I had her meet me at the shop. Darlene tried it on her and said it fit just right."

Stefanie smiled at Breanna, then looked back at Langan with misty eyes. "Thank you, Curt—I mean, Sheriff."

"Make it Curt, okay?"

"All right. Thank you, Curt. And thank you, Breanna, for being the model."

"My pleasure. I hope it fits all right. If not, you can take it to Darlene and she'll alter it."

Curt cleared his throat. "Stefanie, I…ah…asked Breanna what she thought about my buying you something as personal as a dress when we've only known each other since this morning. She said that under the circumstances…with all you've been through today, it would be a proper move."

Stefanie raised up on tiptoe and kissed Curt's cheek. "Thank you."

"You're very welcome," he said. "Well, we'd better head for Russ Cullen's place."

"Missy and I will be praying for you, honey," Breanna said.

"Thank you." Stefanie folded the dress and placed it back in the box. "I'll try it on when I get back."

Lantern light was visible through Russ Cullen's window as the buggy drew up to the front porch.

"I don't like you going in there alone, Stefanie, but I understand why you have to do it. I'll be right here. If something happens and you need help, just call out. I'll come on the run."

"I assure you, Curt, I'm in no danger. Daddy wouldn't harm me."

"Well, I'm here if you need me," he said, stepping down and going around the rear of the buggy to help her down. "You're trembling."

"I'll be all right," she assured him.

Langan leaned against the buggy and watched as Stefanie stepped up on the porch and knocked on the door.

Russ Cullen's features stiffened when he saw his daughter's face. "I don't want to talk to you!"

His eye then caught the sheriff standing at the buggy.

Langan moved toward the porch. "She wants to talk to you in private, Russ. It can't hurt you to give her a few minutes."

"Oh, all right. Come in." When the door was closed, he said, "Come back to the kitchen."

Stefanie followed him and sat down at the table when he gestured for her to do so.

"Stefanie, I...I'm sorry I had to desert you in San Francisco. But I left you with people I knew would take care of you. My life depended on me being able to vanish off the face of the earth, so to speak. Even at this moment, my life is in grave danger. If you convince the sheriff and the people of this town that I'm Will Andrews, I'm a dead man."

Stefanie was so relieved to be acknowledged as his daughter that she burst into tears, leaped from the chair, and wrapped her arms around his neck.

Cullen lightly embraced her.

"Oh, Daddy," she sobbed, "it was so horrible not knowing what happened to you, whether you were dead or alive! Why is your life in danger? Why will you be killed if your true identity is known?"

213

"Here," he said, gently pulling her arms from around his neck. "Sit down and I'll explain it."

Stefanie listened intently as her father told her that shortly after he had married her mother, he had taken up gambling, hoping to make a fortune. It didn't take long before he was a compulsive gambler. By the time Stefanie was two years old, and her mother died, he had no control over his gambling.

This was why he was gone for days and weeks on end, leaving Stefanie with neighbors, both in Mexico and California. He went away to gamble. It seemed his luck was always bad. He tried to quit but just couldn't do it. He would end up giving IOUs to casinos, saloons, and individual gamblers. Then he would run. This was why they had to move so often. He had to elude his creditors, most of whom would have killed him on sight.

The money he had made in carpentry was lost in gambling. By the time they reached San Francisco, so many men were after him that he had no choice but to vanish, leaving his daughter with the doctors at the hospital. He couldn't keep dragging her along with him. She needed a home and stability. He knew the doctors would see that she was taken care of.

He went to Missouri and hid out. He disguised himself by losing sixty-five pounds and growing the full beard. So far, the only person to recognize him was Stefanie.

"Daddy," Stefanie said, "you should tell your story to Sheriff Langan. Since you've broken no laws, he'll protect you from the gamblers and casino owners who are after you."

"No, Stefanie! If Langan knows who I really am, it will leak out. The men who are after me will find me. I'm a dead man if they do." He looked her square in the eye. "Honey, you have to tell Langan that you were mistaken. Russ Cullen is not your father."

"But Daddy, that would be a lie. I...I can't lie to the sheriff."

"Why not? It'll save my life."

"There has to be another way. I became a Christian two years ago. Jesus lives in my heart. I can't just out-and-out lie."

"Stefanie, if you expose me, you'll be guilty of my death when I'm murdered."

Stefanie bit her lip to suppress the tears. She studied her father's features for a long moment. "All right, Daddy, I won't expose you. I'll handle it with Sheriff Langan."

"That's my girl," Cullen said, patting her shoulder. "You're doing the right thing."

"Daddy, in all my growing up years, we never went inside a church building. We never talked about God or Jesus Christ or heaven and hell. Dr. Carroll gave me the gospel and led me to the Lord. I'm saved now; I want you to be saved, too."

"Honey, I have my own ideas about life, death, and eternity. I've investigated religion and found it a sham."

"Daddy, I agree. Religion *is* a sham. But there's a world of difference between religion and salvation. All of us are sinners and responsible to Almighty God for those sins. There's a hell for sinners who die unforgiven by Him. But there's a heaven for those who will allow God to cleanse them and forgive them of their sins through the shed blood of His Son. That's what the cross of Calvary was all about. You—"

"Honey, listen, it's time for you to go. The sheriff is going to get tired of waiting out there."

"But, Daddy—"

"Go on, now. We don't want to irritate the law, do we?" Cullen ushered his daughter toward the front of the house as he spoke.

"Can we see each other from time to time, Daddy? Now

that I've found you, I want to spend time with you."

"We'll work that out later. Right now, you have to convince the sheriff that you were mistaken—that I'm not your father."

Curt wondered what was going on inside the house. It suddenly clicked in his mind that Russ Cullen lived only a few doors from the house where Hector Thompson had lived. He attempted to shrug off the coincidence, but it continued to pick at the back of his mind. Then came to mind Russ Cullen's size. The man would weigh about a hundred and sixty to sixty-five pounds—the same weight Langan had figured for the man who had thrown the bodies of Thompson and Lenny Pinder in the river.

He wondered what boot size Cullen wore.

Suddenly the door opened, diverting his thoughts.

Stefanie appeared first, then Cullen behind her. As Stefanie started across the porch, Cullen looked at Langan and said, "We got it all settled, Sheriff. Stefanie will tell you about it. Thanks for bringing her by."

With that, Cullen closed the door.

Curt helped Stefanie into the buggy, then climbed in on the other side. He snapped the reins gently and urged the horse onto the street.

"Well?" he said, as they moved slowly toward the corner.

"Curt," Stefanie said, "I've been through an awful lot of emotional stress today. I'm totally exhausted. Could we talk about it later?"

"Sure, we can talk about it tomorrow. But would you just answer one question for me?"

"What's that?"

"Is Russ Cullen your father?"

Curt Langan knew by her silence that he had his answer.

"I really don't want to talk about it anymore right now, Curt." She paused, then, "Martha and I were discussing you today. She brought up how terribly Sally Jayne had hurt you. I want you to know how very sorry I am that you were hurt so deeply."

"I appreciate that, Stefanie. But I'll tell you what..."

"What?"

"Becoming acquainted with you has already helped shove Sally and the pain she brought on me to the back of my mind."

Soon they pulled into the Goodwin driveway. Curt helped Stefanie from the buggy and walked her around back to the cottage.

When Stefanie saw the cottage well lit up, she said, "Those two...they're waiting up for me."

"Sounds like them."

At the edge of the porch, Curt and Stefanie stopped and faced each other. Their eyes met by the lantern's soft glow.

"I'm so glad you came to Denver, Stefanie."

"I am too," she said. "I'm glad I met you today...and I'd be glad even if you hadn't had to save my life for us to meet."

"That makes me feel good."

"Well, I guess I'd better let you go. Tomorrow you can get back to protecting the town. I...I don't know how to thank you, Curt. For saving me from an awful death...for being so kind and good to me...for buying me that beautiful dress."

She raised up on tiptoe and planted a soft kiss on his cheek. "Good night."

"Good night. I'll see you some time tomorrow."

"I'd love it."

When the door closed behind Stefanie, Curt hurried to the

buggy at the front of the big house, touching the spot on his cheek where she had kissed him.

"Curt, ol' boy," he said to himself, "today you met the woman of your dreams."

Breanna and Missy were indeed waiting up for their new friend. They were sitting at the kitchen table clad in their robes. Both stood when Stefanie entered.

"So how did it go?" Breanna said.

"I had a wonderful time with Curt," Stefanie said, and smiled.

"You know what she means," Missy said. "What about Russ Cullen?"

"I've had a pretty rough day, ladies. I just don't feel like talking about it tonight. I need to go to bed."

"We understand, honey. You can tell us about it whenever you're ready. You can stay here and rest tomorrow, or you can come and work at Dr. Goodwin's office. Choice is yours."

"Oh, I'd love to go to the office. A good night's rest and I'll be ready for a full day's work."

A short time later, as Stefanie lay in bed with the darkness all around her, she pushed her father's demand that she lie about their relationship from her mind and prayed for his salvation.

Then her thoughts went to the tall, handsome sheriff. She had never met a man like him. Before drifting off to sleep, she whispered, "Curt, if you'll give me a chance, I'll love you the way you thought Sally Jayne did."

✦

The Goodwin Clinic was a busy place the next morning. When the doctor had taken care of patients who needed his attention, he told the nurses he would leave the others with them. He must talk to Russ Cullen and see if indeed they were going to be ready for the equipment due by rail on September 15.

It was near ten o'clock when Goodwin returned. Letha Phillips was counseling an elderly woman in the outer office. Breanna and Stefanie were stitching up a cut hand for one of the construction workers, and Missy was finishing a small bandage on a young boy's finger while his mother stood by. There was no one else in the waiting room.

Dr. Goodwin observed Missy's work and pronounced it excellent. Soon all the patients were gone and the nurses were cleaning up the examining and surgery room. Dr. Goodwin came in from his private office, smiling broadly, and holding a telegram.

"Good news, ladies," he said. "A telegram was delivered to me while I was at the hospital. It's from Mary Donelson. She's getting away from Philadelphia a few days early. She'll be arriving in Denver on Monday, September twelfth!"

"That'll put her here three days before the equipment arrives," Breanna said. "This is going to work out great."

At the same time Dr. Goodwin was telling his nurses about Mary Donelson's telegram, a tall man in black passed through the doors of the Federal Building a few blocks away.

Two deputy marshals came out of Solomon Duvall's office

and headed down the hall. Both smiled when they saw the man with the bone-handled Colt .45 slung low on his hip.

"Good morning, Mr. Stranger," Deputy Howard Katterly said.

John Stranger smiled. "And good morning to both of you. How's the deputy U.S. marshal business?"

"Never slow, as you well know. When you going to put a badge on and join up, Mr. Stranger? You're working for Chief Duvall most of the time anyway."

"I like it better this way. Leaves me free to do other important things that come along."

"I can understand that, sir, but I've heard it said that if Chief Duvall were to retire, President Grant would appoint you chief of this district in his place."

"I'm flattered," Stranger said with a grin, "but I don't think Chief Duvall is anywhere near ready to retire. Speaking of the chief, is he in his office?"

"Yes, sir."

"See you later, gentlemen." Stranger moved on down the hall and turned in at the U.S. marshal's office. There was a young deputy at the reception desk who recognized him and rose to his feet. "Good morning, sir. Welcome back."

"Thank you. I need to see Chief Duvall if he's not tied up."

"There's no one in his office at the moment, sir. Let me tell him you're here."

The deputy knocked, stepped part way in, and said, "Mr. Stranger is back, sir, and would like to see you."

"Send him in!"

Solomon Duvall was out from behind his desk in a hurry, shaking the tall man's hand.

"Well, John, did you get him?"

"No, but I know where he is. His trail led me right to him.

I thought you might like to be in on the arrest."

"Where is he?"

"Right here in Denver. In fact, right under your nose."

"What? Where's he holed up?"

"He isn't holed up. He's a prominent businessman." John reached in his shirt pocket and pulled out a folded slip of paper. He showed the chief the pencil sketch of a man's face and asked, "Know him?"

Duvall's jaw dropped. "Well…yes! It's Russ Cullen. His construction company is building the new hospital."

"That's right. Russ Cullen, alias Bill Gregg. I picked up his trail at Garden City. It took me to several other Kansas towns, Chief, and it was a bloody trail. By the time I followed it to Dodge City, I learned that Gregg has murdered almost every man he owed gambling debts to."

Duvall shook his head in astonishment. "Russ Cullen is Bill Gregg. Wait'll Sheriff Langan finds out."

"Going to be a shocker, isn't it?"

"It already is to me! So where'd you get the sketch?"

"Dodge City. When I was inquiring around town about Gregg, I ran onto a professional artist named Elson Humberd. He had gambled in the same saloon where Gregg and a professional gambler named Lowell Jessup had played poker several times. Humberd had heard about Jessup being murdered here in Denver and told me he'd bet it was Gregg who did it. Jessup told some of his friends he'd heard Gregg was headed west, and he was going to ride him down and collect the money Gregg owed him. Humberd made the sketch for me."

"Well, it's Cullen, all right. You bet I want to be in on the arrest. Langan will, too. Let's go see if he's in his office. The three of us will move in on Cullen…uh…Gregg together."

19

CURT LANGAN HELD the artist's sketch in hand with Steve Ridgway, Solomon Duvall, and John Stranger looking on. "This brings it all together, gentlemen. It was Cullen—Gregg—who murdered Lowell Jessup. Hector Thompson lives a few doors from Gregg. He and Lenny Pinder no doubt saw Gregg kill Jessup, and somehow Gregg found out about it."

"He's quite a liar, too," Stranger said. "He arrived in Denver, telling everyone he had been in business in El Paso, Texas, and came here when he heard of Denver's boom. From what Chief Duvall tells me, the man knows the construction business, but he wasn't in El Paso. He came here from Kansas, looking for a place to hide. No doubt he hired men along the way and told them to go along with his El Paso ruse."

"Well," Langan said, "let's go pick up Mr. Gregg. Chief Duvall, you're the one with all the warrants for his arrest. You do the honors."

"Gladly."

Russ Cullen was in the surgical room, checking the finished construction work for any flaws. His back was to the door and he was on his knees, examining the storage area beneath the counter, when he heard footsteps.

He looked up to see three men enter. Each wore a badge on his chest.

Chief Duvall stopped just short of the surgery table and said, "Bill Gregg, you are under arrest for murder. You will come with Sheriff Langan to be held in the county jail until you face Judge Roger Surrat in Denver County Court."

"Wh—what are you talking about? Who's this Bill Gregg? You know me. All of you know me. My name's Russ Cullen."

"We also know that Russell Cullen is only an alias. You are wanted in California and Kansas on sixteen counts of murder."

"And right here in Denver on three more," Langan said. "Lowell Jessup, Hector Thompson, and Lenny Pinder."

"You've got the wrong man, Chief! I'm a contractor...a businessman. I'm no murderer!"

Duvall took the sketch from his pocket, unfolded it, and turned Gregg's own likeness toward him. "This is you, isn't it?"

"Looks like me, yeah, but that doesn't prove anything. I'm telling you, Chief, you're barking up the wrong tree." Gregg inched his way closer to the surgery table. "I came here from El Paso to put my construction company on the map. I—"

"You're lying, Gregg," Langan said. "You came here from Kansas to elude the law and the men who are dogging your tracks to collect gambling debts. That's what Jessup was here for. You murdered him. Now, let's go."

Gregg seized the table and flung it at the lawmen with all his might. Duvall was knocked off his feet, and the other two were thrown off balance.

Gregg wheeled and darted toward the corner door, only to be confronted by a tall man in black. Gregg's head bobbed as if someone had slapped him in the face. He recovered quickly and barreled toward the man, ejecting an animal-like roar.

Stranger planted his feet and swung an iron-hard fist with precision. It caught Gregg on the jaw, lifted him off his feet, and landed him on his back. He was unconscious before he hit the floor.

Reid Shelby, who had been jailed several days earlier, had been taken to the territorial prison at Canon City by two of Chief Duvall's deputies the day before. When Bill Gregg came to, he sat up on his cot, blinked, and rubbed his aching head. He was the only prisoner in the jail.

Movement caught Gregg's eye as Steve Ridgway rose from a shadowed corner and called toward the office, "Sheriff! He's awake now!"

Ridgway stepped up to the barred cell door. When Gregg looked up again, three men had entered the cellblock. He recognized Sheriff Langan and Chief Duvall. Then it came back to him. The third man was the one who had put him down and out.

Langan moved up to the bars beside Ridgway, peered sternly at Gregg, and said, "How about coming clean now, Gregg? Stefanie is your daughter, isn't she?"

Gregg said nothing.

"Look, Gregg," Langan pressed, "you're going to hang. You might as well be honest for a change. You are Stefanie's father, aren't you?"

A cold glare was Gregg's only reply.

Langan turned to Stranger and Duvall. "I'm going over to the clinic. Stefanie is probably there. I need to tell her we've got her father locked up."

"I'll go with you," Stranger said. "I want to see Breanna."

Steve Ridgway was left with a mute prisoner as Chief Duvall left for his office and the other two headed for the clinic.

Breanna embraced John in front of everybody at the clinic and then introduced Stefanie to him. After the introductions, Curt took Stefanie into the small supply room and closed the door.

"Curt, what is it?"

"Stefanie, I…I have something to tell you, and it's not going to be easy. I hate to do it after the kind of day you had yesterday, but you have a right to know."

"Know what?"

"I know you couldn't answer my question last night because Russ Cullen had you in a tight spot."

"What do you mean?"

"I asked you straight out if he is your father. Your silence gave me the answer. Tell me I'm wrong."

Stefanie bit down on her lower lip. "I…"

"Maybe it will help if you know that I have him locked up in jail on murder charges."

"What?"

Curt took her hand and told her about Bill Gregg's killing career, and about John Stranger being sent to track him down. He explained about the artist's sketch, and how it led Stranger to Gregg, also known as Russ Cullen.

Curt put an arm around her shoulder. "He has another name, too, Stefanie—Will Andrews. Am I right?"

Stefanie burst into tears and could barely speak. "Yes, Curt. The man is my father. He told me last night that if I let it be known Russ Cullen was Will Andrews, he would be found out by wicked men who are after him, and they would kill him. I...I didn't answer you last night because I would have had to lie to cover for him."

"I'm so sorry you have to know, but your father is going to hang, Stefanie. He's wanted on sixteen counts of murder in other territories, and on three right here in Denver."

"How soon will they...hang him?"

"It'll be up to the judge, I'm sure it will be within a few days."

"Curt..."

"Yes?"

"I want to see him. Will you take me?"

"Of course."

John Stranger had explained the whole thing to Dr. Goodwin and his nurses by the time Curt and Stefanie came out of the store room. They all went to her as she held on to Curt's arm.

Stefanie couldn't stem the flow of her tears as she said, "After thirteen years, I just found my father...and now I'm going to lose him."

Breanna wrapped her arms around Stefanie and spoke softly into her ear. "Honey, the Holy Spirit lives in you. He will give you comfort like no mortal being can do."

"Yes, I know He will." She went to a desk drawer and pulled out her purse and Bible.

Stefanie clung tightly to Curt's arm as they walked to the jail.

"Stefanie..." Curt said. "Though your heart has been crushed in a different way than mine, I know how it hurts."

She looked into his eyes and said, "Thank you for trying to feel my hurt with me."

When they reached the sheriff's office, Steve was there to meet them. Curt explained that Stefanie wanted to see her father.

"I would like to see him alone, if I may," she told Curt. "Are there other men in the cells?"

"No, he's the only prisoner we have. I'll take you to the cell block, then leave."

When they stepped into the cell area, Curt picked up a straight-backed wooden chair and placed it in front of the cell door. "Your daughter wants to see you alone, Gregg. Sit here, Stefanie. When you're through, just come on back to the office."

"Thank you, Curt," she said, smiling faintly.

Gregg's dull gaze settled on his daughter.

"Daddy, I believe I deserve the truth from you."

Gregg picked up a small stool from the corner of the cell and placed it next to the bars. He sat down and looked at her glumly for a long moment.

"Stefanie," he began solemnly, "I told you last night that I became a gambler shortly after Ellen—your mother—and I were married."

"Yes."

"That was in Philadelphia."

"I never knew that before now."

"I know. By the time you came along, I had already had a lot of bad luck and run up some horrible debts. A year or so later, your mother became ill. Medical bills mounted. To pay them I gambled more, but lost more than I won. By the time she died when you were two years old, I had gamblers and casino owners hunting me. I knew that if they found me, and I couldn't pay, they would kill me. So I took off with my little girl and ran to Mexico."

"Those are my first memories."

"You already know the rest of the story. I told you why I took off the weight and grew the beard. I even stopped gambling, Stefanie. For several months, at least.

"I was making my living at construction and carpentry. Then I drifted into Dodge City. In a weak moment, I went to a saloon and sat down at a poker table again. As usual, my luck was bad. I was up to my ears in gambling debts and had to leave town fast. When I came here to Denver and started building the new hospital, I quit gambling once more. My men could tell you that I did."

"But what about all those men you murdered?" Her father's features turned to stone. "Are you going to tell me that all these murder charges are false? That the lawmen are wrong?"

"I don't want to talk about it."

Stefanie was quiet for a moment, then she said, "Daddy, you never told me what Mother died of. What kind of illness was it? Where can I find her grave? Is it in Philadelphia?"

His lips formed a thin, hard line.

"Tell me, Daddy. I have a right to know."

It was evident he was not going to tell her.

"What is your real name?" she asked.

"Bill Gregg. I changed my name to Will Andrews when I took you to Mexico."

"Then what's *my* real name?"

"Sarah Lynne Gregg. I changed Sarah to Stefanie and told people your name was Stefanie Lynne Andrews. I got to thinking about those men who were trying to track me down. It was better that I give you another first name since they might learn I had a daughter named Sarah. That would help throw them off."

"Daddy," she said, choking on the word, "why won't you

tell me what caused Mother's death? Please. I need to know."

He set his jaw and gave her a cold look. "I don't want to talk about it. Just put it out of your mind."

Stefanie reached into her purse for a small Bible. "I want to read you something, Daddy," she said, flipping to the New Testament.

"Put that away. I don't want to hear it."

"Daddy, listen to what Jesus said. 'For God sent not his Son into the world to condemn the world; but that the world through him might be saved. He that believeth on him is not condemned: but he that believeth not is condemned already, because he hath not believed in the name of the only begotten Son of God.' Do you understand, Daddy? Jesus didn't come into the world to condemn sinners. They were already condemned. That includes *you*, Daddy. Just as it did me. I was condemned already because I had not put my faith in Jesus to save me. But when I opened my heart to Him—"

"I don't want to hear it!" His whole countenance suffused with anger.

"But Daddy, you're going to die on the gallows. You need to be saved. Jesus—"

"Stefanie!" He articulated his next words coldly and precisely. "I don't want to hear another word of that stuff! Now, or ever! Do you hear me?"

"But Daddy—"

"Listen to me! I don't want anything to do with God or Jesus Christ or that Bible! And that's final!"

"But Jesus went to the cross—"

Gregg jumped to his feet, grabbed the bars, and shook them. "Shut up!" he yelled. "Shut up! Shut up! Shut up!"

Curt Langan charged through the door. "What's going on in here?"

"Get her outta here, Langan! I don't want to hear any of that religious fanaticism! I don't believe any of it! Get her out of here!"

"Come on, Stefanie. You can't help him if he refuses to listen."

Stefanie closed her Bible, heartbroken. She didn't think she could walk the few feet to the door by herself, and she let Curt guide her. She stopped once more and looked over her shoulder. "Daddy," she said, as her voice cracked, "if you die lost, we'll never see each other again."

"Get out! Get out!" he roared.

Breanna Baylor was excited as she prepared dinner with Martha Goodwin and Missy. The Goodwins had invited the Carrolls and John Stranger to dinner, wanting to make things special for them as they met each other for the first time.

The Carrolls arrived a little early, which gave Dottie some time to help in the kitchen. James and Molly Kate amused themselves in the parlor, looking at an old Goodwin family photo album.

Also in the parlor were Drs. Goodwin and Carroll, who were discussing Russ Cullen's arrest.

Goodwin said he had talked with the Cullen construction crew, and had been reassured that everything would move forward as planned. They would choose a foreman from among themselves.

"Good," Matt said. "I sure wouldn't want to see it come to a halt now."

There was a knock at the front door, and Goodwin went to answer it. Breanna came from the kitchen, hurrying through the parlor. The other women were on her heels.

"Welcome, John!" Goodwin said, as the tall, broad-shouldered man filled the doorway. "Come in. We've got some excited people waiting to meet you."

Breanna dashed up and embraced him. "Hello, darling."

"Hello, yourself," he said, tweaking her nose playfully. "You look gorgeous tonight."

"Thank you," she said, then turned to face the Carrolls, who were standing in a line together. Breanna took John by the hand and led him to her family.

"Wow, is he ever tall!" James whispered to his sister.

"Like Goliath!" Molly Kate whispered back, looking at Stranger in awe.

"John," Breanna said, sounding a little out of breath, "I want you to meet Matt."

The two men shook hands, and Matt felt the power in Stranger's grip.

"And Dottie..."

Dottie moved to Stranger and smiled up at him. "Hello, John."

Stranger embraced her discreetly. "It's so good to finally meet you, Dottie. Breanna has told me so much about you."

John's attention then went to the two wide-eyed children. He bent over and extended his hand to the boy. "James, I sure am glad to meet you."

James gave his small hand to John's grip and said, "Same here, Uncle John!"

Stranger laughed. "Uncle John, is it? I like that!"

James looked at his mother, smiling from ear to ear. "See, Mom! Molly Kate and I told you he'd like us to call him that!"

Stranger turned his attention to the little bright-eyed girl and dropped to one knee. "And this is Molly Kate. My, aren't you the pretty one! And don't you look just like your mother and your Aunt Breanna."

Molly Kate nodded, feeling a bit overwhelmed by the stature of John Stranger.

"Since I'm your Uncle John, could I hug you?" the tall man asked, looking her square in the eye.

Molly Kate nodded shyly.

Stranger wrapped her in his arms and kissed her cheek. Then he reached into a side pocket and pulled out a handful of hard candy. "Here, sweetheart," he said. "You can start on this after supper."

"Thank you." Molly Kate accepted the candy in both hands.

Stranger turned back to James and filled his hands too. "*After* supper, pal, okay? I wouldn't want to get in trouble with your mother."

"Yes, sir! Thank you!" He paused, then said, "Uncle John…?"

"Yes?"

"Could…could I give you a hug, too?"

During the meal, James looked across the table and asked Uncle John about all the outlaws and gunslingers he had put in the ground and how many he had put behind bars.

Stranger winked at Dottie and Matt and told the boy some quick, wild tales.

While James was digesting this information, Molly Kate gathered up her courage. "Uncle John, I saw those silver round things you gave Aunt Breanna. What are they called, Mommy?"

"Medallions."

"Mm-hmm, those. Aunt Breanna showed me the ones you

gave her. They really are pretty. Do you have any more?"

John smiled and reached into a coat pocket.

"Molly Kate!" Dottie scolded.

John laughed and produced a silver medallion with a star in its center and Scripture emblazoned on its circular edge. "It's all right, Dottie. She's just a typical female!" John placed the medallion in her tiny hand. The little blonde wrapped her arms around Stranger's neck and planted a kiss on his cheek.

James eyed the medallion with admiration, but said nothing.

Stranger grinned at him and reached into his pocket a second time. "James, would you like one, too?"

The boy glanced at his mom and dad.

"It's all right, son," Matt said.

James quickly shoved back his chair and stood up. "Did you want a hug and a kiss from me, too, Uncle John?"

There was a round of laughter as John gave James his medallion.

20

THE COLORADO MOON was clear-edged and pure against deep blackness as Curt Langan and Stefanie Andrews, and a few other young couples, strolled along the South Platte River.

Curt and Stefanie had been invited to dinner at the Goodwins but politely turned down the invitation, not wanting to intrude when Breanna Baylor's family met John Stranger.

Soon they came upon a bench beneath a huge cottonwood tree. "Would you like to sit down?" Curt asked.

"All right," Stefanie said, and gave his arm a squeeze.

A soft breeze blew across the moon-dappled surface of the river, ruffling Stefanie's hair and blowing dark wisps across her forehead.

Curt looked at her in the silvery light and thought his heart was going to burst. He wanted to blurt out that he loved her, but felt it would make him look like a fool. They had met only yesterday.

Though Stefanie was happy to be with Curt, the signs of the burden she carried were visible.

Curt took her hand. "Steffie...Stefanie—"

"Oh, Curt. Only one other person has ever called me Steffie. A girl whose home I stayed in while Daddy and I lived in Los Angeles. We were such good friends. You can call me that, if you wish."

Curt smiled. "All right, I'll call you Steffie. Somehow I just made up that nickname for you in my mind before I fell asleep last night."

Stefanie wanted to tell him what meaning he was putting into her life, but she couldn't find the words.

"I'm so sorry for the pain your father has caused you," Curt said. "I wish it could be different."

"Thank you, Curt."

"I've only been a Christian for a short while, but I've learned a whole lot in that time. Breanna has taught me a great deal, and I've learned so much from Reverend Larribee. One thing I've learned is that whenever the Lord allows His children to go through a deep valley, there's always a mountaintop just ahead."

"I've never thought about it that way," Stefanie said, looking into his eyes. "But it does sound like our wonderful Lord."

"Mm-hmm. You know, I went through a real deep valley with Sally Jayne."

"Yes."

"Well, Steffie, I want to tell you that meeting you is my mountaintop after that deep valley. And I'm...well, I'm glad for the valley because it makes this mountaintop that much more wonderful."

"Speaking of valleys and mountaintops," she said softly, "I am both in the valley and on the mountaintop right now. I'm hurting way down deep over my father, but being here like this with you is my mountaintop."

Curt felt his heart start to drum. He swallowed hard and ventured into unfamiliar territory. "Steffie, do you...do you believe in love at first sight?"

"I know it's possible, Curt. Because yesterday morning when I looked into your face in the middle of the street...I fell in love with you."

"Oh, Steffie," Curt said, "I fell in love with you at the same moment."

He took her in his arms, looked deeply into her eyes, and kissed her tenderly.

On Friday, September 9, Bill Gregg faced judge and jury in a packed courtroom. Stefanie sat in the second row with Breanna and John on one side and Missy on the other. Sheriff Langan stood directly behind Gregg near the judge's bench.

Irrefutable evidence from California and Kansas authorities was enough to convince the jury. But Sheriff Langan's testimony of the boot size and approximate weight of the man who had dumped the bodies of Hector Thompson and Lenny Pinder in the river, along with the fact that Gregg had tried to escape when put under arrest by Chief U.S. Marshal Solomon Duvall only added to their conclusion that Gregg deserved to hang.

The jury was out less than ten minutes and returned with the only possible verdict: guilty of murder.

Stefanie shook like a leaf in autumn wind as her father stood before the judge and was sentenced to die on the gallows at nine o'clock the following Monday morning.

Sheriff Langan escorted Gregg, hands cuffed behind his back, from the courtroom. As they approached the row where Stefanie sat, she burst into tears and moved toward her father. Langan stopped, giving Stefanie an opportunity to speak.

"Daddy, please think about what I read to you from Scripture. Please. Turn to the Lord before it's too late!"

Gregg gave her a disgusted look and turned to Langan. "Get me out of here."

Breanna wrapped her arms around Stefanie and held her tight as sheriff and prisoner left the building.

John Stranger patted Stefanie's shoulder and said, "Breanna told me about your father's refusal to talk about the Lord. I'll follow them to the jail and see if I can get anywhere with him."

"Oh, thank you, Mr. Stranger. Thank you!"

Some thirty minutes later, John entered the Goodwin clinic where Stefanie was helping Missy file patient records. Stefanie looked at him with hope in her eyes.

"I'm sorry, Stefanie," John said. "He wouldn't stop swearing and screaming at me. I couldn't get a word in edgewise."

She lowered her eyes and said, "Thank you for trying, Mr. Stranger."

During the next two days, Stefanie tried to see her father, but she received the same treatment as before.

At 8:45 on Monday morning, September 12, a large crowd gathered at the gallows set up on the east edge of town next to the cemetery. In the crowd were Solomon Duvall, John Stranger, and Reverend Lin Larribee. First Baptist Church's pastor had tried to talk to Bill Gregg before he was taken from the jail, but he met with the same hateful barrage of words Stefanie and John Stranger had experienced.

↑

At the Goodwin cottage, Breanna, Missy, and Martha were with Stefanie. Breanna was on her knees before Stefanie, holding both of her hands.

"Honey...Martha, Missy, and I love you. We wish we could take the pain you're feeling right now. We would gladly do it, but we can't. But please know that we're hurting with you. And even more, your Jesus is hurting with you."

Stefanie burst into tears, wailing as if her heart would burst. Breanna embraced her, and the other two laid tender, loving hands on her shoulders.

"Oh, Breanna! I wish my mother were here! I wish I could have known her!"

"Yes, I wish you could have, too. Maybe...maybe she was a Christian and you'll meet her one day in heaven."

"I've thought the same thing so many times since I came to the Lord, but there's no way I can ever know in this life." She drew a shuddering breath. "It's so awful! After all these years, I just found Daddy. And now, I've lost him again...this time forever."

Stefanie's heartache touched the three women, and they wept with her. When their weeping diminished to sniffles, Breanna took Stefanie's hands again and looked at the grandfather clock. Four minutes after nine.

"Stefanie, let's pray."

Breanna held Stefanie's hands in a firm grip as she prayed for God's special grace, peace, and strength. After praying earnestly for several minutes, Breanna said, "Lord, I've found it true in my own Christian life that after every valley, there is a mountaintop—and Lord, You know that Stefanie needs a mountaintop. Give it to her, I pray. Fill her heart right now with Your wonderful peace, and turn Your sunlight of love into her life by lifting her very soon from this dark valley. Please, Lord. Touch her wounded heart with Your wounded hand, and give her the peace that passes all understanding. I ask it in the wonderful, marvelous, powerful name of Jesus. Amen."

Missy left Stefanie's side long enough to pull some hankies from a drawer. She passed them out and the women talked quietly of the wonderful peace that only God could give.

Moments later, there was a tap on the door. Martha went to answer and quietly let Curt Langan and John Stranger in. Curt moved toward Stefanie, and she stood up to meet him. He cupped her face tenderly in his hands.

"It's over, Steffie."

She laid her head against his chest and wrapped her arms around him. He held her close, but noted that she did not weep. Breanna noticed it, too.

"You have that perfect peace, don't you, honey?"

She nodded and pressed even tighter against Curt. "Yes. It's like Jesus has wrapped His nail-pierced hands around my heart and taken the pain away. It's...it's the peace that passes all understanding."

"Only a child of God can have that kind of peace, Stefanie," John Stranger said. "And Stefanie, let me tell you something. The Lord never takes anything away from us but that He gives us something else in its place. You have lost your father so quickly after finding him again, but the Lord will give you someone else to take his place."

Stefanie managed a weak smile and looked into Curt's eyes. "He already has given me someone else, Mr. Stranger. Do you want to tell them, darling?"

Curt grinned lopsidedly and said, "I know this may seem

strange to your ears, since Steffie and I have only known each other a few days, but we believe the Lord has chosen us for each other. Some people don't believe in love at first sight, but we do. It's happened to us."

"*Some* people may not believe in it, Curt," John said, "but *I* do. I fell in love with Breanna the instant I laid eyes on her."

Breanna stroked his face. "Well, it took me just a little longer to fall in love with you...probably a few hours, anyway."

Martha and Missy laughed. Breanna went up to Stefanie and hugged her. "I'm so glad for you."

Then Breanna turned to Curt. "And I'm so glad for *you,* Curt."

"Thank you, Breanna. I know Steffie is God's good gift to me."

"*Steffie,*" Breanna said. "That's cute. I like it."

Breanna clasped her hands together. "Well! John tells me he's been asked to go and see Chief Duvall right away, and Drs. Carroll and Goodwin want me to go with them to Union Station. Our new head nurse, Mary Donelson is coming in at 11:15."

"Whoops!" Missy gasped. "I'm supposed to be at the clinic by 11:00. Dr. Goodwin will have my hide!"

"I'll stay here with Stefanie," Martha said. "That is, if she's staying."

"I thought if she felt like it, I'd have her go with the doctors and me," Breanna said. "Would you like to do that, Stefanie?"

"Yes. I'd like to be among the first to welcome Mrs. Donelson to Denver. Do you want to come with us, Martha?"

"I'll be meeting Mrs. Donelson at a special affair we've got planned for her," she said. "I think I'll go back to my housework."

"Well," Curt said, "I've got to get back to the office and do some of that boring paper work sheriffs have to do."

As everyone filed out the door, Stefanie put an arm around Breanna and whispered, "Thank you for being such a wonderful friend. I love you."

"I love you, too," Breanna whispered back.

At 11:15, the train from Chicago rolled into Denver's Union Station. The big engine chugged to a halt with a screeching of steel against steel and the sound of clanging bell. Doctors Goodwin and Carroll stood on the platform with Breanna and Stefanie.

"Do you know what she looks like, Dr. Goodwin?" Stefanie asked.

"She sent a daguerreotype of herself in the first letter," he replied. "From what she said, it was done recently. So I'm sure I'll know her when I see her."

"You already told us she's in her late forties, if I remember correctly," Stefanie said, her eyes scanning the passengers as they got off the train. "Do you know her hair color?"

"Dark, from the description she gave of herself when she filled out the application. The daguerreotype showed some gray at her temples."

"Is that her just now stepping off car number two? The lady carrying the beige overnight bag?"

"Oh, yes!" Goodwin said, moving toward Mary Donelson.

Breanna and Stefanie let Dr. Carroll precede them so he could catch up to Goodwin.

Mary Donelson was well dressed all the way from her fashionable lace shoes to her plumed hat. Stefanie felt a small leap in her heart as she gazed at the woman who would become her head nurse. There was something about her she couldn't quite put her finger on, but it made her feel warm. Stefanie hoped they would become good friends.

When Goodwin and Carroll had introduced themselves, Goodwin turned to the two young women. "And this is Miss Breanna Baylor and Miss Stefanie Andrews, Mrs. Donelson. I thought you might feel more comfortable to have a lady or two here to meet you. Breanna is actually a visiting C.M.N. working out of my office. She's going to be working at the hospital for about three months to help us get it running smoothly. Stefanie is also a C.M.N. She came to us recently with Dr. Carroll and his family from San Francisco."

Mary smiled winsomely and reached for Breanna. They embraced lightly, then Mary held her by the upper arms and said, "A visiting nurse. I thought about moving west to do your kind of work when my husband died four years ago. But it never happened."

"Well, you're here in a much higher position," Breanna said. "And I want to welcome you to Denver and Mile High Hospital."

"Thank you, dear." Then Mary embraced Stefanie in the same manner, and said, "I've read the information Dr. Goodwin sent me about Dr. Carroll. Did you work with him at the asylum?"

"On my off days, I did, ma'am. My main job was at City Hospital, but I always worked at the asylum as much as I could."

"And she did a marvelous job, I might say," Matt Carroll said. "That's why I brought her here. She's very good at what she does."

"Glad to hear it." Mary studied Stefanie's slightly swollen, bloodshot eyes. Her forehead crinkled in a frown. "Honey, do I detect that you've been crying?"

Stefanie glanced at Breanna, who said, "Stefanie's father just died, Mrs. Donelson."

"Oh, I'm so sorry." Mary touched Stefanie's arm. "Please forgive my prying."

"You weren't prying, you were only showing concern. There's nothing to forgive."

Mary asked no more, and Breanna felt the less said about Bill Gregg's death the better.

"We'll let you ladies ride together in the back seat," Dr. Goodwin said, as he offered his hand to Mary.

On the other side of the buggy, Matt helped Breanna and Stefanie into the rear seat. Just as Dr. Goodwin was extending Mary's overnight bag to her, it slipped from his fingers and hit the ground, popping open. Several items fell out, including a Bible with a chestnut-colored leather cover.

"Oh, I'm sorry." Dr. Goodwin bent down and put the objects back in the bag, but not before Breanna saw the Bible.

"Oh, Mrs. Donelson, what a beautiful Bible!"

"Thank you. It was given to me by my Sunday school class at my church in Philadelphia. I taught a ladies' class. They presented it to me on my last Sunday there, a week ago yesterday. Would you like to see it?"

"Oh, yes!"

Breanna flipped open the Bible and noted what nice print it had. As she was closing it, her eye caught the front flyleaf. Little notes had been written from each lady in Mary's class. Some of them mentioned that it was Mary who had led them to Christ.

"Look! Not only has Mrs. Donelson been a Sunday school teacher, but she's also a soulwinner!"

"Oh, Mrs. Donelson!" Stefanie looked at the older woman with joyful eyes. "You're a Christian!"

"Sure am, honey. Jesus saved me many years ago, and it's been wonderful to walk with Him!"

"Well, I'm pleased to tell you, ma'am," Breanna said, "that so is everyone in this buggy!"

"Praise the Lord!" Mary said, popping her hands together. "This is more than I could have hoped for!"

"*You* are more than *we* could have hoped for, ma'am," Matt Carroll said. "It'll be wonderful having a Christian at the head of my nursing staff!"

John Stranger left town that day on a mission for Chief Duvall.

The medical equipment arrived on schedule, and the builders—minus their boss—raced to put the finishing touches on the bulk of the building so the hospital could open as planned on Saturday, October 1.

During the next week, Dr. Carroll hired six male attendants, two for each shift, along with receptionists, cooks, and janitors.

Mary Donelson proved to be even more than the doctors expected. She won everybody's hearts, and under her leadership the nurses were prepared for the big opening. A special friendship was growing between the head nurse and Stefanie and Breanna.

On Friday, September 23, Curt and Stefanie were having supper together at Mamie's Café. During the meal, Stefanie grew quiet for a moment, then looked at Curt across the table and said, "You remember me telling you that Daddy said my real name is Sarah Lynne Gregg."

"Yes."

"I suppose I should go by that name."

"No need," he grinned. "You're Stefanie Lynn Andrews to everyone who knows you. You'll always be my special *Steffie*. Sarah just wouldn't fit."

She smiled at him.

"But Steffie…well, I *would* like you to change your *last* name, though."

"You mean lay aside Andrews and go by Gregg?"

"No. I mean lay aside Andrews and go by *Langan.*"

"You…you're asking me to—"

"Yes."

"To marry you? To become your wife?"

"Yes."

Other customers in the café were looking on as Stefanie stammered. "Oh, Curt! I…I don't know what to say. I—"

"How about just saying yes?"

"Well, yes…yes, of course I'll marry you! *Yes!*"

As she spoke, they both left their chairs and delighted patrons watched them embrace.

"Steffie, you've made me the happiest man on the face of the earth!"

John Stranger returned the following day with his prisoner in tow, and turned him over to Chief Duvall. The chief then had one of his deputies escort the outlaw in handcuffs to Curt Langan's jail.

Stranger visited Breanna for a few minutes, then headed for his hotel. He came upon Curt and Reverend Larribee talking on the street. They greeted John, and Larribee asked if he would preach both services tomorrow. The tall man said he would be glad to, then excused himself and went on his way.

An hour later, Curt and Stefanie sat in Reverend Larribee's office and told him they wanted to marry on Saturday, December 3. This would give them little more than a three-month courtship. They asked their pastor if three months would be proper for a Christian couple. Larribee told them that since they were both mature adults, it would be both proper and acceptable.

Curt then asked if John Stranger could have a part in the ceremony. Larribee said he would love to have John in on it if he was going to be in town then.

With the engagement official, the happy couple asked the pastor to announce it in church the next day. Larribee did so, just before presenting John Stranger for the morning sermon.

When the service was over, Curt and Stefanie were swarmed by their friends. Among them was Mary Donelson. She was already feeling a special attachment to Stefanie, and she expressed her congratulations with warmth and joy.

The well-wishers also included John and Breanna.

"John," Curt said, "Steffie and I would like to ask a favor of you."

"Name it."

"Will you have a part in our wedding ceremony? We asked Reverend Larribee, and he said he'd love to have you perform it with him."

"You'll have to be sure and be home on December third," Breanna said.

Stranger laughed, put an arm around Breanna, and said to the engaged couple, "I'm deeply honored. And I will make it a point to be here on December third."

"Great!" Curt said.

Then Stefanie turned to Breanna. "Will you be my maid of honor?"

21

ON THURSDAY, SEPTEMBER 29, John Stranger rode out of Denver on another mission for Solomon Duvall. As always, Breanna Baylor felt as though a part of her went with him.

The next morning, Dr. Carroll met with his entire staff and finalized preparations for opening the hospital. All of the doctors had patients who were in need of hospital care and would admit them just as soon as the hospital doors were open on Saturday.

Opening day, at 7:00 A.M., nine patients were admitted, and the real work began. By late afternoon, two expectant mothers were admitted, and before midnight, Denver had two new citizens.

Within ten days, the hospital was running at 75 percent capacity, with patients from as far away as Cheyenne City to the north, Pueblo to the south, Grand Junction to the west, and eastern Colorado almost to the Kansas border. Dr. Carroll pushed the construction workers to hurry and finish the rest of the hospital.

Though her schedule was hectic, Breanna found time to spend with Dottie and the children, who had moved into their new house three days after the hospital opened.

Curt Langan and his future bride spent as much time together as their jobs allowed and found their love growing stronger and deeper every day.

Mary Donelson managed the nurses well, and after a month of getting used to each other, Dr. Carroll and his entire staff worked together as if they had done so for a long time.

During the first week of November, Lawrence Bartlett brought in his young wife, Melinda, who was in her seventh month of pregnancy. She had started hemorrhaging at home the previous week, and Lawrence had rushed her to the hospital. Dr. Moon had skillfully averted the miscarriage, and after three days, sent her home.

This time, Lawrence brought Melinda to the hospital late at night with the same symptoms. Dr. Moon was sent for and worked on her until sunrise, finally managing to stabilize her condition. He waited until Mary Donelson arrived for her shift at 6:00 A.M. before leaving the hospital. He would barely have time to go home to shave and eat breakfast before he was expected at his office.

Mary was glad Stefanie Andrews was working the day shift. After a month of working with Stefanie, Mary had the utmost confidence in her medical knowledge and ability to handle difficult situations. She assigned Stefanie a few other patients to care for, but her main patient would be Melinda Bartlett.

During that day, Stefanie left Melinda for only minutes at a time, checking her regularly for any sign that she was going to miscarry. It was almost two o'clock in the afternoon, time for the next shift, when Mary Donelson entered Room 10 to find Stefanie standing over Melinda, holding her hand. The patient was quite pale.

"I'll tell Donna Wygant to be sure one of the nurses stays close to Melinda just like you have," Mary said to Stefanie.

Donna was in charge of the nurses who worked the 2:00 P.M. to 10:00 P.M. shift.

Melinda gripped Stefanie's hand with what little strength she had. "Please don't leave me, Stefanie! Please! I...I'm so scared. I need you!"

Mary laid a tender hand on Melinda's forehead and said softly, "Melinda, it's time for a shift change. Stefanie's been on her feet for eight hours. She must go home and get some rest. You know Nurse Wygant. She took good care of you on her shift when you were in here last week."

"But...but not like Stefanie. I need her, Mrs. Donelson. Lawrence's job takes him out of town. He won't be back until about eight o'clock tonight. Please let her stay, at least for a little while."

"Mary, it's all right," Stefanie said. "I'll stay with her. I wouldn't rest too well anyway, knowing the condition she's in. It'll free up a nurse to care for other patients, too."

"Please, Mrs. Donelson," Melinda said. "She can sit down beside my bed. She doesn't have to stand up. I just want her with me a little longer. She...she read to me from the Bible and showed me about Jesus dying on the cross for me, and I asked Jesus to come into my heart and save me. I'm a Christian now, and I know Jesus is with me. But I need Stefanie to stay with me for just a little longer."

Mary glanced at the Bible lying on the bedstand. She smiled and said, "Melinda, I'm so happy you've received Jesus into your heart. That's the greatest thing that could happen to you. And I understand your wanting Stefanie to stay with you. She's a wonderful young woman. Tell you what...if Stefanie is staying for a while, I'll stay, too. When she's ready to go, we'll leave together."

"Thank you. Oh, thank you."

"Melinda," Stefanie said, "it's time for your sedative. Dr. Moon wants you to get plenty of rest."

"But even if I go to sleep, you won't leave me, will you?"

Stefanie squeezed her hand. "No. Mary and I will stay until you wake up. But soon after that, we'll have to go."

While Stefanie was administering the sedative, Mary left to talk to the other nurses who were coming on duty. When she returned, she found the patient resting peacefully and Stefanie holding her hand.

Mary tiptoed in and whispered, "She asleep?"

"Just about."

"I told the other nurses not to come in here until we let them know we're leaving."

"Good. You go ahead and sit down."

Moments later, Stefanie eased her hand from Melinda's grip and joined Mary at the window.

As Stefanie sat down, Mary said, "You're the ideal nurse, Stefanie. I wish all of them had your traits."

"You flatter me."

"I *admire* you is what I do."

Stefanie glanced at Melinda to make sure the sedative had taken effect. She was sleeping soundly.

"Honey," Mary said. "I keep meaning to ask you about your father. He had just died the day I arrived. What took him?"

Stefanie looked down at her hands. "He…he was hanged, Mary."

The head nurse stiffened. "Oh, no! I'm sorry. I just seem to stick my nose in where it doesn't belong."

"It's all right. You're not being nosy. You're simply showing concern and interest. Daddy was hanged for murder."

"Oh, you poor child! Is your mother still living?"

"No, she died when I was two years old. I don't remember her at all."

"Sounds like you've known your share of troubles. Dr. Carroll told me about your battle with the Bay Area Strangler in San Francisco."

"That was quite an ordeal."

"I'm sure it was. And Dr. Carroll told me how you saved the man's life and even tried to win him to the Lord before he was executed." Mary turned to look toward the bed and noted that Melinda had not changed position. "Stefanie, since we've got some time, tell me about your childhood. Did your father remarry after your mother died?"

"No. My first recollections are of living with Daddy in Mexico."

"Mexico! Why Mexico?"

Stefanie found herself telling Mary Donelson the whole story—her father's gambling addiction and the grief it had caused; how he deserted her in San Francisco when she was twelve; how she had met him again just days before he was arrested for murder. She wept as she finished the story, saying how wonderful God had been to bring Curt Langan into her life...and the Carrolls, Breanna Baylor, Missy O'Day, the Goodwins, and now...Mary Donelson.

Mary rose from her chair and wrapped her arms around Stefanie. "You've had a rough life, but it looks like the Lord is making it better now."

"No question about that. I love my job here...and I'm so glad you're my head nurse." She paused to brush tears from her cheeks. "I'm glad you're my friend, too."

Mary kissed her cheek.

"And Mary..."

"Yes, dear?"

"Breanna's been such a good friend since I came here. She's tried to mother me some, but she's more like a sister, since we're not far apart in age. I'm twenty-five, but since I had to grow up without my mother, I guess I still need some mothering. Could...could I sort of adopt you as my mother?"

It was Mary's turn to shed tears. "Stefanie, I'd love that...if I could sort of adopt you as my daughter."

As the two women embraced, Mary said into Stefanie's ear, "I used to have a daughter."

"Really?"

"Mm-hmm. She was taken from me when she was very small."

"Oh, I'm so sorry. How did she die?"

Mary was about to speak when Melinda moaned loudly and pulled up her knees. Mary rushed to pull back the sheet and saw blood.

"She's hemorrhaging profusely, Stefanie! Go send one of the male attendants to Dr. Moon's office and bring him here fast!"

Dr. Eldon Moon dashed into the reception area of the hospital and ran hard for Room 10. He shoved the door open and hurried into the room. Flora Richards was making up the bed.

"Melinda Bartlett?" he said.

"She...she died, Doctor," Flora said, a quiver in her voice. "But Mary and Stefanie were able to save the baby. It's a girl."

"Where—"

"In the nursery."

"Thank you," Moon said, and returned to the hallway.

The doctor entered the nursery to find Stefanie in a rocking chair, holding a tiny form in a blanket. Mary stood over her.

"Melinda died, Doctor," Mary said. "She was farther gone

than any of us realized. Even if you had been here, you couldn't have saved her. But as you can see, we were able to save the baby. Little girl. She's quite small, of course. Doesn't have any eyelashes or eyebrows yet, but the rest of her seems to be all there."

Dr. Moon checked the baby and agreed with Mary's evaluation. By all appearances, the baby would be fine. When they told him that Lawrence would be arriving about eight o'clock that evening, Moon said he would be there to meet him and tell him what happened.

The baby was left in the care of the other nurses, and at 5:30 that afternoon, Mary and Stefanie left the hospital with mixed emotions. They had lost the mother, but they had preserved the life of the child.

As they stepped outside into the light of the lowering sun, Mary said, "Stefanie, if you hadn't cared enough for your patient's soul to tell her of Jesus, she'd be in hell now. Bless your heart, you *did* care…and at this moment, Melinda is in the arms of Jesus."

Weeping softly, Stefanie said, "All the glory belongs to Him. If He hadn't saved me, I wouldn't have cared about Melinda."

"Praise His name," Mary said with a sigh.

Mile High Hospital's unfinished section was completed on November 15. One wing of the new section was for mental patients.

During a light snowstorm the very next day, six new nurses arrived by train from eastern cities and were immediately put to work.

Both Drs. Glen Wakeman and Newt Stratton had patients with emotional problems. They had been treating them under stressful circumstances, and the families had been caring for them at home. As soon as the new wing was ready, two elderly women and a man in his early forties were admitted, much to the relief of their families.

Since Dr. Carroll's main work had been psychiatry in San Francisco, he took personal charge of the mental wing and called upon Stefanie Andrews to help.

Stefanie gave tender care to the three mental patients and worked in the main part of the hospital as well. In her quiet moments, she dreamed of her wedding and thought of the small house Curt had bought. In their spare time, the two of them were redecorating it.

On Monday, November 28, there was a dusting of snow on the ground as the day shift came to work at 6:00 A.M. Mary Donelson greeted her nurses as they came in one by one, along with the day receptionist, Kathryn Conner, cooks Eldridge Mansfield and Charlie Crawford, and attendants David Halden, Michael Adair, Ervin Dodd, and Jake Fields.

Breanna and Stefanie were among the nurses. They came through the door together, and Stefanie smiled when she saw the head nurse. "Good morning, Mom."

"Good morning, daughter," Mary said.

Veronica Clyburn came through the door and stomped the snow off her shoes. "Well, Stefanie, five more days and you take the big plunge."

"I'm so excited I can hardly stand it!"

"Is your dress finished?"

Stefanie looked at Mary. "I've got it almost done. We'll have a fitting tomorrow evening."

"It's so sweet of you to make Stefanie's dress," Breanna said.

"Well, what's an adopted mom for?" Mary said with a chuckle. "I'm having a wonderful time doing it."

"And I'm having a wonderful time letting her!" Stefanie said.

Dr. Carroll came in, giving the crew a mock scowl. "What's all the frivolity here? Don't you people know there's work to be done? Let's hop to it!" He winked at Stefanie and said with a sly grin, "I happen to know there's a bunch of men in town who are planning to kidnap the sheriff on Friday and not bring him back till Monday!"

Stefanie jutted her jaw. "If they do, I'll send John Stranger after them. He'll tie them in knots so they have to stick a comb between their toes to groom their hair!"

The group had a good laugh and went to work as the night shift filed out the doors and went home.

Dr. Carroll and Stefanie walked toward the mental wing. His custom was to look in on his patients first thing every morning. As they moved down the hall, Carroll said, "You mentioned John Stranger. I haven't heard Breanna say where he is right now. Will he be here for the wedding?"

"He said he would, Doctor. Breanna hasn't heard anything from him since he left several weeks ago, but I'm trusting him to keep his word. I do so want him to have a part in the ceremony. And I'm so happy Dottie is going to sing for the wedding. She has such a lovely voice. I'd have Breanna sing too, but since she's maid of honor, she's going to be pretty busy."

"Be pretty hard for her to do both. And Stefanie..."

"Yes, Doctor?"

"I want you to know that I'm very pleased and highly honored you've asked me to give you away in place of your father."

"Well, like I told you, Doctor, you are my father in the Lord, just as the Apostle Paul said he was the father of those he had led to Christ in the church at Corinth. No one can ever take your place. You have a very special spot in my heart because you led me to Jesus. I can never thank you enough."

They were almost to the mental wing when they heard loud voices behind them.

"You go on and see to the patients," Carroll said. "I'll find out what's going on."

Moments later, Stefanie was coming out of one room and heading for another when she saw a husky bald-headed man with a bleeding head being wheeled into the surgical room. Dr. Carroll walked alongside, holding a towel against the head wound, and Clint Byers followed.

Clint stopped at the surgery door. He noticed Stefanie and waved to her, and she hurried toward him.

"Hello, Clint. Did you bring that man in?"

"Yes. I was coming home from down in New Mexico…for your wedding, you know. I took off a couple days earlier than planned to spend some time with Missy."

"Can't blame you for that. So what about that man and his bleeding head?"

"He caused some real trouble on the train. Lost his temper over virtually nothing and tried to throw a man off. It took two other men and myself to subdue him. One man had to use a fire ax to knock him out. Hit him with the flat of it, of course, rather than the blade. Happened just before we arrived in Denver. I told Dr. Carroll how the man acted, and he said he'd be placed in the mental wing after his head's sewn up."

"Do you know his name?"

"One of the men who sat by him on the train said it's Hugo Forge."

↑

The hospital's kitchen was located in the main section of the building, right next to the doors to the mental wing. An hour and a half after Hugo Forge had been taken into surgery, Stefanie was coming out of the kitchen with a tray of hot tea. She saw Dr. Carroll with Forge, who was stretched out on a cart. Attendants Jake Fields and Michael Adair were with him.

"Is he hurt bad, Doctor?"

"Not really. Clint probably told you how he got hurt."

"Yes. He said he thinks Mr. Forge is mentally off balance."

"Sounds like it from the way he was acting on the train. It took forty-three stitches in his head. He's still under the ether, but we're taking no chances. We'll also use the leather straps. He looks like he could wrestle a grizzly and come out the winner. He's running a fever. I don't think it has anything to do with his head gash. My guess is he had the fever when he got on the train."

"I'll get some cold water and bathe him. Maybe it'll help cut the fever."

"Good," Carroll said. Then to the attendants, "Jake, you and Mike strap him in leathers when you put him on the bed. Stefanie will take care of him. I've got some pressing things to do right now."

Soon Stefanie was alone with Hugo Forge. He was beginning to come around, and she was bathing his neck and chest with cold water. His wrists and ankles were strapped to the bed with thick leather belts.

Stefanie heard soft footsteps behind her and turned to see Mary Donelson and Breanna.

"Dr. Carroll told us about him," Mary said.

Hugo's eyes were still closed, but he was moaning and rolling his head from side to side.

"Big guy, isn't he?" Breanna said. "Dr. Carroll said Clint Byers and a couple of other railroad men brought him in."

"I'm glad we've got him in leathers," Mary said. "Maybe I should get one of the attendants to come and stay with you, Stefanie."

"It's all right, Mary. The attendants are busy."

"Well, one of us would stay with you, but we've both got our hands full. I've got to get back to the nurse's station."

"I'll be in room twenty-six, next to the kitchen, for about an hour, Stefanie," Breanna said. "If you need me, just give a holler."

"I'll be fine."

Mary and Breanna left the room, and Stefanie continued to work to bring down the man's temperature. Within another five minutes, he was pulling at the leather straps, and his moans were turning into growls.

The water was getting warm and Stefanie left to replace it. Moments later she returned with fresh water from the hospital's well outside and saw that his eyes were open.

Forge glared at her and strained hard on the leathers.

Stefanie set the pan of water on the bedstand and laid a hand on Hugo's shoulder. "Please settle down, Mr. Forge. Nobody's going to hurt you. You're at Mile High Hospital. Dr. Matthew Carroll stitched up the gash on your head. You're going to be fine."

The man's head trembled as he lifted it from the pillow and pulled against the straps. Through gritted teeth, he growled, "I want outta here!"

"We can't let you out, sir. You've had a severe blow to your head, and you're running a high fever."

"I want outta here!" he yelled. "Get these straps off me! I want outta here!"

"Mr. Forge, please. I'm trying to bring your fever down with cold water. You must calm yourself."

Suddenly the right wrist snapped free. Before Stefanie could move, his fist struck her in the midsection, and she collapsed on the floor. She fought to catch her breath and started to get up. She saw that the madman had snapped the leather on his left wrist and was now clawing at the buckles that held his ankles.

Stefanie clutched at her stomach and used the wall to get to her feet. She opened her mouth to yell, but nothing came out. When she pushed away from the wall, her knees gave way and she dropped to the floor.

Stefanie forced herself up. Her breath came in spurts, high in her chest, and caught as if she had swallowed something. But she was finally able to let out a high-pitched scream.

Hugo Forge was off the bed now, lunging for her with fire in his eyes.

Stefanie pushed toward the door and broke free into the hall just as Breanna came running from room twenty-six. David Halden and Michael Adair were right behind her.

Stefanie avoided the hand that grabbed for her, and darted for the kitchen door. In her panic, it seemed the safest place to go. The kitchen door was still swinging as the madman plunged after her. Stefanie ran past cook Charlie Crawford, a small man in his late fifties, gasping, "Charlie, run! He's out of his mind!"

Crawford picked up a butcher knife. Stefanie yanked open what she thought was a door that led outside, only to face a storeroom.

She turned around to see Hugo Forge bat the knife out of

Charlie's hand and smash him to the floor with a huge fist. Charlie went down and didn't move.

Just then David Halden and Michael Adair burst through the kitchen door. Hugo wailed and punched Halden so hard he backpedaled into Adair, and both tumbled into the hall.

Hugo headed for Stefanie, holding the butcher knife in his right hand. Stefanie felt her heartbeat pounding at the back of her eyes, on top of her head, in her throat.

Suddenly she was in his grasp, her neck in the crook of his left arm, the sharp blade of the knife at her throat. "You're my ticket outta here, nursie!" he said, forcing her to the door and into the hall.

Several nurses had collected in the hall, including Mary Donelson, who had sent a nurse on the run to get the sheriff. David Halden was still down, but Michael Adair was on his feet, trying to decide what to do.

Hugo took a step down the hall, dragging his hostage in a vise-like grip. "I'm leavin' here! Anybody tries to stop me, I'll cut her throat, y'hear me?"

"You don't have to take Stefanie," Adair said. "Just go. We're not gonna try to stop you."

"I don't believe you! She's goin' with me so's nobody comes after me! Now get back, or I'll slit her throat!"

Stefanie's stomach wrenched with fear and her legs would hardly hold her up. Only Hugo's powerful arm kept her from crumpling.

Suddenly Mary Donelson leaped in front of them. "Mr. Forge, if you think you need a hostage, take me instead."

"Get outta the way, nursie, or I'll cut this woman's throat, *then* take you with me!"

No one had noticed Breanna Baylor, who had dashed past the kitchen door when the trouble started. She remembered a pile of building materials the construction workers had left behind the mental wing, and had slipped out to find something to stop the massive man.

The rest of the staff watched, wide-eyed, as Hugo backed down the hall, half-carrying Stefanie with him. Mary was afraid to say any more for fear he would indeed kill Stefanie.

Just then Breanna appeared behind Forge, bearing a three-foot length of lead pipe. She shook her head at the others to not give her away.

Hugo seemed to get even more agitated and bawled, "Get outta my sight—every one of you! Out of my sight!"

As the staff people scattered, Breanna rushed up behind Forge and swung the pipe with all her might. Hugo started to turn, but never saw who or what hit him. The lead pipe cracked his head with a horrible thud, and he went down, taking Stefanie with him. The butcher knife clattered to the floor.

Before anyone had time to move, Sheriff Langan and Deputy Ridgway came racing down the hall, guns drawn. When Curt saw Forge in a heap, he holstered his gun and lifted Stefanie to her feet. Mary told him and Steve what had happened.

Dr. Carroll had been away from the hospital on a personal errand and returned in time to see the attendants picking up the unconscious Hugo Forge. This time, Dr. Carroll ordered him put in chains.

As the staff workers went back to their duties, Stefanie went up to Breanna and wrapped her arms around her. "Thank you for saving me, Breanna."

"Yes, Breanna," Curt said. "Thank you, thank you, thank you."

From the corner of her eye, Stefanie saw Mary standing by. She let go of Breanna and went to embrace her. "You did a brave thing offering to take my place as hostage."

Mary kissed her cheek. "That's the least a mom can do for her daughter."

Curt stepped close and said, "Will I get a kiss too when I become your adopted son-in-law?"

Mary laughed, let go of Stefanie, and kissed the sheriff on the cheek. "You don't have to wait till then, Curtie Pie."

"Curtie Pie!" Steve said, laughing. "Hey, everybody, my boss's name is Curtie Pie!"

Langan fixed him with a steady glare and said, "You tell that to anybody outside these walls, pal, and your name is mud!"

22

LATER THAT MORNING, Mary and Stefanie stood over a sedated Hugo Forge. Mary felt his brow. "Your cold water treatment is paying off. His fever's definitely down. Dr. Carroll's diagnosis has to be right—he's got some kind of internal infection. He'll just have to wear it out."

"Well, he's strong enough to do that, I'm sure."

Mary looked at Stefanie more closely. "I want you to come down to my office and rest for awhile. You look a little peaked."

"I'll be all right. The blow I took in the stomach sort of weakened my knees, but I'm feeling better now."

"Since I'm the boss, I insist that you go to my office and sit down for a half hour or so."

"Or I'm fired, is that it?"

Mary smiled and took a playful swat at her. "No, I'll just turn you over my knee and give you a good motherly spanking. Come on. Hugo will be fine."

Breanna stopped the two nurses as they were heading for Mary's office.

"Stefanie," she said, "I just received a telegram from John. He's in Cheyenne City and will be home day after tomorrow. He wanted me to let you and Curt know he'll be here for the wedding."

"Wonderful! Thank you. I'll tell Curt."

When Mary and Stefanie reached the head nurse's small office, Mary stepped in behind Stefanie and closed the door. The top was glass, but there was a curtain when Mary needed privacy. She pulled the curtain now. "There. No one will even know you're in here. Have a seat over there and relax a bit, okay?"

Mary started to leave, but saw tears begin to pool in Stefanie's eyes.

"Honey, what is it?"

Stefanie sniffed and brushed at the tears that were about to spill. "I'm beginning to realize just how soon the wedding's going to happen, and I...I just wish my mother could have been here for it."

"I do too, sweetheart."

"I wish I knew if I'd meet her one day in heaven. She probably wasn't a Christian, though, since Daddy wasn't." Stefanie rose from the chair and hugged Mary's neck. "But I'll have *this* mom in heaven with me forever!"

Mary held her tight. There was a tap on the door and Mary went to see who it was.

"It's Dr. Carroll," Mary said, and opened the door for him.

Dr. Carroll glanced at Stefanie and saw her wiping tears. "Sorry for the interruption. I need to talk to you about a couple of things, Mary, but there's no urgency. We can talk later. Anything I can do to help?"

"Stefanie's just reacting to the Hugo Forge incident, Doctor. I brought her here to rest for awhile."

Dr. Carroll nodded, sensing that Stefanie needed Mary more than he did at the moment. "You just stay with her. I'll get one of the other nurses to fill in for you at the nurses' station until you let me know otherwise."

"Thank you, Doctor."

Mary closed the door and said, "Sit down, Stefanie."

There was another chair near the one Stefanie was using. Instead of sitting behind her desk, Mary sat there.

"Since we've got a little time," Stefanie said, "there's something I'd like to know."

"All right."

"It's about your little girl. I asked you the other night how she died, but we were interrupted and you didn't get a chance to answer."

Sadness touched Mary's features. "My daughter didn't die, honey."

"But you said she was taken from you when she was very small."

"She was. Literally. My husband ran off with her when she was two years old."

"Why did he do that?"

"Because I became a Christian."

"Really? That was the reason?"

"We lived in Philadelphia, and a widow who lived next door to us invited me to attend a revival meeting. The evangelist was one of those 'hell-fire-and-brimstone' kind. For the first time in my life, I really understood the gospel. The Holy Spirit shined His light into my spiritual darkness, and I saw that Jesus had gone to the cross for *me*. He had shed His precious blood for *me*...died for *me*...and had risen from the dead for *me*. I went to the altar at the invitation. The pastor's wife went with me to be sure I understood. I opened my heart to Jesus that night, Stefanie."

"How exciting!"

"But...my husband was a blatant infidel," Mary said with a sigh. "When I went home and told him I had become a

Christian, he acted like a crazy man. He cursed God, cursed the Bible, and cursed me. Then one morning he was gone, and so was my little girl. I've never laid eyes on them since. I tried to locate them—went to the state and federal authorities—but they could find no trace."

A strange tingling flooded over Stefanie, and her heart began to pound.

"Mary...what was your little girl's name?"

"Her name was Sarah Lynne. Lynne with an *e.*"

"Was it...Sarah Lynne Gregg?"

Mary's eyes widened. "Why, yes. How did you know?"

For a few seconds Stefanie couldn't speak, and her voice was unsteady when she finally found it. "Just before my father was hanged, he told me something I had never known—that we had once lived in Philadelphia. When I was very small."

"Really?"

"Yes. He had always told me that my mother's name was Ellen Marie Andrews, and that she died when I was two. But he never told me how she died, nor would he tell me where I could find her grave. Daddy's real name was Bill Gregg. He told me just before he was hanged that he changed his name to Will Andrews when we left Philadelphia after my mother died. He said my name was Sarah Lynne Gregg, and he changed it to Stefanie Lynne Andrews when we went to Mexico."

Mary was finding it difficult to breathe. Trembling, she said, "My name is Mary *Ellen.* And my...my little Sarah Lynne had a birthmark shaped like a butterfly on the bottom of her left foot."

Stefanie bent over with shaky hands and removed her shoe. "You mean a birthmark like this?"

They rushed to hold each other and wept for joy. Stefanie sobbed over and over, "You're alive! You're alive! You're alive!"

"Only the great God of heaven could have brought us together, my darling daughter," Mary said.

There was silence then as they savored the moment of restoration and thought about God's unfathomable goodness.

Then Mary said, "Honey, after you and your father had been gone seven years, I had him declared legally dead, and I married a wonderful Christian man named Jack Donelson. We had no children together. He died four years ago from pneumonia. I never considered marrying again. I just buried myself in my nursing career."

Stefanie embraced her mother again. "This is almost more than I can stand, Lord. I found my father after thirteen years, then lost him again. Now You've brought my mother to me, and I no longer have to wonder if she was a Christian. I know we'll have an eternity together in heaven with You. Thank You! Oh, thank You!"

On Saturday evening, December 3, there was snow on the ground in Denver, Colorado. But the cold, biting air did not affect the warm atmosphere inside First Baptist Church as a capacity crowd watched Dr. Matthew Carroll walk Stefanie down the aisle and give her away to a proud and happy Curt Langan.

As the couple knelt after taking their vows, John Stranger offered a heartfelt prayer, asking God to bless their union and to keep His mighty hand on them.

Mary Donelson sat in the second row of pews, weeping with joy and pride as the bride and groom kissed and Reverend Larribee pronounced them husband and wife.

Then Dottie Carroll stepped up to sing a song of dedication

to the Lord. Just before she sang, Dottie turned and looked at Breanna. When their eyes met, Dottie mouthed: "One of these days it will be you and John!"

Breanna smiled and met John's eyes.

When the song was finished, the pastor said, "Ladies and gentlemen, it is my pleasure to introduce to you Mr. and Mrs. Curt Langan!"

An hour later, after the reception, Curt and Stefanie put on their coats and stepped outside into the frosty night air, laughing as they ducked the shower of rice from well-wishers.

John and Breanna stood arm-in-arm and watched the bride and groom climb into a waiting surrey and ride away.

"It's great to see those two so happy," John said. "After all they've been through, they sure deserve it."

Breanna wiped her tears and said, "Yes, thank the Lord, their every dream has been fulfilled."

OTHER COMPELLING STORIES BY
AL LACY

Books in the Battles of Destiny series:

☛ *A Promise Unbroken*

Two couples battle jealousy and racial hatred amidst a war that would cripple America. From a prosperous Virginia plantation to a grim jail cell outside Lynchburg, follow the dramatic story of a love that could not be destroyed.

☛ *A Heart Divided*

Ryan McGraw—leader of the Confederate Sharpshooters—is nursed back to health by beautiful army nurse Dixie Quade. Their romance would survive the perils of war, but can it withstand the reappearance of a past love?

☛ *Beloved Enemy*

Young Jenny Jordan covers for her father's Confederate spy missions. But as she grows closer to Union soldier Buck Brownell, Jenny finds herself torn between devotion to the South and her feelings for the man she is forbidden to love.

☛ *Shadowed Memories*

Critically wounded on the field of battle and haunted by amnesia, one man struggles to regain his strength and the memories that have slipped away from him.

☛ *Joy from Ashes*

Major Layne Dalton made it through the horrors of the battle of Fredericksburg, but can he rise above his hatred toward the Heglund brothers who brutalized his wife and killed his unborn son?

☛ *Season of Valor*

Captain Shane Donovan was heroic in battle. Can he summon the courage to face the dark tragedy unfolding back home in Maine?

Books in the Journeys of the Stranger series:

☞ *Legacy*

Can John Stranger bring Clay Austin back to the right side of the law...and restore the code of honor shared by the woman he loves?

☞ *Silent Abduction*

The mysterious man in black fights to defend a small town targeted by cattle rustlers and to rescue a young woman and child held captive by a local Indian tribe.

☞ *Blizzard*

When three murderers slated for hanging escape from the Colorado Territorial Prison, young U.S. Marshal Ridge Holloway and the mysterious John Stranger join together to track down the infamous convicts.

☞ *Tears of the Sun*

When John Stranger arrives in Apache Junction, Arizona, he finds himself caught up in a bitter war between sworn enemies: the Tonto Apaches and the Arizona Zunis.

☞ *Circle of Fire*

John Stranger must clear his name of the crimes committed by another mysterious—and murderous—"stranger" who has adopted his identity.

Books in the Angel of Mercy series:

☞ *A Promise for Breanna*

The man who broke Breanna's heart is back. But this time, he's after her life.

☞ *Faithful Heart*

Breanna and her sister Dottie find themselves in a desperate struggle to save a man they love, but can no longer trust.

☞ *Captive Set Free*

No one leaves Morgan's labor camp alive. Not even Breanna Baylor.

Available at your local Christian bookstore